WH
SHE
KNEW

BOOKS BY KAREN LONG

Cry for Mercy
Perfect Little Dolls

KAREN LONG

WHAT SHE KNEW

bookouture

Published by Bookouture in 2021

An imprint of Storyfire Ltd.
Carmelite House
50 Victoria Embankment
London EC4Y 0DZ

www.bookouture.com

Previously published in 2017 as *The Cold Room*

ISBN: 978-1-80019-264-5
eBook ISBN: 978-1-80019-263-8

For MJ

PROLOGUE

Eleanor Raven had visited the abandoned fairground before but fortunately not under the same circumstances. She stood at its entrance and contemplated climbing the narrow steps and entering the dilapidated ghost train. The world she found herself in was silent and dark, illuminated only by a row of tea lights placed there by her killer.

The battered trolley car leaned precariously on several feet of rusted track, which disappeared through an arch into darkness. A canvas tarpaulin separating the ticket area from the ghost train was painted with overlapping images of ghosts. These were not tempered images of floating white sheets with darkened eyeholes; rather they appeared like vapid souls roiling straight from the pages of Dante's *Inferno*, each face twisted into a rictus of pain and fear. Eleanor knew that if she looked more closely she would see herself emerging from the dark, alongside Lee Hughes' other victims.

Her killer stepped out of the shadows, his nondescript features and slender frame at odds with the murderous chaos that enveloped him. Eleanor watched his arm sweep theatrically in a wide arc, drawing her attention to the surroundings. 'This is *all* for you,' he pronounced grandly.

She knew exactly why she'd been brought here. Lee Hughes was going to murder her and display her body as a testament to his artistic vision.

Just behind the arch, hidden by skeins of cotton gossamer, a large metal hook swung from a central wooden beam attached to a length of industrial chain. A carmine red lipstick and neatly folded transparent plastic bag, ready to display her corpse, had been placed on a small table.

For almost a year, Eleanor had balked at the sight of her killer. Her throat would close and she would feel a surge of panic as she tried to back away from her inevitable death. But this time, strangely, she felt completely calm.

'Eleanor?' came a distant voice. 'Can you see the others?'

Slowly she looked around her and shook her head. 'No, I think they're gone,' she replied.

'Is Hughes still there?' asked the voice.

She nodded, not taking her eyes off him.

'Are you afraid?' asked the voice.

She paused, trying to register her feelings.

'This is important, Eleanor. Are you afraid?'

She paused and considered. 'No,' she replied. 'Not anymore.'

Eleanor walked over to the canvas and began to tear it from its anchor points. Hughes let out a cry of anguish but she carried on, shredding the images with her hands. The faces of the dead – her dead – were beginning to blur and disappear.

'What are you doing, Ellie?' asked a familiar voice from her childhood.

She stopped and looked behind her. Hughes was gone and in his place stood a boy. The boy was naked and his skin bore the green and black bands of putrefaction. He looked exactly the same as he had on the day she'd found his murdered body, lying beneath a pile of rubbish sacks.

'I have to let this go, Caleb,' she said sadly.

'Am I to go as well?' he replied anxiously.

She took a step towards him and considered her lost friend. 'I have to move on.'

'I won't exist anymore?' he asked quietly.

She shook her head and closed her eyes, listening to the voice of her psychiatrist as he counted backwards from ten. 'I don't want to come here anymore,' she whispered.

'Please open your eyes,' Caleb pleaded. 'Look at *me*.'

But Eleanor Raven kept her eyes firmly closed. There would be no more conversing with the dead.

'Three... Two...' said Dr Seb Blackmore. 'And on the count of one I want you to open your eyes... One.'

Slowly, Eleanor opened her eyes and focussed on her feet. She had lain in this chair every week since her attack at the hands of Lee Hughes, sometimes in a hypnotic state, sometimes just talking. Initially reluctant to comply with the decision that she needed psychiatric help, she had started to approach her anger, addiction to self-harming and inability to form a trusting relationship with anyone other than her ex-partner Mo, with increasing equanimity.

Seb gave her a few minutes to readjust before questioning her, watching for signs that the hypnotherapy had had an adverse effect.

'What did you see?' he asked quietly.

Eleanor sighed and readjusted her position. 'I was at the fairground.'

'Was he there?' Seb asked, scrutinising her.

She nodded. 'Yes, both Lee Hughes and Caleb.'

The psychiatrist waited.

'I don't want to keep them alive anymore,' she said flatly. 'I'm done.'

Seb twisted the beaded leather bracelets on his left wrist.

'Are you still visiting Toby Adams?' he asked carefully.

Eleanor sighed again. 'I saw him a month ago and he's requesting I continue with the visits. He claims he has new information for me.'

Seb nodded. 'And how do you feel about that?'

Eleanor shrugged. 'A little indifferent I guess. I don't *think* he has any more hidden bodies. His last two confessions were duds.'

'Is it possible that he doesn't want to let go of you?'

She nodded. 'He found out I had been… dead and…' Eleanor fell silent.

Seb waited.

'He found out that Lee Hughes had murdered me and was then obliged to restart my heart, so that he could kill me under more *creative* conditions.'

'How did that feel?' he asked quietly. 'That's the first time you've ever used the word "murder" to describe those events.'

Eleanor thought for a moment or so. 'How do I usually refer to it?'

'You say killed. It's less emotive, more impersonal.'

'There you go… I'm cured. Ready and able to sally forth and be murdered again, for the greater good of the city.'

'Is that the only reason Toby still wants you to visit and interview him?'

Eleanor believed it was unlikely that Toby would be standing trial for the murder, preservation and display of a known fourteen women and three men over a twenty-some year period any time soon, because he was insane. He was being kept in the isolation wing of Milhaven maximum-security prison, where a dedicated psychiatric team from all over North America was producing papers on him by the ton. Eleanor had been encouraged to visit him as she was one of the very few people he would speak to – with everyone else he maintained a mulish silence.

'I think he does see me as someone he would have liked to have as part of his collection.'

'He's a serial killer that confesses a desire that he'd had the opportunity to murder you.'

She smiled. 'When you put it like that!'

Seb closed the gap between them and lowered his voice. 'I think we've gone as far as we can in your rehabilitation.'

Eleanor looked at him expectantly.

'I've signed you off the Serving Officers Psychiatric Assist Programme,' he said. 'Are you comfortable with that?'

She took a moment to process this information. 'No more sessions?'

'Unless you want to carry on that is?' he teased.

She smiled. 'Thank you.'

CHAPTER ONE

Patrol officers Millie Goldsmith and Sonny Maitland had, between them, amassed over thirty-five years of active service, the greater part of this having been spent on the smoothing over of domestic altercations. So, when a call came in at 7.15 a.m. from an angry neighbour stating that, 'The asshole at number thirty-four is raising merry hell… *again*!' the two cops sighed and headed out on their last journey together.

The small, semi-detached house in the Jamestown region of Toronto was unremarkable, except for the hideous yells and smashing sounds coming from behind the façade. Millie approached the front door and knocked, while Sonny gathered some facts and a great deal of opinions from the neighbour, Al Perkins, who'd called it in. This strategy, which was to cost them their lives, had been adopted early in their partnership. What they hadn't considered was that the nature of this domestic incident was beyond either their fire or negotiating power.

The first bullet was delivered with astonishing accuracy from behind the closed front door, denying Millie Goldsmith the option of any evasive action. It entered just below her left eye and destroyed all eloquent brain regions before exiting through the lower right occipital lobe. The post-mortem conclusion was unequivocal: PC Goldsmith was technically dead before her body fell backwards and down the wooden porch steps.

Sonny, whose conscious self was desperately trying to keep pace with his body's subconscious attempt to save him, watched as his hand unholstered his Smith & Wesson, prepped, aimed and began to fire steadily at the figure that had just emerged from the building. Unlike his partner, Sonny took his fatal bullet in the throat, which allowed him to savour several precious moments of introspection before the final tunnelling of his senses.

Al launched himself towards the furthest corner of his porch, skidded round to the side entrance of his home and dived under his kitchen table, grabbing the house phone as he lunged. However, his second call to emergency services was surplus to the stacked calls already being taken from Maple Drive's other distressed inhabitants.

*

DI Eleanor Raven and her partner Laurence Whitefoot had been minutes away from the scene when the call came through, which placed them as the primaries when the dust had settled. Eleanor pressed her index finger into her left ear to block out the siren wail, Laurence's imaginative swearing as he jockeyed the car through chaotic early morning traffic, and the persistent instructions emanating from their radio.

'Are you listening?' bellowed her commanding officer Marty Samuelson into her right ear.

'Yes, sir,' she replied.

'You and Whitefoot observe, assist and keep out of the way of the firepower. I'm coming down.'

Before she could stress that this would probably be unnecessary and that the attendance of ninety per cent of Toronto's emergency capability was more than enough to guarantee the best possible outcome, he disconnected.

Toronto, having learned the hard way that it was neither immune to, nor necessarily prepared for, situations involving stand-offs with high-calibre weaponry, had invested in an Emergency Task Force equipped to deal with these matters 24/7. The 'high-risk' tactical team, which had been deployed within seconds of receiving the alarm, was now descending onto the area in a fleet of black SUVs.

'What's your position?' asked the team leader. Eleanor could picture him talking calmly into his headset as he scrolled through the data downloading onto his in-car screen.

'We're on Rowan Drive, heading for the back of the property,' said Eleanor, adjusting the earpiece.

'Okay,' began the team leader, 'we've got the negotiator and three overhead snipers getting into position…' There was a pause as he received an update. 'We'll have 360° coverage on the house in the next five minutes but have no visuals or identification of either the occupants or the armed suspect as yet.'

'Officers Maitland and Goldsmith?' asked Eleanor through gritted teeth.

'They're gone.'

She cleared her throat.

There was a pause as the team leader read a new bulletin. 'Okay, there's a possibility that the shooter is a marine, a Lieutenant Eddie Myles. His commanding officer has confirmed he's AWOL and he's likely to be in possession of a C7 automatic rifle and a Browning 9mm.' He ignored Eleanor's despondent sigh. 'His estranged wife Angela moved into the property nine months ago and there's an active restraining order out on him.'

Eleanor massaged her forehead. 'Children?'

'Three all aged under seven. We're calling phones now. Get me something I can work with.'

Eleanor held her badge aloft to the heavily armed task force officer approaching quickly from her left. Unable to see his eyes, or any other flesh for that matter under his grey-and-black protective clothing, she opted for clarity of intent.

Using hand signals, he gestured to the roof of the house. 'You can't be sighted if you keep to the area marked by the kids' swing and the open gate over there.'

Eleanor made a quick check of the parameters and motioned to Laurence to move towards them.

'Al Perkins is the neighbour who called it in and witnessed the shooting. Communicate only with team leader on one,' he said, pointing to his radio. Then, giving her the thumbs up, the officer hoisted his rifle and moved silently along the side of the building until he'd lined up his offensive position.

*

Keeping low, Laurence approached the side door and let himself in. Al, who was still hunkered under the table, let out an involuntary scream. He instinctively made a tamping gesture with his hands. 'It's okay, Mr Perkins. I'm Detective Laurence Whitefoot and we're here to keep you safe and ask you some questions.'

Al's eyebrows shot up wildly on seeing Eleanor enter the small kitchen.

'From the top, Mr Perkins,' said Eleanor brusquely, indicating that he stand up.

Al inhaled and clambered out nervously. 'The guy next door, he's a marine or some such.'

'Lieutenant Eddie Myles?'

Al nodded. 'They used to live on the base but his wife, Angie, left him and moved in here with her kids.'

'You know her?'

'My wife gets on with her. She babysits the kids when…' His voice trailed off and his face grew white. 'They're in there, aren't they? They never went to school.' He was becoming agitated.

'We don't know who's in there yet, Mr Perkins. I need to understand what you saw and heard, up to and including when the two officers were shot and killed.'

Al nodded. 'My wife went to work at six this morning but I don't go in till later, so I tried to get back to sleep for an hour but the goddamn noise was coming through the wall…'

'Could you hear what was being said?' Eleanor asked.

'He called her a whore. I could make *that* out. She was yelling back. Not screaming, just yelling.'

'Did you hear the children? Were they crying or shouting?' asked Eleanor carefully.

Al shook his head. 'I don't think so. I would have…' He paused, as if unsure of exactly what he would have done under those circumstances.

'Did you clearly identify the man who shot the officers?'

'Yes! It was him; her husband.'

'Eddie Myles?'

Al nodded doubtfully.

'What was he wearing? Could you see his face?'

'He was dressed in combat gear. The green camo stuff and the biggest goddamn rifle I ever saw.'

Eleanor leaned closer to him. 'How many times have you seen Eddie Myles before?'

Al was flustered; a line of sweat appeared above his lip. 'Once. I saw him once – briefly.'

'So why are you sure that the man you saw shoot the two officers was Eddie Myles?' she asked, her eyes narrowed.

Al shook his head. 'I can't be sure but he *looked* like the guy the cops hauled off last time he came round and started yelling.'

Eleanor glanced at Laurence and they both listened to the silence, punctuated only by a distant siren. 'When did the yelling stop?'

'After the cops were shot.'

'Tell me *exactly* what you saw.'

*

Eddie Myles finally opened a dialogue with his negotiator at 9.13 a.m. His voice was unwavering and his thought processes lucid, if not rational. He apologised unreservedly for the deaths of the two officers but he was apparently on a 'war footing' and, as such, collateral damage was inevitable.

The team negotiator had long since learned that the only feeling he would allow into his dialogue with an armed and dangerous suspect was his instinctive knowledge of when things were going to blow. So far, the tipping point hadn't been reached.

After refusing to talk to his commanding officer, who was being flown in from the base, Myles offered to send out his three children but would not allow Angie to leave. His plan was for an unarmed female officer to stand at the bottom of the porch steps, next to the body of Millie Goldsmith, and receive the three children. Myles gave his word that the children and officer would be safe, but on the question of allowing what little remained of Millie's bloody face to be covered, he was resolute. He said it would teach his children the consequences of their mother's betrayal.

If it ensured their safe retrieval, the negotiator would go along with this. There was a team of psychologists whose task, over the coming years, would be to erase the horror of this day for the children; his only job was to save their lives.

*

Eleanor Raven removed her jacket and tightened the straps on her body protector while the team leader explained the procedure to her. She would be unarmed, as the team's psychologist advised that a marine would look for concealed weapons and if Myles suspected she was carrying, he might kill her and the children. She nodded and tried to ignore Laurence's increasingly anxious body language. The only thing she needed to focus on was making sure that the children – Becky, Sam and baby Aden – were escorted, as quickly and quietly as possible, across the 200 yards that separated the porch from the safe zone. Five armed assault specialists would cover Eleanor, prioritising the safety of the children and her above all other considerations.

Eleanor nodded. She was ready. She raised a warning finger to her partner and mouthed, 'This is my job.' A wafer-thin microphone and transmitter were taped to her chest and tested.

Eleanor walked with Laurence over to the safe zone and waited in deafening silence for the command. There was nothing more to be said.

At the team leader's nod, she raised both hands over her head and began to walk slowly towards the front porch of 34 Maple Drive. She allowed herself a momentary glance at the body of Sonny Maitland, which lay sprawled across the path leading to Al Perkins' house, noting that his hand was still locked around his weapon.

Millie Goldsmith had not been spared any dignity in death. Her legs were spread-eagled on the steps, the remains of her head acting as a wedge on the bottom rung, preventing her body from sliding onto the ground.

Eleanor stopped and waited. She could feel the sharp nag of lactic acid building up in her raised arms and an overwhelming desire to close her eyes.

Cautiously, the door inched open, revealing a child's hand at the midpoint and above it the muzzle of what was, in all probability, a C7 semi-automatic rifle, identical to those aimed back at it.

*

'Stay calm and lower your breathing,' said the team leader into the microphone as he monitored Eleanor's raised heartbeat, which echoed through everyone's headset.

The child's hand slid back through the crack in the door, leaving only the rifle and a dark shadow.

Suddenly, the negotiator's tone and body language changed. 'You have my word.' He nodded to the team leader and cupped his hand over the phone, 'He's releasing the three children.'

*

Eleanor was trying to control her breathing in an effort to lower her increasing adrenaline levels. She didn't want the last representation of her living self to be seen shaking uncontrollably.

The barrel of the rifle slid back inside as the door opened slowly. The children were still in their pyjamas, with red eyes and hair mussed from sleep. None of them looked back as they took in the scene. The eldest child Becky held the baby on her hip, just as her mother would have, her right hand firmly clamped around her younger sister's.

'Becky, my name's Eleanor and I want you to walk towards me.' She tried to smile and relax her features into an expression that would make the girl feel safe but felt the wrong muscles working.

'Don't move forward,' warned the team leader in her earpiece. 'Coax her to you.'

'Becky, I need you to walk over to me, so I can take you somewhere safe,' Eleanor said carefully. But the child was frozen to the spot, her eyes glazed and uncommunicative.

'You *have* to get her to walk towards you,' said the voice in her ear, with greater force.

She tried again. 'Becky, the baby's getting cold. Can you bring him over to me so I can get a blanket and some warm milk?' She fought the urge to lunge towards the children and grab them.

Becky pursed her lips and squeezed the baby closer. His face was buried in his sister's shoulder, a fist balled tightly around her long, dark plait.

'She's in shock, Raven; you *need* to get her to move,' said the team leader.

'Becky, I want to make you safe but you have to walk towards me. I can't climb the steps.'

Becky's eyes began to focus on her.

'I *can't* come to you. You have to bring Sam and Aden to me. Do you understand?'

Becky nodded and spoke to her sister. 'Don't look at the sleeping lady, Sam… Do you understand?'

Sam stared back at her and began to cry.

Eleanor nodded encouragingly to Becky. 'We're going to walk towards the big black car behind me… just us, okay?'

Becky furrowed her forehead and glanced back at the door, which was still slightly ajar. She faced Eleanor. 'Is Daddy coming too?'

Eleanor swallowed and listened to the team leader say, 'Not just yet…'

'Not just yet,' she repeated. 'When you walk past the lady, I'm going to pick up Sam and carry her. Will you tell her that it's alright? I don't want to scare her.'

Becky whispered to her sister.

'*Hurry it up, Raven*!'

'Ready?' she asked.

Becky moved tentatively towards the steps, pulling her sister with her. Eleanor was aware that her raised hands were lowering, eager to grab the children as they moved within reach.

With excruciating caution, Becky led them down the steps, keeping her sister's face pressed into her chest, so she couldn't see the dead officer, but the baby was slipping and she had to relinquish her handhold to reposition him.

In the fraction of a second that she was adrift, Sam turned on her heels, ran back to the front door and began to hammer on it, sobbing for her mother. Eleanor, aware of the team leader's warning voice, bounded past Becky and flung her arms round the little girl.

Time ground to a sluggish thump as the door opened to reveal Eddie Myles, his face obscured by the rifle. Eleanor let the little girl slide to her feet, pushing her gently behind.

'Take out the earpiece,' he snapped.

It was with some relief that she dug it out of her right ear and let it drop to the floor, silencing the team leader.

'I'm unarmed,' she said quietly.

He shrugged his left shoulder.

'May I take Sam over to get warm?' she asked cautiously. 'She's frightened.'

Slowly, he lowered the rifle sufficiently to reveal his eyes. They were dark, angry and unreadable. Eleanor blinked but would not lower her gaze from his.

'I'm turning away from you and intend to walk your children over to a safe area. Will you allow me safe passage?'

There was a pause as he considered this before pushing the front door closed with his foot. For a fraction of a second her eyeline was level with the bullet hole and its corona of blood splatter. In a decisive motion, she swung Sam up into her arms and grabbed the hand of Becky, who was standing transfixed on the lower step, and walked briskly towards the safe zone.

Their reception was organised and swift. The team paramedic checked over the children as they were wrapped in blankets and ushered towards the waiting ambulance.

Eleanor felt a grip on her arm, steering her to one side.

'I'm the team psychologist,' said the woman, 'and I want you to be with me during Becky's debrief. If she won't speak to me, I'll need you as a trust figure to step in. You okay with that?'

*

It took less than three minutes of gentle probing for the psychologist to indicate that Eleanor take over. Becky's eyes were focussed on the middle distance, her jaw tightly clamped.

'Becky, we really need your help,' said Eleanor quietly, lowering herself to the child's level. 'We need to know what happened this morning so we can help your mom.'

Becky's eyes saccaded nervously to the left before she returned her gaze to Eleanor's.

'Can you tell me where your mom is? Is she alright?' The child's expression became granite. 'Did Daddy hurt her?' she questioned softly.

Sam inched her way forward on the stretcher, bringing herself closer to Eleanor. 'Daddy put Mummy in the bed... But she wasn't asleep,' said Sam, her voice shaking as she tried to find words for the unspeakable.

Eleanor caught her breath. 'How do you know Mommy wasn't asleep?'

'Don't!' yelled Becky. 'Daddy said we mustn't tell or—'

'Or what?' Eleanor pulled Sam closer to her chest. 'What did Daddy say would happen?'

Becky dropped her eyes. 'Something bad... He made us promise.'

'Sam, how do you know Mommy wasn't asleep? Was she hurt?' she asked carefully.

Both girls were silent, scarcely breathing. Eleanor glanced at the taut face of the psychologist.

'He said Mommy was asleep and tried to close her eyes.' Sam placed her two index fingers on her eyelids, by way of explanation.

Eleanor felt her throat tighten. 'Did Mommy's eyes close?'

Becky let out a howl of misery as Sam shook her head.

*

'How sure are you?' said the team leader, his eyes moving from Eleanor to the psychologist. 'You understand the implications? No hostage and I end the siege.'

'She's dead,' said the psychologist with conviction. 'And Myles *will* kill himself.'

He paused for a moment, allowing her a second or two to reconsider. He turned to Eleanor. 'Your gut?'

'He killed her.'

The team leader turned to the negotiator, who had been hovering on the periphery. 'The doc thinks Myles killed his wife. Can you get me proof of life?'

He shook his head slowly. 'He broke off twenty minutes ago and won't pick up.'

The team leader turned away from them and spoke into his microphone. 'Snipers, any change?'

There was a moment's silence as the team leader reflected. 'You understand the consequences and potential fallout if we move in? So, I am *repeating* my question. Have you enough information to believe that Angela Myles is dead?'

There was silence.

'Is it both of your beliefs that Myles will kill himself following the murder of his wife?'

Eleanor and the psychologist both nodded, but the negotiator took a couple of seconds before committing.

As the team leader raised the microphone to his lips, the muted crack of a pistol shot came from the direction of 34 Maple Drive.

*

Laurence Whitefoot had followed the proceedings on his earpiece from the sanctuary of Al Perkins' side entrance. He covered the garden and the front lawn. His instructions were simple: shoot anyone resembling a heavily armed suspect and avoid shooting anyone who could be a city employee. He'd been relieved that, so far, the only sounds from the siege break had been of the door-smashing type. No further gunfire had been heard and the general radio traffic had been mainly 'Clear!' and 'Safe!'

*

Angela Myles' body was found in the bedroom and deemed beyond medical intervention; as to the whereabouts of Eddie Myles, there was no clue.

'Where the hell is he?' snapped the team leader into the collective earpieces of the equally mystified officers searching for Myles. The house had been scoured from the loft space to the ground floor and not even the two enthusiastic German shepherds had managed to locate him. Attention was now being paid to the exit routes, and the officers whose task it had been to spot them were responding in tight, defensive phrases.

Eddie Myles had vanished.

*

'What the hell's going on?' hissed Laurence as Eleanor took up position next to him. 'No one came past me.'

'It's because he's still in there,' said Eleanor as she opened the kitchen door and slipped inside. 'Is your house identical to number thirty-four?' she asked Al Perkins as he peered out from under the table.

'Yeah. Have they got him?'

'Is there a crawlspace?'

Al screwed up his face. 'There is, but you can't really call it that! You couldn't get into it, it's just—'

'Can I access it through the house?'

'No… Hang on. There's a metal cover in the laundry room.'

'Show me.'

*

The team leader was losing patience. There were now four Kevlar-plated tacticians, himself, Eleanor Raven and a malodorous canine standing in the small laundry room of number thirty-four. He felt hemmed in, both literally and figuratively. 'You think Myles is in the crawlspace?' he whispered to Eleanor as they both stared at the two-by-two-foot metal floor-plate, positioned to the right of the washing machine.

'He's in there,' she replied.

The team leader shook his head. 'Okay, set it up. How big and how deep is it?'

'It extends the full length of the house and averages between two- and maybe two-and-a-half-feet deep,' Eleanor responded.

'And you think he's crammed himself in there? How?' hissed the team leader.

'He was determined,' she replied calmly.

*

As the floor-plate lifted, the unmistakable waft of gunfire left little doubt as to where Eddie Myles had fought his last battle. A light was dropped in and then, after the dog was finally silenced, a mirror was rotated in the hole. It reflected nothing of interest, other than heavy undulations of compressed soil and what were, in all likelihood, recent drag marks.

'Can we get the dog in there?' asked the team leader, massaging his forehead.

'To what end?' Eleanor asked.

He turned to her with some irritation. 'I don't want to lose another officer.'

'You think a Marine would miss?' Eleanor waited as he ground his jaw. 'Myles is dead.'

'Light it up in there,' snapped the team leader.

Within seconds, the fibre-optic camera picked out what appeared to be a motionless booted foot. Even stripped of all body protection, none of the ETF bulking out the small laundry room were under six foot or 100 kilos. Several of them began to hurriedly remove their webbing.

'I'll go in and confirm,' said Eleanor, pulling off her jacket and body protector. For a brief moment she thought that there might be some sort of gender politicking but the team leader had had enough. 'You're armed?'

She nodded and politely refused the helmet offered to her. 'How did Myles do it?' she asked the nearest officer.

'Feet first, so he could replace the cover. Then he'd have rolled onto his belly and pulled with his hands and forearms, pushing with his toes. We'll slide you in face forward. Torch in left; weapon in right. You good?'

Eleanor nodded and manooeuvred herself into position. With alarming speed she was tipped and gently inserted into the crawlspace.

A heady amalgamation of loam, cordite and urine hit her. She has few doubts that Myles was dead; whether he'd had time to set an ambush charge was anyone's bet.

She could see his feet flicking in and out of the light as she edged forward. Progress was considerably slower than she'd imagined due to the dryness of the soil, which forced her to lift and place her body, more than drag it.

She was within an arm's length of Myles but couldn't make out more than a shadowed outline.

'Lieutenant Myles? I'm Detective Raven and I need to know if you've been injured.'

She shone her torch in the direction of his head but he must have either found or created a hollow in the earth, as his head and torso were below the light's penetration.

Bringing her face level with his motionless chest, she reached for his hand. His fingers were warm but unresponsive, allowing her to extract the clasped pistol and place it beyond his reach.

As she felt for a pulse she was surprised to feel a soft, uncoordinated flutter. Eleanor pushed her arm over his chest, cracking her head on a joist as she did so, and shone the light on his face. Lacking the elbow room for a temple shot, Myles had placed the muzzle under his chin, probably leaving just enough of his hindbrain to allow his autonomic system to pitch a last-ditch struggle against the inevitable.

Eleanor wasn't completely sure why she slipped her hand into his. It was possibly because he was beyond judgment now. None of the complex emotions that had triggered this maelstrom of destruction were left, so any comfort was wasted and undeserved. But a deep atavistic need for her own redemption, undiminished by the year of therapy, made her take his hand. She wondered, as his circulation faded, whether he could have chosen a different path given an opportunity for retrospection or negotiation? Maybe everything in his life had always pointed to this moment and every step he, his wife and the two officers had ever taken were simply moving them towards this collective destiny.

The fluttering stopped and Eleanor turned her head towards the light bleeding in from the laundry room and reported simply, 'He's gone.'

There was a palpable change in the atmosphere.

'Excellent work, Raven,' yelled the team leader into the crawlspace, his head blocking out the light. 'Now ease yourself away from the body and make your way back.'

Usually indifferent to morbid fears, Eleanor felt a rising tide of claustrophobia. The soil was heavy and cloying, and the joists above her felt oppressive. She took a gulp of air and began to scrabble towards the square of light, propelling herself forward with an ungainly flopping motion.

Suddenly, she was yanked backwards: something had her and was pulling her by the waist. Eleanor must have expressed her fear as the team leader yelled, 'You okay? Raven?'

'Yes!' she gasped. 'I've got my belt snagged on a joist. Give me a minute.'

'Need a hand?'

'I *need* to get a grip!' she muttered. 'You're blocking the light!'

Snatching at her belt and transferring weight onto her left hand, she fumbled to unfasten the buckle and free it from her trouser loops.

As her supporting hand sank into the loose soil, she could feel something rubbing against her fingers. She stopped struggling and concentrated her senses on the object. The torch held between her teeth, she carefully pushed away the surrounding material to reveal the skeletal remains of a human hand.

CHAPTER TWO

There were no wisecrack defence strategies while the bodies of the two officers were scrutinised, bagged and gently placed into the morgue vehicles. Marty Samuelson personally assisted with the lifting of each body onto its respective gurney – a gesture not wasted on any of the demoralised workforce. He was now deep into what looked like an intractable conversation with the Chief of Police.

Eleanor watched with interest as he and the Chief repositioned themselves as scaffolding equipment was deftly manoeuvred through a window into number thirty-four. The majority of the ETF had departed, leaving a pared-down crew to hand over the reins to Toronto Homicide. In their place were two morgue vehicles and three Crime Scene trucks, complete with heavy dismantling equipment. Large tents were being erected on the front and rear lawns to contain the flooring that was being torn out of the laundry and surrounding rooms, and a structural engineer had just arrived to complete the health and safety check. It was an expensive undertaking and Marty's ameliorating hand gestures didn't seem to be winning over the Chief, whose body language was ratcheting up the already tense atmosphere.

'How long before we can get in?' asked Laurence, handing her a coffee.

Eleanor stared at his profile. His hair and beard were streaked with grey and his face was, more often than not these days, dulled with a petulance that she didn't really understand, or probably care to. 'What's the matter?' she asked quietly.

He didn't turn, but by the tightening of his jaw she could see there was an issue and that it would be making its unwelcome appearance in the very near future. She gave him a moment and then carried on. 'I'm waiting for a nod from the safety guys. But first—'

'I thought we'd come to an agreement about sharing information and intent?' he said pointedly.

Eleanor sighed. 'You're right.'

'It's *my* job to have your back,' he said tightly.

'I agree, but there was plenty of back-watching going on down there.'

'You could have been killed!'

'Only if the floor collapsed onto me. Myles was dead,' she replied emphatically.

'But you didn't know that for sure.'

The guilt twinge passed and she felt herself revving up for a snippy response but took a deep breath and counted, just as Seb Blackmore had taught her.

Marty stormed over. 'Run this past me again,' he hissed, waving respectfully as the Chief's car pulled away.

Eleanor opened her mouth, but her boss hadn't finished airing his outrage.

'*Because* this is how it sounds to me. You were here to *back up* ETF…' Marty's finger was beginning to wave round in an effort to locate the source of blame. 'And managed, within the space of twenty minutes, to locate not only *one* crime scene but to acquire a second for good measure!'

'Yes, sir,' replied Eleanor.

'Why were you under the floor in the first place? Weren't there about seventeen highly trained and appropriately waged city employees, whose task it was to be under the floor-space, rather than you?'

'I offered, sir,' she replied simply.

Marty leaned forward, his finger thrust menacingly at her chest. 'You didn't *offer*, Raven! You muscled your way into someone else's jurisdiction and that level of nosy self-promotion will be the undoing of you.'

Eleanor smiled. 'I have to agree, sir.'

'So where'd this hand come from?'

'There's nothing to indicate that the skeletonised remains could be linked to Eddie Myles' actions,' said Eleanor calmly. 'These are probably two separate crimes that just *happen* to occupy the same location and discovery day. It's probably just a coincidence, sir.'

'Hmm,' he growled. 'Until I've concrete proof that this is an unconnected crime, I want you and Whitefoot on both cases. You close this as soon as possible. Understand?'

'Excuse me?' interrupted a tall, angular man holding out his hand to Eleanor. 'I'm Dr Benjamin Grenson… I'm your forensic anthropologist.'

Marty growled, 'Are you on loan or payroll?'

Grenson leaned towards him and said cheerily, 'No such thing as a free lunch.'

Eleanor watched with interest as her boss declined to engage and walked stiffly away.

'Hmm, what rattled his cage?' the academic asked casually.

'I suspect a death tally of two long-serving officers and one mother of three with no opportunity to find out why,' said Eleanor pointedly.

Grenson looked around with an air of mystification. 'I was only informed about skeletal remains on the phone.'

The sun had long set by the time Eddie Myles' body had been extracted and removed to the morgue. Up to this point, the first team allocated to the Myles shooting had flooded the small house with exclusion tape, camera equipment and a heavy presence. The upstairs rooms had been sealed and the only remaining area still being investigated was the laundry room, or rather what remained of it. The floor had been taken up, as had that of the adjacent kitchen, which had been stripped of all furniture. Myles' body had been located beneath the far end of the kitchen; the skeletal remains were found halfway between, under a partition wall, now on the 'to be removed' list.

The extraction process had been time-consuming and torturous, as each team tried to retain the integrity of the separate crime scenes. After one technician slipped off a galley plank and left two large footprints, inches away from the exposed bones, a cull of extraneous workers took place, which further drew out the proceedings.

'Right!' said Dr Grenson, slapping his hands together. 'I think we're ready to begin. I have your numbers and I'll call you when I've got something.'

'I was going to stay for a while,' Eleanor replied, glancing at her watch.

'Nope, this is better on my own. I've got a couple of research assistants on their way and I'm surrounded by patrol officers.'

Laurence was silent as he drove them back to HQ. Ordinarily Eleanor would have been disinterested in the cause, but after months of therapy and rehabilitation following her last two cases, she had committed to becoming more 'open' and 'nurturing', initially in the hope of being taken off the Serving Officers Psychiatric Assist Programme, but now it had become a lifestyle choice. 'Something's bothering you,' she asked cautiously. 'What?'

'Nothing,' he replied, taking the corner onto Dundas Street too quickly.

'Is that a "nothing" but keep asking?' she tried.

'No!' he snapped.

'Alright, but if you want to—'

'I'm being dragged into court,' he said.

Eleanor took a moment or two to process this. 'Why?'

'Mags wants either the apartment, or for me to buy her out… *and* she wants Monster,' he spat.

'Why go to court? Can't you negotiate?' she added cautiously.

'I don't want to give up the apartment – or Monster.'

Eleanor was struggling with this concept. 'But you don't *like* the dog.'

'*That's* not the point!' he said, through pursed lips. Laurence slewed the Taurus into one of the bays and yanked on the hand-brake. 'It's making me very tense.'

Homicide, although well-staffed due to the clocking on of the night crew, was subdued. Detective Timms was sitting at his desk, behind mounds of paperwork littered with empty cups and Styrofoam food cartons. He looked defeated and heavy.

'How's it going?' he asked Eleanor distractedly, loosening his tie.

'There needs to be a neck on the block for Myles and I'm designated finger pointer,' she replied.

Timms slumped back heavily into his seat and nodded. 'I graduated with Sonny Maitland. He was a good guy.'

'I'm sorry,' she replied, pouring herself a coffee.

'Anyway, what are the odds of finding a graveyard?' he asked.

Eleanor contemplated this. 'I'd say the odds are pretty slim but…' She shrugged.

'You thinking Myles had buried someone there earlier?'

She shook her head. 'Seems bizarre, especially as he hadn't had any access to the house. But what are the odds of finding an unconnected "just happened to be there" body next to that of someone who just happened to have murdered three people; four if you include himself?'

Timms narrowed his eyes. 'I'd say that the world is a mysterious place and maybe coincidences are just that.'

She raised her eyebrows and nodded. 'Maybe.'

'And this is for you.' Timms handed her a square of memo paper. 'Just what you needed after today, huh?' he added, rifling through the empty food wrappers with an air of optimism.

Eleanor sighed and placed the memo into her back pocket.

'You know my thoughts on not letting go of cases.' He leaned towards her, waving a rediscovered half-eaten sandwich from hours earlier. 'That guy's given up what he had and now he's yanking your chain and *that's* dangerous. You can get addicted… drawn into a world that's safest left behind bars.'

Eleanor nodded.

'So,' he said, through a mouthful of food, 'take my advice and *don't* call back.'

For a brief moment Eleanor surprised herself by toying with taking his advice, but there were only so many new leaves that could be turned over in one lifetime.

Wandering back to her office, she noted the time of the incoming call from the correctional officer at Milhaven, Ontario's maximum-security prison, and the subject of the call: Toby Adams, who believed he had some information that 'might interest her'.

It was late and she needed a bath and thinking time, so closing the door on her office and zipping up her coat, she headed for her car. She'd just de-misted the windscreen and pulled onto the street when her phone rang.

'Detective Eleanor Raven? I'm Rachel Gilbey, Dr Grenson's assistant. He asked me to call you and let you know that we've found something,' the young woman explained cautiously.

'On my way,' Eleanor replied, turning the car around.

*

'That's it,' said Dr Grenson. 'We've fine-toothed the area and there's nothing else to report.'

Eleanor stared at the hand, which had been placed on a steel tray ready to be put into a plastic evidence bag. The fingers had been pared back to the bone, but the palm and wrist were held together by brown leathery skin, which gave the appearance of an ill-fitting glove.

'How far have you excavated?' she asked, glancing at her partner, who had squatted down on the wooden galley plank and was studying the remains.

Grenson waved his hand expansively. 'This house is primarily built on rock. The crawlspace is filled with topsoil, which would have been brought in by the builders. There's about a foot of soil and then rock, which is what you'd expect in this area of the city.'

'Okay, so that means it would have been difficult to bury a body here,' said Eleanor.

'Without excavating equipment I'd say almost impossible,' he replied. 'And if you look closely' – he spread some of the soil apart, using a trowel – 'it's very moist and compacted. If a body had been buried here, even taking into account animal activity et cetera, we'd have uncovered it. What you've got here is what you see.'

'A hand?' said Laurence, without expression.

'*Ex*actly,' enthused Grenson.

'It looks as if it's been hacked or sawn off the arm,' said Laurence. 'Any idea how long it's been down here?'

'Ah,' said Grenson. 'It's highly unprofessional to take a guess. I have to analyse soil and—'

'We'll accept a guess for the moment,' said Laurence quickly.

'Then I'd say about a day.'

Both Eleanor and Laurence turned to stare at him.

'You believe this hand was buried or placed here about a day ago?' asked Eleanor incredulously.

'That's a non-quantified assumption and you'll have to wait for me to conduct the forensic autopsy. But there's no soil adherence, no insect activity, nothing that would indicate it had spent anything other than a cursory time here.' He pointed to the hand. 'That specimen has been air dried. There's no way that has been anywhere near this environment. Well, certainly not for any period of time.'

He smiled cheerily and then, in response to the two detectives' unhappy expressions, asked, 'Is that a problem?'

CHAPTER THREE

Eleanor slid quietly into the morgue suite, nodding deferentially to Dr Mira Hounslow, who was about to conduct the autopsy, and positioned herself next to Laurence. The naked body of Eddie Myles lay on a gurney. His skin was pale and blood-spattered; his hands were taped inside brown paper evidence bags and lay by his side.

'Dr Hounslow, I'll need a complete material collection from Lieutenant Myles' hands,' Eleanor stated.

'Is this for ballistics?' snapped Hounslow. 'Because I am well aware—'

'No, ma'am, this is for a separate investigation and the material will be analysed by forensic pathology.'

Hounslow nodded curtly, adjusted the microphone, which recorded her autopsy notes and, after testing it to her satisfaction, began the external examination.

The autopsy findings were fairly unequivocal, as the bullet's path was traceable by inserting a length of dowel from below Myles' chin and allowing it to slide easily through the gaping hole at the back of his skull. The small-calibre bullet casing had been collected at the scene and would be matched to the pistol extracted from his hand. What remained of his brain was carefully scrutinised by Hounslow for signs of visible lesions that may have given a physical justification for his actions.

Having drawn the necessary fluids, Hounslow removed the stomach, collecting its contents into a large jug. Dictating recognisable food items into the microphone she paused, her brow furrowed. 'Detective Whitefoot, perhaps as a former medical professional you might like to cast your eye over this,' she said carefully. 'What would you say these two objects were?'

Laurence looked carefully at the two small, pale, pea-shaped objects, his face darkening. 'Have you checked his wife?'

Hounslow shook her head. 'She's scheduled for later today.'

'What have you found?' Eleanor asked Laurence quietly, while Hounslow spoke to her technician.

'Follow me,' said Hounslow as she dropped her latex gloves into the bin and left the room.

The body of Angela Myles lay on a gurney inside a body bag. The attending technician, after breaking the plastic seals, unzipped the bag and exposed her corpse, which bore the clear bruising and petechiae associated with strangulation. He then carefully unbuttoned and pulled aside the shirt, exposing her breasts.

'I don't understand,' said Eleanor, staring at the body.

The pathologist shook her head. 'I'll run all of the necessary DNA checks but I'm fairly certain that the two nipples extracted from the stomach of Lieutenant Myles will be those missing from his wife.'

*

Eddie Myles' autopsy lasted another hour, during which his body was photographed, X-rayed, sampled and dissected but, apart from the obvious means and cause of his death and the presence of Angela Myles' nipples in his stomach, there was nothing unusual about the body.

Hounslow sighed as she peeled off her gloves. 'This post-mortem is at an end; all subsequent findings will be reported as soon as possible.'

Eleanor nodded. 'Officers Maitland and Goldsmith?'

'I will be conducting their autopsies this afternoon,' she replied quietly.

'*Not* in here, I hope,' said Eleanor, her voice dangerously low.

Hounslow's body language became rigidly defensive. 'I do not apply any form of moral judgment in this room, Detective. Truth knows none; neither do I,' she replied acidly.

'*Not* in the same room as him,' she said steadily.

Laurence studied Hounslow's face, unsure if she would engage with his partner, but the medical examiner remained silent, making a small, almost imperceptible nod.

Laurence followed Eleanor through the security doors and into the atrium. 'What was that about?' he asked with disbelief.

Eleanor was silent, apparently somewhat bemused by her own emotional declaration. 'It seemed to matter.'

Laurence looked at her askance for a moment or two. 'Ok*aay*... You want me to drive?'

*

Canadian Forces Base Borden was just under two hours' drive away. Eleanor handed the keys over to her partner and settled herself into the passenger seat.

'Have you ever seen that sort of behaviour before?' Laurence asked, pulling out into the traffic.

'Cannibalism? No, never,' she answered. 'I've read a couple of articles but I've never encountered it.'

'What about the hand? You think we're looking at a pattern?'

Eleanor stared at the buildings, noting that, despite the fact they were still weeks away from Christmas, most of the shops featured tinsel-strewn snow scenes. 'Give me your thoughts,' she said, closing her eyes.

'Okay, Myles is angry, suffering from some form of PTSD and blames his wife for leaving him. He doesn't acknowledge that his changes in behaviour are connected to her leaving him.'

'You can be *less* textbook,' muttered Eleanor.

'He's not private about killing Angela. It's a show – he has the whole of Toronto watching.'

'So no room for a military hush-up,' interrupted Eleanor.

'But he effectively buries himself in the crawlspace, so he's still in control, even in death.' Laurence paused, still mulling over the scenario. 'He knows he'll be found and, providing the hand *was* deposited by him and isn't a weird coincidence, it has to have meaning.'

She nodded. 'Like a talisman, or…'

'Or something that inculpates him, or someone else. He *wants* us to uncover what happened.'

Eleanor gestured to a large bilingual sign ahead, announcing that their arrival at Base Borden was 'most welcome'.

Their reception at CFB Borden was cool to frosty. Despite being expected they were forced to sign in their weapons and pass through three layers of interrogative security before meeting Myles' commanding officer. Laurence pointed out that if they'd applied the same amount of enthusiasm for procedure *before* Eddie Myles' departure yesterday, neither he nor Raven would have to be there today.

Captain Raymond Willard's office was a study in minimalism. No family photographs, no trophies or any hint of sentimentality, no decoration or comfort. Eleanor noted with surprise that throughout the conversation Willard did not refer to Myles by anything other than his rank – 'the lieutenant in question' – and didn't remove his cap. The temperature of the room was, in her estimation, only marginally above freezing. All of the windows were open and the radiators were turned off. Whether it was usually this inhospitable, or made so for their benefit, Eleanor wasn't sure.

'Which of you is in charge of the *civilian* investigation?' asked Willard pointedly.

'Well, it depends on which investigation you're referring to,' said Eleanor. 'We're here to find out why Eddie Myles was able to pop out of this high-security establishment carrying a C7 rifle, which is anything but a subtle weapon, along with a couple of handguns.'

Willard's cheeks were beginning to redden. 'That investigation is already underway here,' he spat.

'We are also here to investigate who owned the severed hand that Myles brought with him.'

'I have absolutely no idea what you are referring to. What hand?'

'A partially skeletonised hand was found next to Lieutenant Myles' body. It appears that he'd positioned it there himself, but we're still awaiting scientific evidence. It would be helpful if you could supply us with a list of any missing soldiers,' said Eleanor calmly.

'That will be simple. There are none,' said Willard.

'What about those who fell in battle? Eddie Myles saw action several times, which may have been a contributing factor,' she replied firmly.

'I can assure you that any repatriated soldiers were given full autopsies and buried with military honours. It would be *impossible* for any body parts to have been taken.'

'As *impossible* as it was for a member of your division to commit the multiple murders of his wife and two officers?' Eleanor suggested.

There was a tense silence.

'Eddie Myles was being treated for PTSD and we need the full details of who treated him and where. Perhaps we could take a look around Lieutenant Myles' room, while you have a think about all this and put together the documentation we've requested,' said Eleanor, getting to her feet. 'Then we'll need a quiet area to interview his colleagues and any close friends he may have had.'

A considerably more amenable Sergeant Morton escorted the detectives through the maze of corridors and checkpoints leading to Eddie Myles' room. 'May I say how devastated we all are here. That one of our own should—' began Morton.

'Duly noted,' said Eleanor dismissively. She pulled on a pair of latex gloves as they approached a door sealed with official police tape, then raised an eyebrow to Morton.

'Military police sealed the room last night, after checking for a possible explosive device.'

'Find anything?'

Morton consulted his clipboard. 'It was declared clear by bomb disposal experts Lucas and Brine, and then sealed by the MP. There's nothing to indicate whether anything else was removed from the room.'

'*Removed*?' queried Eleanor. 'That would be contrary to protocol, wouldn't it?'

'It would, ma'am,' responded Morton, without missing a beat. 'I was confirming, through my last statement, that protocol *had* been observed.'

She stared at him, nodding sagely. 'Good to know. So who searched this room?'

Morton looked back at his sheet. 'Lieutenant Lucas and Corporal Brine, ma'am.'

'*They* were the bomb experts. *Who* searched the room?' asked Eleanor with growing irritation.

'I imagine that the MPs would have checked it, ma'am.'

'Put on the top of your "To Do" list that I'd like to see those MPs before I leave.'

Using a small knife from her multi-tool, Eleanor sliced through the warning tape and entered the darkened room. She switched on the light and looked around. Laurence followed her, indicating that Morton should stand by the door and not touch anything.

'You sure someone lived here?' asked Laurence. 'Because this is a new level of spartan.'

The room was devoid of any personal items. The bin was empty and there were no marks on the wall indicating where posters or photographs might have been pinned. The wardrobe contained a neatly pressed set of fatigues, a dress suit, two T-shirts, three sets of briefs and three pairs of socks laid on a shelf. Every item was clean, pressed and folded to geometric perfection. A pair of boots, their caps gleaming, was lined up in the corner of the wardrobe and stuffed with newspapers to maintain their shape.

A knock at the door drew their attention. Morton stepped outside and after a moment or two returned. 'Your scene of crime officers have arrived and are being escorted over.'

'Excellent,' replied Eleanor, continuing to look around the room. 'How long did Myles live here?'

'He was rehoused here after his marriage broke down.'

'Why?'

'I don't know, ma'am,' Morton replied.

'Did he ask to be moved out of married quarters or did he lose the right to be there?'

'I'd have to look that up, ma'am.'

Eleanor opened the small cabinet above the sink and surveyed the empty shelf. 'There are no personal items in here, Sergeant, or marks left to indicate that anyone used this room.'

'I can't explain that, ma'am. This was the lieutenant's room and, to my knowledge, he was in physical residence here on the night before he murdered his wife.'

Eleanor looked at him with renewed interest. 'How'd you know?'

'I have the adjacent room,' Morton replied. 'I heard him in here.'

'He was your friend?' she asked.

Suddenly Morton's demeanour changed – his neutral expression slipped into something less controlled. 'No, ma'am. He was not.'

'How long did you know him?'

'Three years.'

Eleanor nodded. 'Long enough to get to know him and formulate an opinion of his character.'

'Yes, ma'am,' Morton said quietly.

'And what *was* that opinion, Sergeant?'

Morton's cheek twitched and his jaw tightened. 'My opinion was that he was… unhinged.'

'Was that an assumption based on the past three years, or after the revelation that he'd committed multiple homicides?' she asked, scrutinising him.

A muted conversation moving towards them announced the arrival of Crime Scene Investigation. Eleanor stepped closer to Morton. 'I'd like to speak to you in more detail after we've cleared up here.'

Susan Cheung, bleached out by her white bio-suit, entered the room. 'How're you both doing?' she asked carefully, looking around the small room.

'All good here,' replied Eleanor as she ran through the procedure for the search. 'Sergeant Morton, I'll need you to bring Dr Cheung over to Myles' original married quarters after she's finished here.'

'Of course,' he replied. 'Are you ready?'

Leaving the building, Laurence surreptitiously dropped behind the Sergeant, leaving Eleanor room to question him.

'You have opinions on Eddie Myles. What are they?' she asked, fastening her coat in response to the increasingly temperamental weather.

'He was an efficient soldier,' Morton answered vaguely.

'Uh-huh,' she replied as his silence lengthened. 'I'm an *efficient* shopper, Sergeant. It's not a helpful phrase.'

He smiled. 'No, ma'am, I guess not. Myles joined our company three years ago and he seemed okay. Had no problem with the training, or the duties. He didn't like leaving his wife on base... but I didn't hear anything weird said about her. Just that he missed her.'

'I thought you special forces guys tend not to be married,' she said gently.

'I'd say around two-thirds of us are single, for various reasons. Maybe it's the job... Or the type of person that's attracted to the job.'

Eleanor could see the married quarters across the next communal car park. 'You said "unhinged"?'

'He started getting angrier about the sort of missions we'd go on.'

She nodded encouragingly, noting Morton was looking less comfortable.

'Politically?' she suggested.

'Not really. It just felt like it was becoming personal for him.'

'The killing?' she offered.

'You're not asking me about individual assignments are you, ma'am?'

'No, Sergeant. I just need to know what was going on in Myles' head when he planned the destruction of his family.'

'Yes, then. It seemed to me, and some of the other guys, that he was on his own mission.' He stopped walking. 'This was his home from July 2013 to March 2015.'

'Was it empty after Angela Myles moved out?' she asked.

Morton checked his notes. 'It was occupied by Lieutenant Smith, his wife and baby in August 2015, presumably when it was decided that Myles' wife wasn't returning. There aren't enough married quarters to go round, so I guess he was encouraged to vacate.'

'Can you find out who arranged that Myles be relocated, so I can check with them?'

'Yes, ma'am.'

'May we go in?' asked Eleanor, looking through the ground-floor window to see if there was anyone there.

Sergeant Morton knocked on the door. 'I did explain to Mrs Smith that you may need to look around.'

Marianne Smith opened the door to the modest house with a harassed air. Her daughter was bellowing in an adjacent room and continued until she was picked up and bounced by her mother.

'Sorry, she's got a cold,' said Marianne, ushering them into her kitchen. The room was filled with damp clothing being aired. 'The dryer's packed up again,' she said peevishly. 'And with Luke overseas, serving his country, there's no one to take a look at it.'

Sergeant Morton nodded. 'Leave it with me.'

'I never met Lieutenant Myles. The place was empty when we moved in,' she offered.

'Had anything been left here?' Eleanor asked.

'Not *really*.'

Eleanor raised an eyebrow.

'Cleaning stuff, a bucket… Couple of kids' socks. Just the sort of stuff you leave when you move out.' She shrugged. 'Nothing you'd be interested in.'

'Is there any storage space in the house that you don't use? Like a loft or cellar?'

'There's nothing under the house, I don't think. There's a loft but we don't use it. I can't get up there and there's raccoons. I hear them at night creeping around. I'd have sent Luke up there *but* he's overseas,' she said pointedly. 'I tried opening the hatch but it's stuck.'

Eleanor glanced at Laurence. 'We'll look now, Mrs Smith.'

'Oh, great. Top of the stairs and there's a stepladder in the yard.'

The loft space was accessed through a small hatch in the corridor ceiling but it was immovable. Eleanor ran her finger along the architrave, feeling it snag on a sharp point. 'It's been screwed closed,' she said quietly to Laurence. 'From above.'

He reached for his phone.

After Marianne and baby had been bundled off to a friend's house, the cover was removed by one of the crime scene technicians. Cautiously, Eleanor peered inside.

The loft space ran roughly the length of two upstairs rooms, which was about twenty feet by ten. It was evident that Eddie Myles had been occupying the space for some time. A mattress roll and sleeping bag were tucked into a corner, next to a small battery-charged lamp. Cautiously, Eleanor climbed into the space and shone her torch around.

'What you looking at?' shouted Laurence from below.

'Home,' she replied.

Laurence's head appeared through the hole. 'What the hell!'

'Ask Susan to turn on all of the upstairs lights.'

Eleanor turned off her torch. Light bled through small round holes that had been drilled through both the plywood floor panels and the ceiling below. Hunkering down, she lined her eye up with one of the holes. Her line of sight covered the Smiths' double bed. It wasn't a large hole but adequate enough to see most of the bed.

She called to Laurence. 'I'm looking at the double bed. Why couldn't they see me?'

There was movement in the room below and she could see Susan Cheung squinting at the ceiling only feet away from her.

'I've got it!' Susan's finger reached for the eyehole and extracted something. 'It's a plastic membrane. I've seen this before. One side is transparent and the other is opaque. It's white, looks like the ceiling paint.'

'You think he was sleeping here and watching the Smiths?' asked Laurence, from the loft entrance.

'Yup,' Eleanor replied, shining the torch into the corners.

'Hang on,' she said, moving cautiously towards a pile of what looked like plastic bags.

'What have you got?'

'I think, judging by the quantity, we have several months' production of urine and excrement.' Gingerly, she lifted one of the bags and shone a torch on it. 'It looks like something the military would issue. It's a bag, with a self-sealing mechanism.'

Laurence groaned.

There was a pile of clean clothes and several pairs of boots near the mattress. Bottles of water and ration packs were stacked next to two books on military strategy and training. A photograph of Myles' three children and wife was tucked inside one of the books. Ominously, Angela's face had been scratched out.

'Any body parts?' asked Laurence.

'Nothing visible. Susan can tear this apart after I've found out how he got in and out. Go stand outside with Morton and see if you can see anything.'

Moving cautiously round the periphery of the room, she looked for any signs of an exit. It didn't take long for her to locate a hinged panel, positioned on the east wall. The bolts were undone on her side.

Suddenly, she could hear Morton's voice on the other side of the divide. 'Ma'am?'

'Raven, not ma'am!' she snapped.

'Copy. Stand back,' he instructed.

Grey, natural light dimly illuminated the room as Morton squeezed himself through the small opening, which was hinged at the side. Standing next to her, he closed and bolted the panel.

'How?' she asked.

Morton reopened the window and directed her to look closely at the wall below. 'It's hard to see but he's hammered pegs into the external wall. It would only take him a couple of seconds to climb and enter.'

Eleanor looked at the surrounding buildings. 'He ran a risk of being seen.'

'There aren't any windows overlooking this side and the tree gives ample cover,' Morton replied.

Eleanor shone her torch at the mound of bags. 'Lieutenant Myles must have spent a fair amount of time up here, wouldn't you say? Watching another family occupy his house, his bed and his children's room.

Morton scratched his head, bewildered.

'You had the room opposite his, Sergeant. He couldn't have been in two places at once, so why didn't you know?'

'I didn't like the guy, so I steered clear.'

Eleanor looked at him. 'Was he isolated? Depressed?'

Morton shook his head. 'I didn't care to find out,' he answered flatly.

'Okay, so what you've dug up for us so far is effectively nothing!' said Eleanor, glaring at Captain Willard. She opened the manila file in her hand and glanced through the meagre documents within. It contained little more than copies of Eddie Myles' application form to join the unit; his past academic and professional history; some cursory medical forms; a chronology of overseas postings; and a sheet covering a disciplinary hearing four years previously for drunk and disorderly conduct. 'We *know* Myles was being treated for PTSD, so where are the contact details?'

'What you have received is everything I am permitted, by the Official Secrets Act, to give you.'

'That's nonsense!' hissed Eleanor. 'This is a murder investigation.'

Willard lowered his voice, leaning into her personal space. 'You know who murdered the two officers and his wife; there is nothing more to add, unless you're looking for someone to take the fall and…' he added, before Eleanor clarified her mission, 'I can absolutely guarantee that there will be a head on a plate before the month is out.'

'Even if it's yours?'

'Absolutely!' he replied, his steady gaze fixed on Eleanor.

The simultaneous ringing of both Eleanor's and Laurence's phones put an end to any further discussion.

'I think,' grunted Susan Cheung as she extracted another sealed bag from under the eaves in the loft space and passed it to a support technician, 'he'd been squirreling this stuff away for months, maybe even years.'

'Years?' gasped Laurence.

'Yup, or else he's collecting for the whole unit.' She stood up stiffly and pulled up her face mask.

'So this guy shits in a bag and then stores it. Why?' asked Laurence, outraged.

'I suspect it's what he's eating,' said Susan carefully.

Eleanor stared at her. 'Show me.'

Susan selected a heavy transparent bag from the second evidence trunk and held it in front of them. Eleanor shone her torch onto it.

'Is that…?'

'It looks like a distal phalanx to me.' She carefully manipulated the bag, which exposed a second bone.

'Human?' asked Eleanor.

Susan shook her head. 'You need a pathologist. Could be bear – they can look pretty similar.'

'You're saying that Eddie Myles was eating people?' asked Laurence, loosening his tie.

'I'd say there was a strong possibility,' answered Susan.

CHAPTER FOUR

Chief Harry Brocker stood at a perfect ninety-degree angle and stared ferociously at the gathered officers. He was silent, waiting for the room's complete attention and recognition of his superior position within the food chain. Despite being in his early sixties and cruising towards retirement, he exuded authority and non-compromise.

'This,' he began slowly, 'is a terrible day. Three days ago, we lost two of our own and today we must find the strength to carry on and serve our city. Officers Sonny Maitland and Amelia Goldsmith have served our people, our nation, and ultimately their consciences. We will *never* forget them or their actions. Neither will we forget to seek and deliver answers to their families; to ourselves and to the citizens of this land. When an officer is shot we *all* feel the pain, and some of the resolve and belief as to why we do this is lost. But I am here to say to you all that this will *not* happen. You *will* be resolved and believe that "To Serve and Protect" is the mantra we live – *and* die – by.'

Brocker waited while the applause exhausted itself. 'Another officer showed her mettle, serving with determination, sacrifice and resolve. Detective Inspector Eleanor Raven put herself in the line of fire in order to save three children's lives. *That* is the action of not just a hero but the action of an officer of Toronto's Police Service.'

With a sweep of his hand, the Chief passed the presentation over to Marty Samuelson and headed for the stairwell, moving between the officers, catching eyes and exchanging nods. He grasped Eleanor's elbow as he strode between her and Laurence, propelling her towards her office.

Opening the door, Brocker was immediately greeted by Monster, who wisely retreated to his bed on gauging the quality of the 'Lie down' command.

'Is that a serving officer?' he asked, looking at Monster with some disbelief.

'He holds a bravery award,' Eleanor said, without committing to the specifics of Monster's curriculum vitae.

'Really?' He paused, digesting the information. 'Excellent.' He focussed on her. 'How are you?'

Unsure of where this might lead, she ventured, 'I'm well, sir.'

He took off his cap, smoothing the fabric and brushing an imaginary dust mote from the peak. 'I hear you're still seeing the psychiatrist.'

'I've just been released from the programme, sir.'

He nodded sagely. 'What you went through last winter was… profound. You must take the time to heal. I want you to know that both Samuelson and myself hold you in the *highest* esteem and we don't want to lose you.'

'Thank you, sir. I don't intend to be lost.' She smiled cautiously.

Repositioning his cap, the Chief took the door handle firmly. 'Good work yesterday, Raven. This find of yours, it's heading back over to the military?'

'We'll know a little more later on today, but it's looking like a civilian matter, sir.'

He nodded and held out a hand, which she shook, noting both its strength and coolness.

'I thought you were dropping Monster off at K9?' Eleanor asked Laurence.

'So did I! But he's been banned,' Laurence replied, opening his desk drawer and rummaging for a staple extractor with more noise than was merited.

'Why?' she asked, surprised.

'Two of the bitches are pregnant and the security cameras show this asshole mountaineering, like Sherpa Tenzing, over ten-foot divides and committing the unspeakable act.'

Eleanor fought off a smile as she opened the door to Johnson, who was manhandling a display board.

'I suspected that you'd need this,' he said, anxiously looking at Laurence who'd begun the process of clearing off the board. Johnson, an officer of little wit or flexibility, was becoming increasingly animated as Laurence began to remove the pins from the Toby Adams murder board.

'That case is not officially closed!' he said, repeatedly uncapping and recapping a dry wipe pen in a gesture Eleanor believed was figurative.

'Not officially, but it's practically over. We are now working a *new* case and that requires board space!' said Laurence, trying unsuccessfully to manage his rising irritation.

'I can bring more temporary boards in,' replied Johnson desperately.

'It's not a goddamn art gallery!' snapped Laurence.

Eleanor ran her eyes over the murder board. It was, she thought, a work of technical brilliance. Each of Toby Adams' victims were positioned laterally, their presumed death dates and identifications linked into a colourful graph and timeline. QR codes had been created so that the secure phones used by the department could scan and be directed to the documents stored on the internal server. If a crime could be worked out purely from the interpretation of written evidence, Johnson had mastered it.

He turned to Eleanor wearing much the same expression as Monster, who was sitting at her feet anxiously watching her eat a croissant.

'You're still interviewing Adams, so is the case closed or not?' he asked peevishly.

Laurence raised a questioning eyebrow in her direction.

Eleanor popped the remaining half of her breakfast into Monster's mouth and stood up. 'I am still communicating with Toby Adams but it's no longer an ongoing case. Photograph the board and box the materials please.'

Johnson looked as if he had more to say, but after absorbing the expression on Eleanor's face, he headed off to the tranquillity of the supplies cupboard.

'What did the Chief want?' asked Laurence curiously.

'I'm not sure, but he asked whether the case was being handed over to the military,' replied Eleanor.

'Is that likely?'

'I hope not,' she said quietly. 'Now let's go and see what Dr Grenson's discovered.'

The anthropology department at Ryerson was housed in the basement of the university, presumably in an attempt to mitigate complaints about the quality of the deliveries and the general aroma that hung about it. Laurence was leaning into Rachel Gilbey, smiling and wafting his hand around expressively. Eleanor acknowledged her rising irritation and tamped it down. 'Miss Gilbey?' she queried.

Rachel shook hands with Eleanor. 'Come on through.'

The warmth, combined with the damp humus smell, made the large, dark room seem oppressive. Tannin-stained bones arranged on a huge table did nothing to lighten the atmosphere.

'Detectives!' trilled Grenson, yanking off a latex glove and rushing over to them.

'Perhaps you'd like to take us through what we have,' Eleanor suggested.

'Absolutely!' Grenson led them over to the table. 'There's a lot of data still to come in. DNA, palynology and soil analysis won't be ready for some days… or dare I venture to say, weeks?' He read their concerned expressions and continued, 'But *most* likely days, as everyone's aware of the urgency of the matter. So, here we have the right hand of a male, probably between his late twenties and early forties. It appears, if you look closely, to have been severed using either an axe or a machete in one single blow. Some of the preliminary results indicate that the hand belonged to someone of southern Asian origin.'

'An Afghan?'

'Feasible. I was going to suggest that, as some of the pollen extracted was *Papaver somniferum* and fennel, so it's not definitive but highly plausible.

'Now, with regard to my theory that the hand hadn't been down in the crawlspace for very long, I feel fairly certain that it had only been there for a few days at the very most, probably less, as the soil taken from Maple Drive doesn't appear in any depth, just surface adherents. It had to have been kept in a dry and mainly insect-free environment, due to the amount of tissue remaining. There's a missing phalanx, just here on the index finger, which looks to have been severed perimortem.'

Eleanor and Laurence stood outside and let the cold breeze clear their heads and lungs of formaldehyde and dust.

'You think we're going to find the finger bone in one of Eddie Myles' poop bags?' asked Laurence with distaste.

'I imagine so,' Eleanor replied. 'If this hand turns out to have been from some Afghan fighter, or heroin dealer, then the chances are we're going to have a battle on our hands to get hold of Myles' mission log, as his commanding officer implied all paperwork was covered by the Official Secrets Act. You need to run that past the DA.' She sighed deeply.

'Where next?' he asked.

'Let's go see what Forensics have uncovered.'

'What have you got?' asked Eleanor, peering through the glass window into the lab, where several technicians wearing full hazmat suits were working their way through Eddie Myles' faecal collection.

'What we've got is a guy with nasty eating habits. And I mean *nasty*,' Susan Cheung offered. 'We're trying to establish how long he'd been collecting his waste and our best guess is eighteen months.'

'Really? How'd he keep this stuff hidden? Or undetected?' questioned Laurence.

'These poop bags are really good,' said Susan. 'We called up the company that makes them and they're designed to be used on field missions where reducing your scent is crucial. The *only* dog that could detect the bag, when it was sealed, was a bloodhound!'

'So what's in the bags?' asked Eleanor.

'Apart from the obvious? Follow me.'

'We need to suit up?' asked Laurence.

'No, you're safe,' she said, leading them down the corridor into a suite of laboratories. 'This isn't all of it by any means.'

Sealed in a plastic container were at least twenty-five evidence bags, each tagged with a barcode and a typed lot number. Pulling on latex gloves from a nearby box, Susan opened the container and extracted the contents.

'These are the bones we've extracted so far.' She began to arrange the bags in an approximate date line. 'Each one is from the same poop bag, which we're assuming was passed at the same sitting, so to speak. We can divide the bags into three lots: urine, faeces comprising of non-human material – i.e. your average meat-and-two-veg dinner – and faeces comprising human material.'

'You've found viable DNA?' asked Eleanor.

'We've got DNA from most of the bones but that's going to take some time to process. From the urine bags there was nothing on the toxicology front, but it depends on how long any substances had been out of his system. Most antipsychotics break down in less than four weeks, and other illicit substances often take twenty-four to forty-eight hours.'

'So he had to have been consuming people here?' asked Laurence.

'Not necessarily,' mused Susan, 'The poop bags could have been brought back from overseas.'

'That's crazy. How the hell did he get them through security? Surely his bags would have been searched, or at least X-rayed?' said Eleanor.

Susan shrugged. 'Maybe the Air Force security regime is different. He was flown straight to Base Borden wasn't he, using military aircraft?'

'How many bones have we got?' asked Eleanor.

'Do you want the total, or the repeats?'

There was a pause before Laurence swore.

It was well into the afternoon by the time Eleanor arrived back at HQ. Entering the office, she was greeted by her ex-homicide partner Artie Morris, known to all as Mo, carrying a full pot of coffee and a bag of his wife's home bakes.

'Hey, Ellie. What news?' Mo asked, easing himself up from Eleanor's chair.

She waved for him to sit down again and poured two coffees. Mo, despite retiring following a massive heart attack three years earlier, worked for the department on an ad hoc basis when he was desperately needed, and when he couldn't stand being at home.

'Is Minnie letting you eat these?' asked Eleanor, helping herself to a large sugary treat.

'Nope,' responded Mo, pushing over the bag. 'She's worried that you guys are working on empty. Anyway, I tried to sneak one down, but this gastric band stops anything *I* want getting past,' he said, grimacing.

Eleanor nodded and tried not to let her appreciation of Minnie's cooking skills show.

'I see many layers of misery on your face. Wanna share?' he said, leaning back into the chair.

She shrugged. 'I've finished with psychiatric counselling.'

'Relief? Or you got more to say?' replied Mo.

She shook her head. 'No, glad it's out of the way.'

'But? I definitely hear a but,' said Mo, using his finger to mop up the scattered sugar.

'I feel—' Eleanor found herself unable to articulate exactly how she felt.

Mo licked his finger and raised an eyebrow.

'Relaxed. Maybe even indifferent.'

'Isn't relaxed a good thing?' Mo asked, searching for more sugary crumbs.

'Yes – maybe,' she said uncertainly. 'I don't feel any anger, or passion any more. It's as if—'

The door opened. Laurence, accompanied by Monster, entered.

'Hey, pup!' enthused Mo, throwing out his arms to welcome the dog.

Laurence examined the bake bag. 'I've just had a long and painful conversation with the DA and he feels we'll have to surrender the investigation to the military.'

'Why does Heidlmann think that?' asked Eleanor, astonished.

'They have jurisdiction. Simple as that!' He gestured a thumbs up to Mo after biting into one of Minnie's cakes.

Eleanor rubbed her forehead. 'Okay, you and Mo have to dig around this afternoon. Find something that will convince the DA that we should keep control over the case.'

'Where will you be?' asked Laurence.

CHAPTER FIVE

It took Eleanor considerably longer than the usual two-and-a-bit hours to drive to Milhaven due to high winds and persistent rain; not that this troubled her. She stopped at the first set of gates and, as she waited for the guard to check her credentials, she wondered why she'd decided to visit Toby again. Milhaven housed approximately 500 of Ontario's most dangerous prisoners, and its grey concrete exterior seemed to suck all the colour from the surrounding area, leaving a grey monotone. Eleanor had contributed several inmates to its interior but none with a higher kill score than Toby Adams.

Toby was brought into the interview room fifteen minutes after Eleanor's arrival. She noted that his girth had widened since his move to Milhaven and his pale, flabby features wore a less haunted air. She prepared herself for his uniquely challenging style of conversation. If she talked too much or exhibited too much movement, he tended to sulk and grow silent. She imagined it was because he liked to visualise her among his collection of dead and preserved 'family' members.

'Toby, you said that you had some important information for me?' she stated quietly.

'How are you today, Detective Raven?' he replied, focussing on the top of her head.

Eleanor sat in silence and waited.

'You seem relaxed and, dare I say, happier than our last meeting?'

'I've finished my therapy.' She watched Toby's face tighten with pleasure as he lapped up her revelation.

'I must say that you're looking well on it. Has your therapist expunged all of those nightmares and feelings of self-hatred you seemed so burdened with?'

'I'm sleeping well, Toby and with a clear conscience.'

Eleanor wondered why she revealed so much to him. She'd justified this exposure by convincing herself that it formed part of an exchange system between them. She gave Toby nuggets of personal information and he, in turn, had confessed to the murder and burial of several more missing women, who would have remained undiscovered if not for her candour.

'You left a message saying you had something important to tell me,' she reminded him.

Toby smiled and made himself more comfortable. 'I've been thinking long and hard about some of the wonderful women I have known over the years and suddenly realised that I haven't mentioned Clarrie Eddow. I haven't… Have I?'

Eleanor stared at him. 'No, I don't recall you mentioning her. How do you spell her surname?'

She listened and then jotted it down into her notebook.

'Toby, the last two names you gave me didn't check out as missing persons.'

Toby looked confused. 'Didn't they? Perhaps you didn't do a thorough search?'

'I am pretty thorough, Toby, as you know,' she replied calmly.

He gave a small shrug. 'I gave you clear instructions as to where I thought they were buried, but perhaps you misunderstood what I meant. Or—'

'Toby, these women don't or didn't exist. Either the names you gave me were false or you've run out of scenarios that will keep me interested.'

He narrowed his eyes and leaned into her, making the warden glance warningly at him. 'Perhaps that is a mutual concept,' he whispered, folding his arms and sitting back in the seat, his lips tightly pursed.

She smiled. 'I have something that might intrigue you.'

He focussed a little more intently on her.

'Why would you eat a part of another person, Toby?'

He raised an eyebrow. 'Which bit?'

Eleanor closed the space between them. 'Fingers, toes, maybe other parts.'

Toby squinted and then began to work his jaw. 'Were they cooked first?'

Eleanor suddenly felt a wave of repulsion and had to glance away from him for a few moments. She had been running scenarios past Toby for the past few sessions, in order, she explained to herself, to get an insight into the criminal mind. When she'd spoken about this to Seb Blackmore, he suggested that she was using Toby to look into the workings of her own mind.

'You find that disgusting,' he stated.

She nodded and looked at him. 'No, they weren't cooked.'

He shrugged and began to stare at his hands. 'I'm sure you weren't this squeamish before you started therapy.'

'Is there a historical precedent for this, Toby? Maybe something you'd come across when you worked at the museum?'

'It's not uncommon historically. A great many civilisations practised cannibalism. We staged a big Aztec and Mayan exhibition at the museum and you know what the public was most intrigued by?' He smirked. 'That they ate the hearts of the dead.'

'Why did they do that?' she asked.

'Some anthropologists feel that it's a way of boosting protein intake. If you don't get much meat, then don't waste any that comes your way. It's also a way of consuming a defeated warrior's strength… But I think that it was most likely a way of getting closer to God. Christians consume the body and blood of their God, don't they?'

'Not literally.'

Toby shrugged. 'Scripture states that unless you eat the flesh of the Son of God and drink his blood, you have no life in you. Maybe that's what your cannibal was doing: seeking life.' His small, pale eyes locked on to hers. 'Or redemption.'

Eleanor mulled this over, allowing a silence to spread between them. 'These aren't modern thought processes. Why else would he do this?'

'I need to think about this,' said Toby vaguely, beginning to drift into his own universe.

She stood up, nodded to the warden and knocked on the door to signal her intention to leave. 'Where can I find Clarrie Eddow?' she asked.

'How can you find what doesn't exist for you?' Toby turned to the warden, who led him through the opposite door and towards his cell.

Eleanor was becoming increasing irritated at having wasted a whole morning pursuing the unreliable thoughts of Toby Adams. The traffic was slowing and she was forced to jump lanes to make any progress. Snatching her phone, she corrected her initial impulse to call Mo and dialled Laurence. 'Any news from the DA?' she snapped.

'Good afternoon to you too!'

Eleanor took a deep breath. 'Sorry. Have you any news?'

'The DA is preparing a petition to allow us access to military files but he's not hopeful. If we want the case to stay in the civilian sector we need to prove that Myles wasn't just scoffing casualties of war. We need a documented suspicion that he preyed on civilians.'

'His wife was a civilian!'

'Mo and I are going through the files to see if there are any recorded homicides that could be linked to possible cannibalistic activity. It doesn't need to be a direct link to Myles, just enough of a concern to overrule the OSA and allow us access to his history.'

Eleanor sighed. 'Anything so far?'

'Early days… Was it useful?'

'Seeing Toby? I'm not sure. He gave me another name. I'm pretty sure he's stringing me along to keep the attention going, like you and Timms said.'

'Give me the name and I'll run it,' Laurence replied.

'Hang on…' Eleanor reached for her notebook but seeing a long line of slowing trucks, checked her rear view and squeezed into the overtaking lane, keeping her eyes on the road. 'Cathy Meadow,' she replied from memory.

'Okay, got it! Drive safe.'

*

'Ellie on her way back?' asked Mo as he took off his glasses and closed the laptop.

'Uh-huh.' Laurence glanced over at him. 'You're tired – why don't you go and have a coffee? Maybe you could combine it with taking Monster out for a pee?'

'You betcha,' said Mo, getting stiffly to his feet.

'Find anything?'

'Some unresolved cases, but nothing in the past five years that would convince anyone with an ounce of legal experience that it's the same MO.'

Laurence leaned back, folded his arms behind his head and raised both eyebrows. 'Go on – try me!'

'Okay,' sighed Mo, opening his notebook and reading. 'May 2011, Louisa Bakersfield, nineteen, prostitute found by the rail track, missing her teeth and fingertips. Case unsolved.'

'That's promising,' stated Laurence.

'Hmm, unfortunately CSI had been televised the evening before, showing a woman who remained unidentified for the same reason. And Eddie Myles was serving in Afghanistan at the time.'

'So unlikely, but we don't want to rule it out. Next?'

Mo turned the page. 'August 2012, Mai Tang, twenty-one, Chinese national studying at Ryerson, found in state of advanced decomp, missing her heart and uterus.'

'Ooh, interesting.' Laurence ran through his notes, jabbing a finger against an entry in his own notepad. 'Eddie Myles was here during August 2012. That's workable – isn't it?'

Mo looked unconvinced. 'No missing digits, only the two organs, which were unfound, as was her Chinese boyfriend who'd mysteriously cleared off back to Shandong where he managed to avoid extradition to Canada but not the wrath of his girlfriend's family.'

Mo pulled on his coat and picked up Monster's lead. 'You're not going to convince anyone that Myles could have been implicated in Mai's death.'

'Give me another,' pleaded Laurence.

'Last one: me and the pup need a break.' Mo consulted his pad, pausing before reading it out.

'Stella Tapley, twenty-eight, discovered in an underpass, asphyxiated, missing her tongue and eyes.'

'Perfect, hang on, when?'

'May 2011, but it's not going to work—'

'It will! Eddie Myles was here in Toronto on compassionate leave. All systems are go!'

'It *won't* work because we have a confession.'

Laurence squinted at him. 'So someone's serving time for the murder?'

Mo slumped back down into the chair. 'I didn't say that.' He rubbed Monster's head and chewed his bottom lip thoughtfully. 'Roma Joe Greene, serving two life sentences, confessed.'

'It didn't go to trial?' asked Laurence.

Mo shook his head. 'We'd already got him for two other murders and the DA didn't want to tie up resources in another investigation. He was happy with the confession. So we let it go.'

'We?' asked Laurence. 'In 2011, you were partnered with Eleanor, weren't you?'

Mo stood up and adjusted Monster's collar. 'I was, but not for this. I was asked to go help out the Hamilton PS.'

'There's a story, Mo,' said Laurence.

'There is!' snapped Mo. 'But I need a coffee before I trawl through that crap again!'

Laurence grabbed his coat. 'I'm buying.'

*

Sergeant Andy Harrison was exhausted. He was losing his lifelong battle with dyspepsia and felt himself sinking into a deep depression. Sonny Maitland had joined Toronto PS the same year as him and they'd shared golfing trolleys and raised glasses together for family births, deaths and marriages for the past twenty-three years. They'd been friends for as long as he could remember and Harrison wasn't sure whether Sonny's noble sacrifice had meant anything in the grand scheme of things.

He opened his second pack of antacids for the day and tried to focus on what the woman standing at the front desk was talking about.

'Shall I wait here then?' she asked with a puzzled expression.

'I'm sorry—' said Harrison, rubbing his chest and stifling a belch. 'Who are you waiting for again?'

'Are you alright?' she asked. 'Shall I get you a glass of water?'

He smiled. 'No, ma'am, but thank you for asking – I'm a little upset.'

The woman smiled sympathetically. 'I understand.'

'You wanted to speak to a detective? Mrs...?'

'I'd like to speak to a detective concerning the awful smell coming from the basement. I've contacted the landlord and he, as usual, is indifferent and so I came straight here.'

'I'm a little lost. Why do you need a detective, Mrs...?'

'It's *Miss* Veronica Sizemore,' she answered tartly. 'I need a detective because the smell is that of decomposition.'

'Detective Whitefoot!' Harrison called, seeing him and Mo heading down the stairs. 'Perhaps you'd like to come and help Miss Sizemore here?'

*

Veronica Sizemore lived in a lacklustre area of Leslieville. The apartment complex was low-rise, neglected and lacking any qualities that might herald future gentrification. Mo stared at the building and then at Monster. 'I'll look after Monster, while you go bag the dead raccoon,' he said, closing his eyes.

Laurence smiled. 'Okay, boss.'

Veronica, who was making her own way home in an ancient 900cc Honda, hadn't yet arrived. Sighing, Laurence zipped up his coat and grabbed his torch and a large plastic evidence bag. He followed the path round to the back of the building, where he was surprised to encounter a fairly palpable odour. He checked behind the dumpsters, which were whiffy but not the source of the distinctive smell. He needed a better nose.

Monster picked up the scent immediately and began to yank Laurence closer towards the back of the building. After a brief distraction, the dog began to bark and scratch at a small steel utility door, positioned to the right of a decrepit iron fire escape.

'What've you found, buddy?' asked Laurence, inhaling what was now the unmistakable stench of decomposition.

'Hey!' shouted an angry voice.

Peering at the open window above his head, Laurence saw a man clad in a grubby dressing gown. 'What the hell's—? Hey, I know you!' bellowed the voice over Monster's persistent barking. The window slammed shut.

'Fabulous,' muttered Laurence.

It took the man less than five minutes to make his way downstairs and catch up to Laurence.

Having stopped only to slip on some shoes, Claddis McAvoy, senior writer for the *Toronto Sun*, stood in his pyjamas and pointed a finger. 'De*tective* Whitefoot!' he intoned, grinning. 'Now, to what do I owe the pleasure?'

'He's investigating the smell,' said Veronica, who had finally arrived on the scene.

'You called in Homicide to locate a dead raccoon?' replied Claddis, with some disbelief.

'It's not a raccoon, it's a body! A human body!' retaliated Veronica, who had obviously spent some time trying to convince neighbours of her theory.

'Oh my God!' exclaimed Claddis with frustration. 'It's a bloody squirrel or something.

'Hey!' he said, shifting tone. 'Raven's not with you, is she? I've still got an active restraining order out on her. She's not allowed within 500 feet of my person,' he continued, peering around nervously.

'Where's the caretaker?' Laurence yelled over Monster's persistent bark.

'Good bloody question,' responded Claddis.

Having rattled the locked door unproductively, Laurence kicked it twice in a moment of supreme irritation and felt some measure of relief as it flew open. The smell hit them like slap.

'*Jesus!*' gasped Claddis, pulling his sleeve over his nose.

Monster, on the trail of something good, descended into the gloom of what looked like an old boiler room and began rooting around. Laurence peered into the space, shining his torchlight into the corners, occasionally illuminating Monster's back.

'What can you see?' carped Veronica.

Refusing to succumb to the smell, Laurence stepped into the unlit space and looked around. The floor was littered with pupal casings and it took him several seconds to locate the source of their meal. Hanging from the ceiling were the bodies of at least six dogs. Each was hanging from a rope, which was wrapped around its neck, the end secured around an old metal outlet pipe.

Veronica stared at the dogs, slowly turned and walked away. Claddis McAvoy took her place. 'What the hell! That's *horrible*!'

CHAPTER SIX

A new and ominous sound woke Eleanor before sunrise. An unproductive grinding was emanating from the ancient boiler her landlord had promised to replace several months ago and the subsequent chill in her apartment implied he'd left it too late.

Yanking on a jumper she went to investigate. The boiler was cold to the touch and the sound seemed to be coming from inside, possibly the pump. Sighing, she grabbed the landline and dialled, while peering into the mechanism. 'Hey, Mo, what do you know about boilers?'

'It's Laurence,' replied the voice. 'You dialled the wrong partner,' he said, with a hint of old jealousy.

She paused, confused and then rallied. 'I *thought* I'd called the only guy I knew who understood boilers.'

'Boilers?'

'It's in its death throes. Ideas?'

'Give me twenty,' he replied and disconnected.

She looked at her phone, surprised to find that Laurence's mobile number had replaced Mo's in her head.

Laurence arrived, along with Monster and a well-stocked toolbox, and examined the boiler. She watched with interest as he inserted pliers into the mechanism and carefully withdrew, cleaned and examined small, mysterious pieces of metal. Monster watched with equal absorption. 'Why'd you give up medicine?' she asked.

Laurence smiled. 'I guess I thought detection would be different, more exciting. I honestly don't know anymore. Did you ever doubt that policing was your vocation?'

Eleanor didn't need to pause before answering, but did so out of sensitivity to him. 'No.'

He nodded and she felt a need to qualify the statement. 'There was never a question that I should look at any other career.'

He smiled. 'I suspected as much.'

He grunted as he extracted a final piece of machinery. 'And here's the culprit. It's a broken thermocouple, which is why the pilot light's gone out. We may be able to order one today.'

Before she could express gratitude, her phone rang.

'Yes, sir,' Eleanor said with as much enthusiasm as she could muster for a conversation with her boss.

'Where the hell are you?' snapped Marty voice. 'We had a meeting arranged and *I'm* here!'

'On my way in now.'

'On my way as in running up the main stairs?' he snapped.

'As we speak!' replied Eleanor.

'*Really?*' bellowed Marty Samuelson, stabbing his watch with his index finger. 'What the hell sort of timescale are you working from?' He sat down heavily, pointing to the chair opposite. 'Don't mess around with my accommodating nature, Raven,' he growled, rubbing his tense neck muscles.

'No, sir,' she replied, in a tone she hoped sounded contrite.

Marty raised an eyebrow. 'Whitefoot has talked me through the contents of Lieutenant Myles' loft and informs me that there's a strong possibility he managed to get the hand back from overseas in his luggage. However, according to the DA, who's been on the phone since breakfast, that's not going to pass muster with the judge. The only grounds for shifting this into a civilian court is to find that one of his snacks was local.' He sighed and readjusted his tie. 'Though between you, me and the Chief, if no link was found it wouldn't spoil my Sunday.'

Reading Eleanor's expression, he continued, 'That's not to say that I want to let the military get away with brushing this under the carpet.'

'Two officers and a civilian deserve better than that,' she said firmly.

He nodded his approval but his expression hardened as he broached the next topic. 'Why have I been recommended that you remain on psych's books for another twelve weeks? You hooked on confession?'

Eleanor looked at him with disbelief.

Marty held up a hand. 'Didn't think so. But I guess I don't have to remind you that anything you're working on while you're receiving counselling for PTSD will be compromised in court, and you work on high-profile cases.'

'Dr Blackmore told me that I'd completed the programme and wouldn't need—'

Marty leaned forward and lowered his voice. 'I don't give a damn what he's saying to you. I have been informed, in writing, that you have not shown sufficient evidence of having been' – he mimed air-quotes – '*de-traumatised*. If you can't get released, Raven, I'm going to have to shift you to patrol, do you understand?'

She nodded tightly.

He spoke slowly, emphasising each word. '*Say* what they *need* to hear.' He waited, letting it sink in.

'Right, what's happening here?' He reached for a piece of paper and read the heading. 'Cathy Meadow?'

'She's another Toby Adams fantasy. Johnson checked and couldn't find anything on a missing woman of that name.'

Eleanor moved to stand up but Marty made a tamping motion with his hand. She didn't like the expression on his face.

'I had a visitor yesterday.'

She raised an eyebrow and waited.

'From Internal Affairs and he wanted to speak to you.'

'What about?' she asked flatly.

'He wouldn't say, which failed to endear him to me. So, after getting rid of him, I made a couple of calls. He's a bonding officer.' Marty leaned towards her, examining her face carefully. 'You know what they're responsible for?'

She nodded unenthusiastically. 'They get to decide whether you're fit to serve and protect.'

'Yes, they do, Raven, and if they say an officer is too fragile, too mentally ill-equipped, or too damned fat that they can't chase a perp for at least 500 yards, then that officer is removed from active duty and placed in an office dealing with irate calls from our beloved public. So what have you said to your counsellor that has been picked up by the bondsman and resulted in him wanting to interview you?'

Eleanor looked at him blankly.

'Well, due to the perilous nature of your mental health, I've told Timms to make himself au fait with your caseload.'

'*Au fait* or in charge?' she asked angrily.

'At the moment, *au fait*. Get yourself cleared,' said Marty.

A voicemail message informed Eleanor that Laurence, Mo and Timms were waiting for her in Timms' office. She paused before heading over, pouring herself a large cup of coffee from the shared kitchen and trying to analyse what exactly she'd said to Seb Blackmore that could have resulted in her not being released from the compulsory counselling list. Why was the bondsman so keen to meet up with her? She had opened up to Seb and, to a certain degree, she trusted him. So why was he lying about having recommended her release? Nothing was adding up.

*

Timms' office was blisteringly hot and barely large enough to fit the assembled team. Squeezing past Mo, Eleanor slid into the spare seat next to Timms. Laurence stood next to an easel, which had a large pad of paper clipped to it.

'You all coffee'd up?' asked Timms.

Eleanor gave a clipped nod.

'Okay,' began Laurence. 'This is the intel so far. Lieutenant Eddie Myles had been receiving counselling and medication after three tours of Afghanistan, where he was showing the early signs of mental instability. On his last tour he'd been kept on to train local police in Afghanistan but was flown home after several of his buddies were gunned down by one of the aforementioned Afghan police officers. He'd been kept off active duty for the past twelve months while they tried to fix him. No one really knew what to do with the sorry bastard, and when his wife asked for more help, the military didn't offer any, so, as we've witnessed, Myles took matters into his own hands.'

Timms nodded. 'What was he doing for the twelve months he was back on the base?'

Laurence pushed a page over to him. 'His time was divided between training and soul-searching with his psychiatrist.'

Timms glanced at the piece of paper. 'This is a list of dates. Have we got the name of his psychiatrist?'

'Nope, that's classified, as are his medical notes,' said Laurence.

'How do we *de*classify them?' asked Timms.

'We can't, *unless* we can secure a civilian investigation,' answered Laurence, glancing at Mo. 'We've found a similar unsolved case, involving the removal of body parts, but we have a confession.'

'Roma Joe Greene: name ring any bells?' Mo asked.

'Is that the guy who murdered the prostitutes down in Hamilton?' said Eleanor.

'That's him.'

'Give us the headlines,' said Timms.

'Hamilton police had three dead working girls within the space of six months. All three were found in underpasses, and all three had their eyes and tongues removed. We had nothing. No fingerprints, no semen, nothing: just three dead girls and no leads. I was called in to goose it up a bit just after Stella Tapley was found.'

'How'd you catch Roma Joe?' asked Timms.

'We didn't. He walked in to the station and confessed. Took a polygraph and passed, so he definitely *believed* he'd killed them.'

'You doubt he did?'

Mo held up his hands and shook his head. 'We searched his trailer and found the first two women's DNA in there, along with the missing body parts. Nothing from Stella Tapley, but Roma Joe said he'd done it and that was good enough for Hamilton PS and the DA. But he was never charged with Stella's murder. The DA felt it was safer to charge him for the first two girls, which would ensure he'd stay in for the duration.'

'But you're not convinced?' asked Timms.

'I dunno,' said Mo, sighing. 'There were issues with evidence gathering, and the chain of custody was broken. It'd never hold up to close scrutiny, so Hamilton cut their losses and based their case on the confession and polygraph. Roma Joe was a piece of work. Canada's a safer place for having that asshole behind bars... But did he kill Stella Tapley? I really don't know. At the time I suspected a copycat.'

There was a pause as everyone mulled over the problem.

'You think the DA will allow us to use Stella Tapley as a possible link to Eddie Myles?'

Mo shrugged. 'Who the hell knows? It depends on how desperate he is to have this case in civilian hands.'

There was a short, brisk knock at the door, which Timms waved his hand for them to ignore. 'How about you go see Roma Joe Greene, test the waters so to speak?' he suggested.

'I can do. Not sure what we'll get out of him though,' said Mo.

'Have a chat. If you've *any* cause to doubt his confession, run it up the DA's flagpole. In the meantime, keep looking through the unsolveds for any other likely links.'

There was a second knock on the office door. 'Yes!' bellowed Timms.

When there was no response, he yanked open the door to reveal Dr Ruby Delaware, a small, plump woman with an alarming dedication to pink floral clothing. She let out a yelp and stepped back in surprise.

'Sorry! I thought you were someone else,' said Timms more quietly.

Ruby looked past him at Eleanor. 'May I have a word?'

'Of course – come in,' Eleanor replied, standing up and ushering her into the room. Ruby looked nervously at Timms before taking a place at the table.

'Coffee, Doc?' asked Timms.

'No, thank you. This may not be an appropriate time but I have a few ideas about the case you're working.' She looked expectantly at Timms, hoping he'd take the hint and leave as she placed a folder in front of her.

'We're all interested in any thoughts you've got on this,' said Timms expansively.

'Really?' she asked, unconvinced.

'*Really*,' said Timms.

Eyeing him with trepidation, she began. 'Thank you for sending me the case notes; it made for interesting reading. *Very* interesting. I've never had an opportunity to work on a case of cannibalism before.'

'Glad we could expand your repertoire,' said Timms tartly.

Ruby opened her mouth to respond and then, thinking better of it, made a small moue of irritation and placed her notebook in front of her. 'Are matters still as they were yesterday, regarding the origins of the human materials Lieutenant Myles had consumed?'

'So far, Forensics haven't managed to create either a timeline that would place him in Canada during the consumption, or a DNA profile. So until that happens we have to assume that he ate parts of those he killed, whilst serving overseas,' stated Eleanor, 'and brought the poop-filled bags back to base with him. Angela Myles' nipples were post-mortem injuries.'

'I'll run through my thoughts on that first. Consuming parts of warriors killed in times of war is considered by social anthropologists to be a way of maximising revenge against the enemy. Eating the heart is a way of combining their strength with yours. Whereas eating the brain is a way to absorb their cunning. I imagine the relevance of the fingertip consumed was that it belonged to the trigger finger – maybe Myles saw it as a way of improving his aim.'

Timms sighed loudly and reached for his pastry.

'I understand there was a psychologically traumatic incident while Myles served in Afghanistan.'

Eleanor nodded slowly.

'It would be interesting to know why no markers for his predilection were picked up earlier,' Ruby mused. 'Biting off and swallowing his wife's nipples is the action of a man who considers himself a proprietor. He owned his wife: therefore, if he couldn't have her, no one else could. Swallowing body parts and not cooking them first – which, I would claim, signifies an effort to hide evidence – is a way of *possessing* those he kills. They are only able to live through him. It's referred to as *incorporation*.'

'Well thank God there's a bloody name for it!' snapped Mo, instantly regretting his outburst when everyone turned to look at him. 'Sorry…'

'You okay, Mo?' asked Eleanor with concern.

He smiled and shook his head. 'Dunno. Guess it's been a shitty couple of days. Losing Millie and Sonny was a blow – and seeing those dogs!' Mo was beginning to shake.

Eleanor put an arm round him. 'You're doing too much, Mo. Maybe we should get you home for a while?'

'No, I'm good. I just needed…' he began.

'What dogs?' asked Ruby carefully.

'We were called out to investigate a smell and it turns out that someone had hanged six dogs in an old boiler room,' said Laurence quietly.

'Were they dead before they were hung up?' Ruby asked.

'Thanks, Doc,' said Timms heavily.

Laurence shook his head.

'That,' said Ruby Delaware, placing her materials back in her bag, 'is something that needs investigating.'

'A couple of patrol guys are making enquiries,' said Laurence.

'I would suggest that Homicide investigate it as a matter of some urgency.'

Ruby paused, registering Timms' expression, 'Whoever did that will be moving on to people shortly,' she stated. 'Anyway, those are my thoughts so far. I'm happy to carry on if you need me to.'

'Doc, we'll want you 24/7 on this one,' said Timms.

Ruby looked askance, unsure as to whether there was a grain of truth in what he'd said. Gathering her belongings and handing a copy of her notes to Eleanor, she nodded curtly and, with tightly set lips, left the room.

'You think she's right?' Timms asked Eleanor quietly.

'I'd certainly bear it in mind,' she replied.

Timms was in the process of steering Mo in the direction of the canteen when he cleared his throat. 'By the way, Whitefoot, Margie Beech came looking for you and Monster. Apparently, her working police dog Chance is carrying a litter and she's looking to charge you for the vet fees, which are running into the thousands, but I've improved your survival chances.'

'Oh god! How?' moaned Laurence.

Timms smirked. 'By offering to get the pups bought and housed. After all, Monster is a pedigree "Distinguished Conduct Award" holder and there's a lot of officers that would happily pay well for that privilege.'

Laurence was silent for a moment or two before answering. 'How much are you hoping to get for them?'

'Fifteen hundred bucks a pup. Going rate for police dogs.' Timms opened the door, adding, 'So I'll need his Kennel Club certificate by the end of the week.'

'How many have you sold?' asked Laurence weakly.

'Four, and I've drummed up a *lot* of interest in the others.' He smiled as he walked out with Mo. 'Might have to run it as a lottery.'

Laurence pursed his lips.

'What's the problem? Sounds like a good idea,' said Eleanor.

'Monster's not Kennel Club. He's not pedigree or even close – we picked him up from a shelter.'

'Wow. That is a problem,' she added helpfully.

CHAPTER SEVEN

The boy lay on his bed and listened carefully to the sounds coming from the downstairs room. The man's voice, which was loud, was making a sort of groaning sound. He was familiar with the depth and meaning of the sound. It meant pain and fear. His doctor had told him that learning to understand the emotions behind sounds was a good thing, as knowledge gave him power.

People and animals tended to behave in the same way, he'd discovered. If you threatened them, they would become defensive and threatening back. Or, and this was more interesting to him, they would panic and take on passive responses. Why, he considered, would a living being not fight back?

He'd only known one creature who ever fought back and his daily reminder of this horror filled him with hatred. He knew that if any being threatened him with sound or expression, he would act with aggression. That's what his mother called it, what his old school had called it and now what the doctor called it. *Aggression.*

It had a predictable pattern, which he liked. First his hands would feel clammy and his throat feel constricted, like an irritation that couldn't be located or soothed. Then, if he wasn't distracted, the sense of anger would wash through him like a red tide. Every movement he made could be internally recorded and played back repeatedly, as if he were watching from another room. How did time become so different for him? It was, according to scientists, a constant. *Always*, time and action were the same.

He liked to watch the movement of the clock in his room. It made a dull tick as the second hand moved in sixty measured jerks around the perfect circle. It was a constant.

The sound stopped, which meant that his mother had finished what she was doing with the man. He stood upright, waited till his head cleared, and then pulled on a jumper, coat and gloves and made his way out of the room. He passed his mother's room and walked into the hallway where his boots were, carefully extracting the two balled-up pieces of newspaper, which had to be in them if his feet weren't. This prevented the boots from changing. He hated change. When things became different, he'd feel a sickness inside the pit of his stomach, so he took care not to let anything around him alter in any way.

He closed the door and after pulling on it three times to ensure it was shut, he felt able to move away from the house and into the darkness. He rarely ventured out in the daylight. People were able to see him clearly when the sun was out and what he registered on their faces was disgust. He did not experience that particular emotion, but he had been shown photographs by his doctor of people *feeling* it and he knew that it was bad. It meant that people didn't like or feel comfortable with him. Only his mother and the doctor felt comfortable with him.

The boy didn't like people using his name. It was a way for them to have power over him, so he ignored its existence. He had tuned it out of his brain and was slowly erasing it from his memory. He liked that he was able to do this, to just rub out a thought that was not of use, or made him feel unpleasant.

The boy arrived at the secret place and knew instantly that something wasn't right. He had a queasy sensation in his stomach. Something had changed. The door to the boiler room was always locked. He had the key, so no one else could go in. But the door had been shoved and broken in some way.

He stared at the new padlock device that had been attached to the door. The boy was confused as to how and why it had appeared but it wasn't a problem for him. He always carried several useful items in the pocket of his coat.

Selecting the crosshead screwdriver, he easily removed the four screws attaching the device to the architrave. The door swung open. He inhaled before entering the darkness but something was missing: the sweetness had gone.

Pulling the door closed behind him and turning on his torch, he could see that his animals were gone. He didn't understand. They couldn't have moved themselves, so why would they have gone? He felt unpleasant. The animals were his, and the only way they could have been moved was if another animal had taken them. Something, or someone, had taken what belonged to him and that was making him feel aggressive.

He was distracted by a voice. It was a woman; he was pretty sure of that. He listened: she sounded angry.

'Who's in there?' she said. 'I know you're in there and I'm going to call the police.'

The boy didn't like the police. They had put him in a room on his own and asked lots of questions. When he chose not to answer them, they'd sent him to see the doctor. *He'd* understood why he didn't answer questions.

The woman was moving closer to the door and making more noise. It made his ears ache and he could feel his hands getting clammy.

'Get out of there!' she shrieked. 'I'm calling the police, if you don't…'

Her voice trailed off as she saw the boy and, reacting to him as everyone did, her face twisted into the expression of disgust.

He felt the itch and, as he began to punch her face with his fists, he felt a calmness settling on his troubled mind.

His fists grew slippery as he continued hitting, sliding away from her face, losing momentum. She was making little grunts now, like the dogs did when he'd hanged them from the ceiling in his secret place. His animals were gone but the room would still be a special place for him because he had her now.

He struggled to lift her off the ground because she was heavy and unhelpful. So, grabbing her by the feet, he pulled her through the doorway and down the little flight of steps, enjoying the wet banging sound as her head bounced from step to step. Before he could do anything else, he needed to close the door.

This was *his* secret place.

*

Laurence sat in his car and rested his head against the steering wheel. He'd read the letter sent by Mags' solicitors several times but nothing was going in. He wasn't sure why he felt so deflated by the request to either buy out her half of the mortgage or sell the apartment, or why her sudden desire to have Monster back filled him with panic – after all, the asshole was providing half of Ontario with genetically modified versions of himself. It wasn't as if he couldn't start afresh with a new puppy. It just felt as though starting afresh was all he ever did. He didn't get on with medicine, so he moved to law enforcement. Didn't get on with Mags, so here he was, starting again, *and* he'd just got the damned dog trained.

He balled the letter and flung it into the back of the car, grabbed his coat and headed towards the forensics lab.

'What's the matter?' asked Susan Cheung as Laurence walked into the office.

Laurence smiled. 'Life.'

'Ah,' replied Susan sagely.

'What news?'

'The DNA analysis on the bones won't be completed for another week, but what I can tell you is that most of the plant materials taken from the poop is of North American extraction.'

'That's our first evidence that Eddie Myles could have been in Toronto when the cannibalism took place,' said Laurence.

Susan shrugged. 'I've checked with Base Borden and they make every effort to supply their guys with familiar home food while they're serving overseas.'

'It's a start and we're clutching at straws here,' said Laurence.

'Maybe it's a sign.'

'What sort of sign?' he asked.

'For you to leave it to the military,' Susan suggested carefully.

'That's not an option,' replied Laurence firmly.

As he swung his car into the traffic, Laurence called Mo. 'Hey, buddy, fancy that little trip to see Roma Joe?'

He heard Mo sigh. 'Yeah, guess so.'

*

Roma Joe Greene, despite being just shy of his fifties, walked with the exaggerated swagger usually associated with teenage gang members. His sloping shoulders and narrow features gave him the appearance of a weasel. For a moment or two, Roma Joe seemed to be struggling to place Mo and leaned across the table to study him. 'I know you,' he said slowly. His eyes narrowed, as the mental effort took its toll.

'Detective Artie Morris,' said Mo helpfully. 'I arrested you.'

'You did!' replied Roma Joe, slapping the table. 'I never forget a face!'

'You're looking well. Prison life suiting you?' asked Mo.

Suddenly, Roma Joe looked uncertain, as if a nagging doubt had entered his conscience. 'Can't complain.'

Mo let a silence settle and was curious to see a line of sweat appear above Roma Joe's lip.

'Whatd'ya want?' he asked. 'And who's he?'

'This is Detective Laurence Whitefoot. He'd like to ask you a few questions concerning the murder of Stella Tapley.'

Roma Joe began to fidget. 'Who sent you?'

Laurence looked at him quizzically. 'Who do you think?' He raised his eyebrows.

For a moment Roma Joe looked around nervously, as if expecting someone else to have been secreted in the small, brightly lit prison interview suite. Laurence rocked back on his chair and assessed the prisoner. 'Why'd you confess to killing Stella?'

'Whatd'ya mean?' he asked suspiciously.

Laurence selected three photographs from the folder he'd brought with him and placed them in front of Roma Joe. The first two showed the prostitutes he was convicted of killing. Roma Joe squinted and then nodded familiarly.

'You confessed to killing these two women but why Stella Tapley?'

He pushed forward a photograph of Stella. Her eyes were unfocussed, and the police card with her arrest number and name drooped in her bony hands. She looked a picture of misery.

'She'd never been in your trailer and there was nothing to link you to her, so why'd you confess to killing her?'

Roma Joe pushed the photograph back across the table towards Laurence, crossing his arms defensively. 'I'm not saying nothing,' he stated.

'It's certainly your MO,' said Mo. 'Three working girls all strangled, all found in underpasses within ten kilometres of each other and all missing body parts.'

Roma Joe shook his head and tightened his body language.

'Why take their eyes and tongues?' asked Laurence.

Roma Joe leaned towards them, lowering his voice. 'They said what they shouldn't and looked in too deep.'

'What did they see' – Laurence mimicked his body language and tone – 'when they looked too deep?'

For the briefest of moments, a look of incomprehension flitted across Roma Joe's features. It only lasted for a second before he recovered. 'They saw the cold inside.'

He shifted his gaze to the far corner of the room and it seemed unlikely that any more information would be forthcoming.

'What cold?' asked Laurence, bringing up the volume. 'What was the cold?'

Roma Joe stood up and headed over to the door. 'I ain't got any more to say,' he said decisively, but before he was led out by the guard, he turned to them. 'I keep asking them to see *my* shrink. The one they give me isn't helping. Can you sort that out for me?' he pleaded.

Mo looked at him. 'You don't get to pick and choose in here,' he snapped.

Roma Joe punched himself viciously in the side of the temple: a dull thump echo around the room. Startled, Laurence and Mo gave him their full attention.

'I *need* to see *my* shrink. He *knows* me.'

'Ok*aay*,' said Laurence, nonplussed. 'We'll see what we can do.'

He nodded and let the guard lead him out.

Laurence turned to Mo. 'What the hell did he mean?'

Mo shrugged. 'Not a clue. That's what he was like when he walked in and confessed. Talking rubbish. The only sense we could make of his ramblings was that he'd killed the women.'

*

Eleanor gazed at the phalanx of trucks moving slowly in front of her and sighed. She'd been irritated beyond measure to discover that the name she'd given Laurence to check on the MISPER website had been wrong. So, instead of spending the morning running through the materials they'd accrued so far, as she'd promised, she was breathing in diesel fumes and trundling along in third gear to talk to Toby Adams again. She dialled Laurence and began her explanation.

'What the hell are you going back there for?' asked Laurence, irritated. 'I thought that—'

'Apparently I was wrong,' snapped Eleanor.

'Johnson and I ran that name through MISPER along with several spelling variants and there was *nothing*.'

'*Because* the name wasn't Cathy Meadow; it was Clarrie Eddow!' she snapped. 'Johnson got a hit late yesterday afternoon and let Samuelson know before clocking off,' she sighed.

'How the hell did you get the names mixed up?' asked Laurence.

Eleanor was about to fling a tart response back, but stopped. 'I don't know. I guess I was tired.'

'When are you back?' he asked.

'Afternoon. You?'

'Mo and I are running through the Stella Tapley case to see if there's enough doubt in Roma Joe Greene's confession to allow us to charge Eddie Myles.'

'Any news on the DNA?'

'Another week,' he replied.

She disconnected just as a message, reminding her that she had an appointment today with the psych team, flashed across the Bluetooth display on the dashboard. Why had she made such an inexcusably simple mistake? What was wrong with her?

Eleanor sat in the interview room and waited. Toby Adams was being mulishly evasive about Clarrie Eddow and refusing to offer up likely burial sites. He was lying, but about what Eleanor wasn't entirely sure.

'Toby, you were eager to share your thoughts about Clarrie last time I visited. You wanted me to find her and, I'm assuming, to let you know how she… appears after all these years.'

Toby shrugged and looked away.

'Tell me a little about her. Where did you two meet?'

Eleanor was becoming aware of a deep-seated anger roiling inside her – a state of mind that she'd worked hard, over the past few months, to quash. She closed her eyes and listened to her breathing, a technique she'd acquired during her therapy sessions. She exhaled slowly and saw Toby staring at her curiously as she opened her eyes.

'You seem a little sad, Detective,' he said cautiously.

She smiled at his inability to read people. 'Pressure at work. It would help if I could locate Clarrie.'

Toby bit his lip. 'Do you have a photograph of her?' he asked.

Eleanor reached into her bag, extracted the photocopy and slid it towards him. He studied it for a moment or two, running his finger across the image, lingering on the woman's face and chest.

'She's so beautiful,' he said. 'I first met Clarrie in 2010. It was such a warm evening and she was standing near the old bandstand. The one they demolished over at the park off Spadina. I seem to recall she was painting the benches…'

Eleanor interrupted. 'That was Giselle.'

'No, it was Clarrie I met in the park. I remember it well,' replied Toby, leaning back into his seat. 'She may not have been painting the benches, but she was definitely part of the same rehabilitation programme for fallen women.'

'You met *Giselle*, a transgender prostitute, in 2012, enticed her back to your house, locked her in a cage, murdered her and then preserved her body using a plastination technique. When she began to decay you buried her in the Westex Landfill, where she was subsequently found by one of the site workers.'

She let this sink in before trying a less confrontational approach. 'Okay, so you met Clarrie in the park. How did you persuade her to come back with you?' asked Eleanor, disregarding Toby's expression.

'It was a meeting of minds,' he said pompously.

'This is nonsense. You're lying, Toby. I don't believe you ever met this woman,' she hissed.

'Then why are you showing me this photograph and asking me about her?' he said slowly.

There was a tense silence. Eleanor knew he was about to clam up and she needed to manage the interview more skilfully. 'I'm sorry, Toby. It's been a very difficult week for me and I'm a little on edge. No doubt you had similar days when you worked at the museum?'

Toby needed a few moments to reconnect with her. 'Absolutely. Every day was fraught with little battles and unpleasantries. My colleagues lacked empathy.'

Eleanor smiled sympathetically. 'So you met Clarrie at the park, near your home, in the same place that you met Giselle. Is there any chance that you could have been mistaken about that? Confused the two women? They are both beautiful women, Toby, perhaps—'

'I am *certain* that we met there. Our meeting is the reason I frequented the park and was fortunate enough to meet Giselle there.' He folded his arms defiantly.

Eleanor was losing patience. 'Where did you bury her?'

Toby gritted his teeth and looked away.

'Tell me where she is or this is the last time I'll visit you, and when I'm gone, who will there be who understands your vision, Toby?' She lowered her voice so that he had to work to follow what she said. 'No one other than myself saw your family before you destroyed them. No one can share your reminiscences. The doctors, wardens and officers who speak to you from now on only have words and photographs. They won't share *our* understanding, will they, Toby?'

Minutes passed before Toby switched his gaze to hers. 'The garden was full. She's in the park by the old bandstand.'

'Draw me a map, Toby.'

He stood up and nodded to the guard. 'She's in the rose garden.'

Eleanor sat in the psychiatric clinic's waiting room, not bothering to hide her annoyance. She waited for her call to be answered. 'He's lying!' said Eleanor. 'If I go digging up the park and uncover zip, which is a *certainty*, it'll be considered a complete waste of time and resources. Something you were keen to avoid.'

'Toby Adams is a murderer,' said Marty, on the other end of the line. 'Which means that his whole life is built on lies. Clarrie Eddow has been identified by Adams as a woman he murdered, embalmed and then buried when she began to decompose. She's in our missing persons' files and what *I'm* struggling to understand is why *you*, a homicide detective, are not champing at the bit to go find the remains of a recently murdered female!' His gathering crescendo was beginning to distort through her earpiece. 'Well?'

Eleanor wasn't entirely sure why this logic wasn't appealing to her. 'I agree,' she replied simply.

'Find where the rest of Adams' victims are buried before some family dog does it on our behalf. Are we on the same page, Raven?'

'Absolutely,' she replied, impressed by the speed of Marty's disconnection.

Laurence's name flashed across her phone screen, and she was about to answer when a man sporting three shades of beige and the heavily furrowed skin of a seasoned smoker opened the door and beckoned her.

'Where's Dr Blackmore?' she asked.

'This is the *waiting* room,' he answered in a surprising baritone. 'My office is where discussions are held.'

He walked back into his office and waited for Eleanor to rise and follow.

Eleanor reluctantly entered, glaring at the man who had taken the seat in front of her. He gestured her to sit down, but she paused before complying and looked around the room. The walls were covered in teak-framed certificates, each one a testament to this doctor's competence and expertise. Photographs of the subject wearing academic garb and collecting various scrolls in hallowed halls were spaced along the bookshelves, which held lines of chronological tomes with blue leather spines. It was a shrine to the man's ability and power.

'I am Dr Launceston,' he introduced himself slowly, allowing her sufficient time to absorb his well-evidenced success. 'And I have been asked by both Dr Blackmore and your commanding officer to review your progress and see if we can get you back to work, without the need for support.'

Eleanor narrowed her eyes. 'Really? Well, I've been feeling good since Dr Blackmore confirmed both to myself and my superiors that I no longer *require* psychological support.'

Dr Launceston sat at his desk and put his hands together, as if in prayer, and sighed deeply. 'I have read your case notes and spoken to Dr Blackmore about the significant amount of progress you have made since you started this programme. However, I'm sure you are aware that unless we can absolutely confirm to the bonding company that you are of sufficiently sound mind to be carrying a weapon on the streets of Toronto, then you will be demoted to less volatile areas of police work. I would, therefore, hope that you will cooperate with the team who are dedicating their time to making sure you achieve your aims.' He smiled without softening his eyes.

'What do I need to do?' she asked flatly.

'I'd like to find out a little bit about you,' he said.

'I'm in that file. Read it.'

'That gives a very one-dimensional representation of a personality. It lists the events that have moulded you, not the type or depth of damage they've caused.'

Eleanor flung herself back into the chair and opened her hands. 'Ask away.'

Launceston readjusted his position and smiled at her. 'You are an astonishing individual, Eleanor. Not only did you survive the mental trauma of finding the abused and murdered body of your childhood friend Caleb, you had the strength and determination to turn that experience around and become a police officer. You save and avenge lost souls.'

'That's not how I see myself,' she snapped.

'No? How do you see yourself?' he asked with interest.

Determined not to reveal her true feelings through her body language, Eleanor forced herself to relax and disassociate herself from the conversation taking place.

'I… don't know,' she replied, glancing at her watch. 'My father was a patrol officer; maybe I was just following his example.'

Launceston shook his head slowly. 'You are too independent a woman to follow footsteps. You create your own path, which is why you've received the fastest and highest promotion curve in the TPS. That's right, isn't it?'

Eleanor looked at him, nodding uncomfortably.

'Only someone with astonishing abilities could have made such a meteoric ascent.' He stopped and smiled. 'You're averse to praise.'

'I'd prefer you to stop,' she said.

'Praise is good for the soul,' he said quietly. 'We all need to feel that we are successful – capable of saving lives. Only the other day you were willing to put yourself in danger to protect three children.'

'Any officer would have done the same. It's what we're trained to do,' she said quickly. 'Why am I here?'

Launceston's voice hardened. 'Because since you've learned to forgive yourself, you've grown complacent, lazy and are a danger to those around you.'

CHAPTER EIGHT

Eleanor was woken by the heavy drumming of rain on the balcony outside her lounge window. The cold had forced her from her bedroom and onto the sofa, where a small electric fire had taken the chill off the room the evening before. She desperately wanted a bath, but with no sign of either her landlord or the replacement thermocouple, hot water was a distant memory.

She boiled the kettle and washed quickly and irritably at the sink. It was 6 a.m. and the broadcaster whose job it was to alert Toronto's citizens to the change in weather conditions had adopted a mournful tone, as if the upcoming storms were some sort of biblical punishment on the city. Up to two inches of rain were predicted over the next twenty-four hours, along with high winds and dismally low temperatures. Perfect digging weather, thought Eleanor grimly as she formulated a strategy to gather evidence, gain judicial and municipal permission to excavate and then gather a team to start work.

She felt controlled and it sat heavily on her.

'Is that Jacob Hareton?'

'It is,' came the reply.

'DI Eleanor Raven here; we met a few months ago regarding a community park scheme you were running with the parole board.'

'Of course! How can I help you?'

'Any chance of meeting me at the park for a walk through?' she asked.

'I'm here now. Any good?' he answered enthusiastically.

She glanced at the traffic. 'Twenty-five minutes?'

'I'll meet you at the gate.'

'Check your files to see if you worked with a Clarrie Eddow.'

'Clarrie Eddow,' he repeated. 'Roger that.'

Jacob Hareton stood at the gates of the small park and waved to Eleanor as she pulled her Tauris into an empty bay. He greeted her with a firm handshake as she climbed out of the driver's seat. 'You'll need a toque,' he said.

She smiled and pulled a beanie out of the glove compartment. As he walked beside her, she was surprised by the calmness he exuded. He was tall, red haired and bearded, not dissimilar in height and appearance to Laurence. His skin was weathered and his habit of pulling his beard as he thought relaxed her.

'I've checked my records and called in the name but I've found nothing on a Clarrie Eddow. Was she supposed to have worked here?' he asked, steering Eleanor off the main path towards his small wooden office. 'There was no one of that name working either on the Probationers' Programme, or employed by the Parks Commission.'

'I'm not convinced that she was, but there's a possibility that she's been buried in a rose garden near the old bandstand.'

Jacob raised an eyebrow. 'May I ask if this is also connected to the Adams murders?'

She nodded.

'I followed it in the papers. So, there's a possibility that there's another body and it's buried here?' He shook his head despondently.

'It's a small possibility but one we've got to check out,' she replied.

She watched with interest as he boiled the kettle and prepared two mugs. 'How do you take your coffee?'

'Milk, no sugar… Thank you.' She was about to ask him if they could speed matters up but a sense of heaviness and increasing isolation was beginning to settle on her, so she watched in silence as he filtered the coffee and poured it into two lidded mugs. As he handed one to her, he glanced at her boots. 'Waterproof?'

She nodded.

The park was virtually empty and devoid of birdsong. Leaves whipped along the path as Jacob led them towards the rose garden.

'The area has been landscaped over the past few years, so I'd need to know what sort of time frame you're looking at,' he said, stopping at a small metal gate standing between two waist-high box hedges. 'The rose garden stretched from these gates up to the bandstand, which stood in the middle there.' He pointed to a circular, grassed picnic area.

'When was the bandstand demolished?' she asked, despairing that the area was so large.

'A couple of years ago. If a body was interred here before the demolition then you're talking about a third less ground space. We dug up most of the roses here and there wasn't a hint of anything untoward.'

She smiled. 'Like a body?'

Jacob laughed. 'Like a body.'

They walked the periphery and sheltered under a beech tree as the rain increased in ferocity. 'What's your plan?' he asked.

'We dig,' she sighed.

*

Laurence had less than half an hour to make the meeting with his solicitor. He stared at the yellow Post-it note taped to his desk. It was one of three he'd received over the past twenty-four hours, all of which he was ignoring. The notes all bore the same message. 'Claddis McAvoy of the *Toronto Sun* has been trying to contact you. It is a matter of some urgency.' The last two notes had the word 'trying' vigorously underlined. Laurence speculated vaguely as to whether he should actually call him back, but Claddis was just about the last person, barring his solicitor, that he wanted to communicate with today.

Balling the notes, he flipped them into the bin next to his desk and shut the door firmly behind him.

Laurence sat in the small, cluttered office and waited as his solicitor, Melissa Bedford, fetched a pile of documents.

'Mr Whitefoot, I have to point out, as your legal representative, that Ms Lindhoff is not making particularly onerous or outrageous demands on you,' she said with an edge of exasperation.

Laurence opened his mouth to counter this but Melissa wanted her say. 'You agree that you took out the mortgage for the apartment jointly.' She held up a finger. 'Let me finish please. And that your ex-girlfriend, Ms Lindhoff, took on the majority of payments during your first year as a qualified medical practitioner.'

Laurence nodded, his mouth set in a firm line.

'So, by your own account, Ms Lindhoff paid off the larger share of the payments during the time that you shared the apartment. Following the collapse of your relationship, she continued to pay her half of the mortgage repayments for a full year, only ceasing payments after you insisted that she did so.'

Melissa sighed, took off her glasses and leaned towards Laurence. 'Ms Lindhoff behaved impeccably on the monetary front. She didn't ask you to vacate and sell up immediately. She left it four years, so that you could get yourself into a good financial position. Now she's getting married and wants to release her capital.'

'I don't want to sell,' said Laurence peevishly.

'Then remortgage and buy her out!' Melissa snapped. 'If she is forced to take you to court, you will lose and end up paying considerably more than your compliance would cost you.' She stared at him, willing him to cooperate.

'I'll try to remortgage,' he said slowly.

'Excellent. I've got a colleague who specialises in mortgage advice. I'll forward you his details.'

'What about my dog, Monster?' he asked flatly.

She sighed. 'I can write another letter and invite her to negotiate, but she seems pretty set on getting him back. Maybe,' she added carefully, 'you could have a fresh start, with a new dog?'

*

Eleanor was late for her meeting with the district attorney. Heidlmann was packing his briefcase and he frowned as she entered the room. 'I'm due in court in forty-five minutes, so make this quick and relevant. And before you start, overturning the OSA is nigh on impossible. You'd have to have concrete proof that Lieutenant Myles was murdering and cannibalising members of the Toronto public, otherwise you'll have to allow the military to hold their own investigation and court hearing.'

'We have an unsolved crime that bears a striking resemblance to Eddie Myles' MO,' said Eleanor with exaggerated confidence.

'Oh yes?' said Heidlmann, glancing at her suspiciously.

'Stella Tapley was—' she began, but Heidlmann held up his hand.

'Let me stop you right there!' he snarled. 'Roma Joe Greene is serving two full life tariffs for the murders of Eliza Camp and Sarah Buckley. Stella Tapley's murder was identical in every way to the murders of Camp and Buckley *and* Greene confessed to it. It didn't form part of the trial because the first two were shoo-ins. There is *absolutely* no way I will present that bullshit to a judge.' He paused. 'That's it? That's all you've got?'

Eleanor nodded.

'Wow. I rest my case.'

'You're going to let the murder of Angela Myles, two serving officers and the orphaning of three children go unpunished?' she said angrily.

'Unpunished? Eddie Myles is dead! What else do you want?' Heidlmann snapped. 'Do you think the military court will somehow let this slip? They will investigate, try and punish anyone who they believe enabled Lieutenant Myles to commit his crimes. They will have the ability, the resources and the determination to discover what the hell he was doing overseas and why the psychological assessment didn't anticipate this outcome.'

Checking his watch, he grabbed his briefcase and headed for the door. 'You have no jurisdiction over the military.'

'So they're above the law?' Eleanor asked with outrage.

'No one is above the law!' Heidlmann spat. 'Democracy and freedom have a cost.'

'Accountability is the foundation of this society.'

'You sound like a goddamned student!' Heidlmann sneered. 'The military *is* accountable, just not to you.' He reached for the door handle.

'What if the DNA analysis of the bones he consumed comes back as of North American origin?' Eleanor asked.

'Then' – he opened the door, glancing back at her – 'we can make a case to the judge.'

The door slammed, leaving Eleanor staring furiously at it.

*

The boy lay on top of his bed, soothed by the steady motion of the clock's hands. Dawn had been breaking as he'd made his way back to the house, but he'd felt such happiness and calm that he hadn't cared one jot if anyone had seen him. He'd spent most of the past evening just looking at the woman and gently twisting her body to the left and the right. She belonged to him now. Like the dogs, she would be his, and his alone.

He suddenly realised that the clock had jumped. It was no longer 9.50 a.m.; it was now 10.15. He couldn't recall taking his eyes off the hands. Had something happened?

He felt his anxiety levels rising and sat up ready to take the clock apart, just to make sure that there was nothing amiss. But then he understood why the shift in time had evaded him. It was exactly as his doctor had told him it would be. Time would change when he found happiness. He was right. Time was no longer a constant but a variable.

He was happy. The cold was diminished.

*

Laurence walked into the office.

'So what's the news?' asked Mo as he fed Monster pieces of biscuit.

'My solicitor told me to buy Mags out,' groaned Laurence, slumping into his chair and surveying mountains of paperwork.

'Did you mention you couldn't… or, more to the point, *why* you couldn't do that?' Mo asked.

'Not in so many words,' replied Laurence. 'How's it going to look if I admit to not being able to get a mortgage because I've defaulted?'

'You can't cover it up or hope they won't work it out. It's in the public domain,' said Mo, massaging Monster's back.

'I've tried to remortgage but because I still owe 70K in medical loan fees and I defaulted for three months, no lender will let me buy her out. If Mags has her name taken off the mortgage, I'll lose the apartment and my dog.'

Mo sighed. 'Get some sort of financial advisor – or Timms.'

Laurence looked at him with disbelief. 'Timms?'

Mo wagged a finger. 'There you go, underestimating the man again. Timms owns more real estate in Toronto than anyone else I know. He's been buying and selling for thirty years. He knows how the system works and, if you're really stuck, he's always got a room somewhere he can rent out.' He observed Laurence's nonplussed expression, 'As you will, but Timms is your guy. If anyone can sort out a problem, it's him.

Mo grabbed the ringing phone. 'Yeah? He's on his way.'

Laurence raised an eyebrow.

'Claddis McAvoy is waiting for you in reception.'

Laurence groaned.

The central reception area of Toronto Police Service Headquarters was airy, overheated and noisy. A multitude of indignant citizens waited, in various states of irritation, to have their issues dealt with. Desk sergeant Andy Harrison, seeing Laurence, waved his hand in the direction of Claddis McAvoy, who was pacing energetically.

'I've been leaving messages for you, Detective Whitefoot,' said Claddis with an air of exasperation. 'But obviously you've been too damned busy to call me back.'

'What do you want?' asked Laurence, without applying a conversational salve.

'I came round to give you an opportunity to comment officially to the *Sun's* readers who will, no doubt, be rightly indignant when they read tomorrow's headline, which outlines the lack of police interest and progress in the *Hanged Dogs Saga*,' said Claddis, waving air quotes.

Laurence remained silent.

'It appears that despite cruelty to animals being the number one indicator of psychopathic tendencies in an offender, little has been done to track down the perpetrator of this heinous crime.'

'And where have you got this astute psychological summation from?' snapped Laurence.

Claddis leaned in towards him. 'I contacted Dr Ruby Delaware, who was more than happy to supply me with a definition and to air her concerns about this case being swept under the carpet.'

Laurence deliberately relaxed his features in an effort to disguise his reaction, but judging by Claddis's smirk, he was a split second too late.

'This is an ongoing investigation,' said Laurence, rallying. 'And, as such, no comment can be made at the present time.'

Turning on his heel, he walked briskly back towards the stairs, ignoring his desire to readjust his collar.

*

Eleanor leaned against the door frame of Timms' office, waiting as he processed her account of her meeting with the district attorney.

'What you gonna do next?' he asked, raising both eyebrows theatrically.

'We ask more questions,' replied Eleanor.

Timms nodded. 'Are you still able to access Base Borden?'

'There's a hiatus while the DNA results are analysed. The military don't want to be seen as uncooperative, but they're spinning out their responses, presumably in the belief that it'll be turned over to them as soon as Lieutenant Myles is proved to have been misbehaving on foreign soil. However, I've got permission to interview members of his unit this afternoon.'

'That's good,' he replied. 'Are you any nearer to getting hold of his medical reports and the psychiatrist that treated him?'

'Nope. Classified.'

'There you are. Got a moment?' asked Laurence, sticking his head around the door.

'Sure.' She made to leave.

'Hey, Raven,' Timms said in a low voice.

She turned.

'Why are you sharing all this with me?'

'Samuelson wanted me to keep you informed,' she answered, puzzled.

'Yeah, I get that, but *why* are you complying? It's not like you to give a damn what anyone else wants you to do.'

She smiled. 'Maybe all that therapy has turned me into a better cop.'

Timms didn't look convinced.

Closing the door behind her, she followed Laurence towards their office.

'What's up?' she asked.

'I've just seen Claddis McAvoy, who has a quote from Ruby Delaware stating her disappointment that the TPS has ignored her advice that we should be looking into who hanged the dogs.'

'Ok*aay*.'

'The *Toronto Sun* is going to run it as its headline tomorrow.'

Eleanor opened the door to their room and ushered Laurence in. 'Firstly,' she said, 'Dr Delaware is very unlikely to have criticised the department to a local paper, and secondly, it's unlikely any story will knock off the baying for answers in the Myles case.'

'So, ignore it?' asked Laurence.

Eleanor thought hard. 'You've got patrol officers investigating?'

'Yeah, but they're getting no place fast.'

'Then take an hour or so to show your face and see what patrol missed. I can do Base Borden on my own.'

Laurence nodded.

'You *can* handle this!' she said firmly.

'Yeah, of course,' he responded with uncertainty.

She looked at him. 'Call me when you've checked it out.'

*

Laurence shook the water from his coat and searched in his pocket for a handkerchief. He'd called in at the local police station and had an uninspiring conversation with the two patrol officers assigned to the 'dead dog case'. They had managed to track down one of the owners, who, on hearing of Benji's ignominious end had required medical attention. As none of the remaining dogs had been either chipped or had collars, they had been deemed as strays. Neither officer was any more enlightened as to who had committed the offence, though a local man with a history of animal abuse was under suspicion.

Checking the address, Laurence knocked loudly on Veronica Sizemore's door. He tried again. A cat had started to yowl miserably on the other side. After writing her a brief note explaining that he'd like to speak to her again, he pulled up the letter flap and began to push the note through. But as the seal between corridor and apartment broke, the acrid smell of cat piss stung his nostrils.

Holding his breath, he hunkered down and peered through the letter box. He could make out very little but Veronica's handbag was clearly visible on a chair. He called her name again and knocked. Looking around, he noticed a neighbour's door was slightly ajar.

'Hello? I'm Detective Laurence Whitefoot, Toronto PS, and I'm looking for Miss Sizemore.'

The door inched open, revealing a small, elderly woman. 'I'm Mrs Patel,' she said hesitantly. 'I have not seen Veronica for a while now. I'm very worried.'

'May I ask you a couple of questions, Mrs Patel?' he asked, positioning his ID.

The door closed and the safety chain was drawn back.

'Come in please.' Mrs Patel closed the door behind him and ushered him into her small, immaculate living room. 'She always has a cup of tea with me at 11 a.m. but she didn't call today.'

'Is that unusual?' asked Laurence.

'Very much so. We have been friends for a very long time and we look after each other.'

Laurence nodded.

'You are a detective? Did someone call you?'

He could see that she was becoming distressed. 'No, I wanted to follow up on a concern that she had.'

'The smell! Veronica was very fearful that there was a dead person and when she found out what had happened, she was angry.'

'Did she do something – about the dogs?' he asked carefully.

Mrs Patel's eyes widened. 'What could she do? We are old women!'

'I understand.'

'I have a key; will you go and look?' she asked.

The cat bolted the second Laurence drew open the door. He switched on the light and made his way round the small space, noting that there was nothing untoward. A cold cup of tea sat on Veronica's small dining table, its surface beginning to separate as the milk soured.

'Is everything alright?' asked Mrs Patel quietly as she waited in the corridor.

'She's not here,' he answered. 'Can you step in for a minute and let me know if anything has changed?'

Mrs Patel walked in, wrinkling her nose at the smell. 'Elvis never messes. He must have been in for a long time.'

'When did you last see Veronica Sizemore?' he asked, taking his notebook out of his jacket.

'Yesterday, for our morning cup of tea. She didn't mention that she was going out.' She pointed to a set of car keys hanging from a hook. 'And she didn't use her car.'

Having settled Mrs Patel back into her flat, Laurence locked the door to Veronica's apartment and went to look for her car. He had no trouble finding it. It was parked where Mrs Patel had predicted.

Determined to check that the caretaker had installed a new bolt, Laurence made his way round to the steel door leading to the boiler room. He placed his hand on the door and pushed; the lock held. He reached for his phone, intending to call the caretaker and take another look around, but as he searched for the number, his phone rang.

'Is that Detective Laurence Whitefoot?'

'Speaking.'

'This is Detective Marcus Layton of GTA PS. I'm investigating the death of Joe Greene, aka Roma Joe. Apparently you visited him yesterday.'

CHAPTER NINE

The storm was beginning to subside by the time Eleanor left the city. The wind had dropped but the unremitting rain pattering on the windscreen was making her feel soporific. She'd been trying to clear her mind and formulate an investigative strategy for her interviews at Base Borden but for some reason she couldn't focus her thoughts. If she were to prevent the military taking over the case then she needed to find something concrete that would convince a judge it was a civilian matter, but her mind kept wandering, unable to fix on any one problem. It was as if she couldn't draw on sufficient anger to sharpen her thinking.

Eleanor assessed the man sitting in front of her and concluded that either she was losing her ability to deduce character, or Sergeant Clinton Barber was a master of unreadable body language. Barber's facial expression conveyed polite interest, nothing more. She'd been trying to coax a more emotional response from the soldier but to no avail.

'Let's recap what you've provided us with so far,' said Eleanor, withholding the desire to sigh with frustration. 'Despite the fact that you bunked down with Lieutenant Myles on two of his three trips to Afghanistan, you had no idea that he was consuming finger trophies from Mujahedeen fighters, or planning to kill his wife.'

'That is correct, ma'am,' Barber replied, without a hint of either exhaustion or irritation at having been questioned for the past half hour.

She nodded sagely. 'Or that you suspected he was capable of carrying out these atrocities?'

For a moment the soldier was silent. A furrow appeared across his brow.

'You suspected something was going to happen?' she asked quietly.

He paused to reflect before shaking his head. 'No, I don't think anyone could have anticipated that he'd kill his wife. It's just that acquiring trophies isn't that… incomprehensible.' He looked at Eleanor.

'Maybe you could elaborate on that statement, because chopping off body parts and swallowing fingers is generally not condoned in our society.'

Barber nodded. 'But being on a war footing isn't normal for society. You don't know the specifics but you have an idea of what this sort of unit does, don't you?'

Eleanor leaned towards him. 'I've an idea.'

'The first few men I killed, I had to go and check what they had on them and I remember thinking that taking their lives hadn't affected me. They'd tried to kill us and we got them first. Simple. It took me a few months to realise that was a problem.'

'In what way?' she asked.

'That killing the enemy wasn't making any impression on me. They were nothing. I felt I was losing my humanity, so I tried to connect in some way. The faces didn't bother me; their eyes were dead. It was their hands.' He glanced at his own. 'I'd see their hands and I'd feel kinda close to them. I imagined that their hands had touched a child, or dug a garden – maybe created something good. We were on different sides but we were the same. Warriors.

I didn't regret killing them, but their hands gave me something to ponder on. It helped me feel some remorse, I guess.'

'You think that was the motivation for Eddie Myles?' she asked.

Barber shook his head. 'I can't answer for the man. Maybe he saw too much. He'd been part of the team that trained up the Afghan police to take over when we left.'

'They killed two of your team.'

'Yeah. Myles saw it but we'd seen worse. He got angry – too angry for combat. You need to be detached, calm or you put everyone in danger.'

'You think that could have been the tipping point for him?' she asked.

Barber shrugged. 'Dunno. They shipped him back home pretty damned quick and got him under obs.'

'Did he say anything to you while he was receiving treatment?'

'I hardly saw him, and when he was around, he was quiet.'

'Four people died: who do you blame, Sergeant?' asked Eleanor.

'I'm not qualified to answer that.'

'We all have opinions,' she coaxed.

'That may be the problem,' Barber answered carefully. 'Will that be all?'

She nodded. 'Thank you.'

Barber tapped his cap and moved towards the door, then stopped. 'If there is anyone here to blame, then you can rest assured that it will be dealt with.'

Barber closed the door behind him.

Eleanor rubbed her taut neck muscles, wondering if she were any the wiser as to the reasons why Eddie Myles had been consuming body parts, or why his mental health had snapped, causing a bloodbath. Barber was the last of five soldiers she'd interviewed and they had all said pretty much the same thing. She was getting nowhere fast. Her request for Myles' medical records had fallen on deaf ears so, gathering her paperwork, Eleanor prepared for the long drive back.

Most of the residents of Base Borden seemed to be under the impression that it was their appointed place to investigate Myles' misdemeanour and this made her anxious. Whether their motivation came from a shared sense of responsibility or, more plausibly, because the promised heads on plates were being protected by the brotherhood, she hadn't yet decided.

Eleanor ran across the Base Borden parking lot, fumbling to answer her phone. 'What happened?' she asked.

'I got a call from a Detective Layton from the GTA,' said Laurence. 'He was called in by the governor when Roma Joe's body was discovered in his cell at 6 a.m. Layton says it looks like a suicide as the body temperature indicates he died between 2 a.m. and 4 a.m., a time when he was alone in his cell.'

'Why did Layton call you? Is he suspicious it's not a suicide?'

'No, he's convinced Greene died by his own hand, but because the prison has been taken to court twice this year for not providing adequate protection against possible suicide cases, he wants to be seen to be covering all possible scenarios and by the book.'

'So because you and Mo were asking questions, they want to make sure nothing was said, or threatened, to make him kill himself?' suggested Eleanor.

'I imagine so. Layton says he'll wait for me before he moves the body.'

'You need me?' she asked.

'No, I think it'd be considered pushy to bring in anyone else on a courtesy call.'

She nodded. 'Keep me up to speed… Did he look suicidal to you?' She cleared her windscreen and squinted critically at the clearing sky.

'Not when I spoke to him.'

'Did you chase up the dog crime?' she asked.

'Yeah, weird thing is that the woman who reported the smell has gone AWOL,' he said, starting the engine.

'Really?' asked Eleanor with concern. 'Suspicious?'

'I don't know. Maybe,' Laurence answered uncomfortably.

'Don't leave that one hanging, okay?' she said, closing the car door.

*

The prison was in lockdown by the time Laurence arrived, and irritable banter from the incarcerated prisoners accompanied his trek to the crime scene. Detective Layton was filling in paperwork when Laurence reached him. They shook hands and Layton showed him into the cell, where the pale, naked body of Roma Joe Greene contrasted shockingly with his bulging, blackened head.

'May I?' asked Laurence.

Layton nodded as he handed over a pair of latex gloves.

'This was his towel?' he asked, pointing to the torn and knotted noose attached to the radiator in-pipe at one end and Roma Joe's neck at the other.

'Uh-huh.'

'He was on his own?'

'He was locked in at 9.30 p.m. and the alarm was raised at 5 a.m., when the warden did her rounds.' Layton consulted his notes. 'She always checked each cell on her round, after missing a hanging three months ago.'

'Any chance he had someone helping him?' asked Laurence.

Layton puffed out his cheeks. 'I don't see how. It looks like textbook to me, but presumably the ME will get back to us if anything untoward shows up.'

Laurence hunkered down and stared at Roma Joe's face, aware that Layton's body language was giving a very different message than that of him casually checking his notes.

'Looks as if he tied the ligature around twice and then leaned forward. Guessing it was effective and quick as there's such a marked congestion,' offered Laurence.

He felt the tension lift.

'Agree with that. Seen it before – guy leans his weight into it and…' began Layton.

'You've seen that here?' interrupted Laurence.

There was an uncomfortable silence. 'Yes.'

'You investigated the other suicides?' Laurence probed.

The chill was returning to the cell. 'I did.'

There was a pause. 'Then you'll know what you're talking about. Me, I've only seen hangings before.'

Layton was suspicious. 'Whatd'ya ask Greene yesterday? Something that might have set him off on this… course of action?' he said slowly, pointing to the body.

Laurence shrugged. 'Who knows? Just needed some clarification on a couple of points.'

'On a case that was solved years back?' snorted Layton. 'You looking to reopen? New information come to light?'

'Well I guess we're going to be none the wiser now,' replied Laurence, standing up and peeling off his gloves. 'Have you spoken to any of the inmates?'

Layton adopted a bullish stance. 'I've spoken to everyone that I needed to in order to find out what state of mind the subject was in.'

'And did they back up the idea that he was suicidal?' asked Laurence.

'They didn't give a damn,' replied Layton slowly.

Laurence nodded. 'When's he being collected?'

'Medical examiner's on his way now. Is there anything else I can assist you with?' asked Layton, scowling.

'I'd appreciate the sharing of any information on your case,' suggested Laurence.

'I'm sure you would,' countered Layton.

The day was slipping away when Laurence finally made it back to Headquarters. Mo was sitting at Eleanor's desk running through paperwork.

'Roma Joe killed himself?' asked Mo.

'Looks that way but Detective Layton wasn't very forthcoming,' snapped Laurence, adjusting his headset.

'*Marcus* Layton?' asked Mo. 'He's okay. Pretty solid cop.'

'Should have taken you with me then. You might have got a warmer reception.'

'Swap positions with him. How'd you react if some city cop came stomping all over what you consider to be a slam-dunk, asking the sort of questions you'd never have thought to ask without a prompt.'

Laurence smiled. 'When you put it like that.'

'I'll give Layton a call later, see if I can get a little more information out of him.'

*

The boy wasn't allowed to sit in the waiting area anymore. He was obliged to wait in a small private room adjacent to the doctor's. When it was his turn to go in, he would be called in personally.

'How are you today?' asked the doctor, closing his notebook and scrutinising him. 'You seem – different.'

The boy looked at him. 'I'm not!' he replied tartly. 'I am the same.'

'Really? You look very content. Has something happened?' he asked curiously.

The boy was silent.

'We had a very long talk last time, didn't we?' coaxed the doctor. 'You talked about all the things that made you feel angry. Do you remember?'

The doctor was used to the silences and, after waiting for several moments and cleaning his glasses, he began again. 'Tell me how you're feeling.'

The doctor was disconcerting, seeming to know everything about him, including his thoughts. He never smiled, but neither did the boy.

'Have you been feeling well?' he asked. 'Perhaps you've had a good thing happen to you recently?'

The boy shook his head.

'Let's play our game, shall we?' said the doctor. 'I will say some words that will make you feel either nothing, or something, and you will tell me which ones make you feel good.'

Silence.

The doctor reached over to a metronome he kept on his desk and, loosening the metal arm, pushed it gently to the left, beginning its one-second rhythm. The boy focussed on this. It made him feel comfortable and relaxed.

'Dark…' Tick… Tick… Tick… 'Mother…' Tick… Tick… Tick… 'Room…' Tick… Tick… Tick… 'Close your eyes,' he said slowly and heavily, maintaining the rhythm. 'Close your eyes and listen to the clock.'

*

The doctor readjusted the weight, slowing the beat. 'Can you hear the ticks as they measure the distance from here to your room? The clock is marking time and now it's slowing. The ticks are becoming slower and slower… Are you asleep?'

The boy was still, his eyes closed and his mouth slightly open.

'You are standing in your room and the clock on the wall is about to stop.' The doctor gazed carefully, trying to ascertain his patient's level of consciousness. 'The minute hand is frozen and now, as it moves to meet it, the second hand will stop and then you will be asleep. The only thing you will respond to is my voice. Do you understand?'

'Yes.'

'You are walking into your room... Down the corridor and into the room that only you can open. It's cold. Very, very cold... Can you feel the cold?'

'Yes,' answered the boy.

'It's so cold in the room that you can barely take a breath.'

The doctor watched dispassionately as the boy's breathing became shorter and more laboured.

'The room you have inside you is a lonely room, isn't it? Empty and cold – there is nothing here that will make you feel happy.'

The doctor watched as emotions flickered across the boy's pale features. His lips twitched and his eyebrows rose and fell as he faced his fears.

'But there is some warmth, isn't there? Look into the corner of your room.'

'I can't see anything...' gasped the boy.

'Look again. In the corner, there's a light, isn't there?'

He saw the expression change on the boy's face.

'Yes, I can see it.'

'But there's something stopping you from reaching the warmth, isn't there?'

The boy was silent. His brow furrowed.

'What is it? Look carefully. Is it a person? I think it's a person, isn't it?'

'Yes,' he said doubtfully.

'Who is it?'

The boy was silent, unable to comprehend who he was looking at.

'Who is in the corner, preventing you from getting to the warmth?'

The boy remained stubbornly silent, his breathing belying his distress.

'Move closer and take a look. Who can you see?'

'It's the man!'

'Which man?'

The boy was beginning to grind his teeth.

'*The* man,' he whispered, his lip curling back from his teeth.

The doctor opened his notebook and made a couple of quick notes. 'It's time for you to start waking up,' he said in a more forceful tone. 'Look at the clock. The second hand is beginning to move.'

He began to incrementally speed up the metronome's rhythm.

'The clock is counting you awake. Listen carefully as it calls you back from your room, ten… nine… eight… The feeling of sleepiness is leaving you… seven… six… five… You can feel the heaviness return to your limbs and you will forget that we have spoken about the man, or the room. Four… three… two… It's time to wake up on the count of… one.'

The boy opened his eyes and scowled.

'Are you alright?' asked the doctor. 'You seem confused.'

Silence.

*

His mother always waited in the car for him, not wanting to venture into the building. 'How was it?' she asked distractedly, pulling into the traffic. 'Honey, are you listening to me?' she demanded. 'How was your session?'

The boy turned to look at her. 'Don't call me that.'

She sighed. 'I'm sorry. It's a term of endearment.'

'Don't,' he said, staring at the traffic ahead.

She clamped her lips and tried to lighten the atmosphere. 'What did the doctor say about your medication?' She waited to see if any information would be forthcoming, but sensing his darkening mood, she decided to call the doctor later in the day and ask herself.

*

'Raven?' barked Marty Samuelson, from inside his office. 'Don't lurk! Get in here.'

Smiling, she walked in. 'How'd you know it was me?'

'Police work,' he sighed.

Eleanor checked her watch. 'Bit late for you, sir.'

Marty rubbed his tired eyes and leaned back in his seat. 'I needed some thinking time after meeting with the Chief.' He scrutinised her. 'You making progress with any of your cases?'

She sighed. 'Some and none.'

Marty passed her a folded piece of paper. 'You'd better read this.'

Opening the letter, she saw that it bore the address of the Psychiatric Support Office. It was a copy of a letter sent to Chief Brocker and signed by Dr Launceston. She glanced at Marty, who gestured that she read the contents.

Noting that the subject of the letter was herself, she skimmed over the first paragraph, which mentioned post-traumatic stress disorder several times and outlined the reasons why Dr Seb Blackmore had felt unable to carry on with his approach to her rehabilitation. Apparently, it had been clear to him that the patient was not responding to the therapy. Having assessed the patient, Dr Launceston had no choice but to recommend that Eleanor Raven receive an extended period of rehabilitation and an immediate reduction in responsibilities, until such time as she was deemed competent. She would need weekly therapy sessions with him for the next couple of months.

Eleanor placed the letter carefully on the desk and met Marty's eye. She opened her mouth but he held up his finger. 'What have they got on you?'

She swallowed and cleared her throat. 'Nothing. They have *nothing.*'

Eleanor sat in her car, tapping her fingers rhythmically on the wheel as she ran through her options. Marty hadn't demoted her as such, but it was clear that his hands were tied and it was only a matter of time before the bonding officer caught up with her and she was either suspended or given a desk job. She didn't believe that Seb Blackmore had lied when he told her that he'd signed her off with a clean bill of mental health, but during the hypnotherapy sessions with Seb she had revealed a great deal of compromising information about herself. They'd discussed her addiction to bondage and sadomasochistic sex with strangers: aspects of her personality that didn't shame her but wouldn't be appearing on her CV any time soon.

Ironically, by admitting this to Seb, she'd gained a greater understanding of why she indulged in a practice that should have been the very antithesis of her character. If Seb had divulged this to Dr Launceston and his colleagues, she could be looking at dismissal.

Eleanor's rhythmic tapping of the wheel escalated into anxious rubbing, her palms squeaking as she applied her frustration. Maybe, she thought, it wasn't what someone had on her that was the issue but what *she* had on someone else. But she had no idea what that was or to whom it applied.

CHAPTER TEN

Today was going to be a miserable experience for everyone, particularly for Eleanor – the asshole who'd organised this futile dig. She made a mental note to locate the park's nearest Tim Hortons and keep the doughnuts coming.

As she dressed, she scrolled through her emails and noticed one from a Mr Richard Glass, Toronto PS's bonding officer. She opened it with some trepidation but it was only a request that she arrange a private meeting with him at her earliest convenience.

There were two emails from CSI intimating their displeasure about the dig and their ardent hope that Homicide had checked that the information it had received was both '*accurate*' and '*likely to produce some results*'.

Just as she was about to close her laptop there was a ping. It was a message from Marty, stressing the importance of making what could be discerned as '*progress*' and a demand that she send him regular updates. The world 'regular' was highlighted in bold text.

Slamming her laptop closed and grabbing her coat, Eleanor left one frosty environment for another.

Jacob Hareton was prepared for the invasion and had made sure that the CSI vehicles had access to the rose garden via a circuitous but private driveway. The park had an official 'closed' sign on the gate, which was probably redundant due to the torrential downpour. He greeted Eleanor with a smile, a mug of cooling coffee and a folder filled with details of every employee since 2005 and every community service probationer taken on since the scheme was adopted in 2010. Eleanor glanced through the material and was unsurprised that there was no one matching Clarrie Eddow's description.

'You seem sure there's nothing out there,' said Jacob, adjusting his waterproofs.

'Hmm, never say never but I'm pretty sure there won't be,' she replied thoughtfully.

Jacob's radio beeped and a staccato voice announced the vans' arrival.

The first hour of the dig passed in a flurry of tent erection, hardware selection and a great deal of discussion between Jacob, the lead CSI officer and Eleanor regarding the possible area the body could have been buried in. Fortunately, Jacob was able to provide a documented history of the land usage and development work that had taken place over the last ten years. This enabled the dig team to narrow the space down to a third of an acre that could have provided a gravesite. Using data from the successful exhumations from Toby Adams' garden, there was a consistent pattern to the depth of grave he preferred. By the most optimistic of calculations they would be digging for several days in order to cover the whole area.

It had been hoped that ground-penetrating radar could be used to hint at disturbances, but because the rose garden had been turned over several times in the past decade, it was thought that this would generate too many false positives. So the first location was selected and the team moved in.

Eleanor sat glumly on a foldaway stool and watched as the digging began.

'You're really convinced they're not going to find anything?' asked Jacob, standing next to her.

'I don't believe so,' she answered.

'But you have to go through the motions, however futile, because if there's a tiny chance that he did put a body there, then you have to look,' said Jacob.

Eleanor stood up and thought. 'No, I don't believe you do. To act on the whims and lies of others turns us into slaves.'

'Then call it off,' he said simply.

Eleanor smiled. 'Slavery comes with heavy shackles.'

He returned her smile. 'It does.'

*

'Hello, this is Rula Frears speaking. My son had an appointment yesterday.' She felt her confidence slip as the receptionist's tone changed.

'Yes, he did,' came the taut reply.

Rula cleared her throat and pushed on. 'Has he been prescribed any more of those antipsychotics? It's just that his behaviour is becoming a little – erratic at the moment and I'm sure he's running out of them by now and he hasn't given me another prescription to take to the pharmacy.'

There was a pause on the other end of the phone. 'Let me go and check for you.'

'Thank you, so—'

Taped music began to play as the receptionist put her on hold. Rula looked at her face in the rear-view mirror and rubbed at a line of mascara that had smeared below her eye. She grimaced as she saw how old and worn out she looked.

'Mrs Frears?'

'Yes, still here.'

'Apparently he's already been given his medication. They're a brand we prescribe from the centre and he has enough to keep him going till his appointment on the twelfth. Is that okay?'

'Yes, yes that's fine. I was worrying that he wasn't taking them.'

'If you're concerned I can speak to his doctor?'

'No, no. It's fine. As long as he's already got his prescription then I can check he's taking them. Sorry to have inconvenienced you.'

'Not at all.'

*

Three hours into the dig and sodden CSI officers were beginning to get snippy, particularly with Eleanor. There had been a few false starts when pig bones and what appeared to be a medal from the World War One were located. Eleanor was intrigued as to why Jacob Hareton had been shown the medal and asked to advise its origins. She watched as he carefully cleaned it with his handkerchief.

'It's a Mercantile Marine War Medal.' He turned it over carefully in his hand. 'This officer would have served in a danger zone during World War One.'

Eleanor leaned over to look at it, reading off the rim. 'Lieutenant R. L. Patterson. You think he lost it here?'

Jacob smiled. 'Maybe. Or buried it here.' He placed the medal in her hand.

'You served?' she asked.

Jacob took his time answering. 'I did. Been a civilian for the past ten years and pleased to be such.'

A request crackled through his radio. With a nod he excused himself and walked through the rain towards his office.

The CSI who'd handed Jacob the medal smiled at her. 'He's a good guy. Teaches my kid's hockey class at the weekend. Nothing's ever too much trouble for Jake.'

'He was infantry?' she asked with more curiosity than she'd expected.

The CSI shook his head. 'I think he was Special Forces, not that he's ever said anything.' He sighed, turned and headed back to the dig site. 'Apparently, he earned a few of those himself,' he called back, pointing to her hand.

*

'Hey son, are you upstairs?' bellowed the man.

The boy sat on the side of his bed, wondering whether he could go and visit his special place. He felt agitated and wanted to leave, but there were several more hours of daylight left.

'You there?'

The boy felt the man's noise intruding on his thoughts, making him uncomfortable and angry.

'Are you still up there?'

Even though he'd been warm only a few minutes ago, the temperature in the room was falling. He didn't understand. His hands were turning blue and his teeth were chattering. Then he knew. The man was doing this. The doctor had known that the man was denying him warmth and happiness. The man was coming between himself and the flame.

Decisively, the boy felt beneath his bed for the knife that he kept there. It had a long serrated blade and a heavy bone handle and it felt good in his hand. Unlocking the door, he stepped out into the stairwell, noting the lightness of his footfalls as he headed down to the kitchen.

'Hey, buddy,' said the man. 'I'm making tea – want some?'

Looking at the shape in front of him the boy suddenly felt unsure of how best to kill him. He wasn't feeling his usual physical responses to a situation, just a strange calmness.

The man was waiting and watching, as if he knew that something important was about to happen. 'Are you okay?' he asked.

The only way to bring down something as large and dangerous as the man was to attack swiftly. So pulling his hand from his coat pocket, he lunged forward.

There was a moment of clumsiness when the knife only seemed to graze the man. Aware that he was beginning to work out what was happening and might make some sort of defensive action, the boy put his whole weight behind the knife, feeling the blade disappear into the man's stomach.

Suddenly, he was too close to the man. He could smell his breath and hear the sounds coming from his throat.

Fumbling with the handle, he tried to extract the knife to give him some distance but the man wouldn't yield. He had wrapped his hands around the blade in an effort to keep it in.

So be it, the boy thought, he was in no rush, and backed away, stopping when the kitchen table prevented him. He sat back onto the tabletop, allowing his legs to swing as he watched with intense interest.

The man was now on his knees, his head resting against the fridge. He was holding the knife in with his right hand as he propped up his weight with his left.

The boy heard him making little sobbing sounds as he fought against time. He wondered if he should tell him that time always won: that thinking the next few minutes could prevent his death or offer some hope was ridiculous. Why should he bother? The man meant nothing to him.

*

Eleanor helped the CSI team pack away. There was still two-thirds of the area to dig and with storms scheduled for tomorrow, no one was looking happy.

'How're those shackles holding up?' asked Jacob quietly.

'Too damned heavy!' she hissed.

Grabbing her bag and walking quickly away from the rose garden, she called Milhaven and had made it back to the car before she was connected to the right department.

'I don't care if Toby Adams is unwell. I'll be there in the next couple of hours and he *will* be seeing me.'

She disconnected and, flinging the phone onto the passenger seat, pulled into the traffic.

Her instinct was to grab Toby Adams by the throat and beat an answer out of him; however experience told her that this would be deeply satisfying but counterproductive on the information-gathering front. She bit her lip and settled into the plastic chair to await his arrival.

'I hadn't expected a visit so soon after the last,' said Toby. 'You seem alarmingly wet.'

She nodded. 'We dug, Toby. All day – and there's nothing there.'

He shrugged. 'You seem surprised, yet you said you didn't believe that there was anyone *resting* there.'

Eleanor calmed herself. 'You told me that you buried Clarrie Eddow in the rose garden, next to where the old bandstand stood in the park!'

'No I didn't!' He turned to the guard. 'I'd like to go back to my cell now. I feel very dizzy.'

Eleanor jumped to her feet, causing the guard to make a few twitchy gestures. 'Don't waste my time or patience, Toby. Did you bury a woman in the rose garden?' She was aware that her voice was filling the room.

Toby stood up and made his way over to the door and waited for the guard to unlock it.

Eleanor slammed the driver's door behind her and watched as the world disappeared behind her steamed-up windscreen. Her phone, once she'd turned it back on, had rung almost continuously. Letting out a deep sigh, she pressed the answer button. 'Yes, sir!'

'Is that you, Raven? Only it's been so long since I've heard your dulcet tones, that I've forgotten who you are or why I employ you!'

Eleanor grimaced and waited, assuming Marty would indicate when he needed her input.

'Guess who I'm about to cosy up to? That's right, Chief Brocker! And what do you suppose he'll want a debrief on?'

There was a significant pause. 'The dig, sir?' she offered.

'Correct! And what am I supposed to tell the Chief? That you haven't bothered to present me with any form of debrief for the past twenty-eight hours, despite your promises and my heartfelt expectations, and that I have no goddamned idea what stage we're at in the proceedings? Or—'

'Tell him we've found nothing and won't find anything,' she snapped. 'I've just seen Toby Adams and he's lying – there is no body buried there.'

'So despite him having named a missing woman and indicated where he put her, we're going to call his bluff?' countered Marty, outraged.

'I believe we should stop digging, sir.'

'You can believe all you want, Raven. You and your team will dig until hell freezes over, or we find a body. Is that clear to you?'

She remained silent.

'Raven?'

'Yes, sir. It is clear,' she responded tensely.

Marty made what sounded like a growling sound before disconnecting.

With a sudden surge of rage she slammed both hands on the steering wheel, dropping her phone into the footwell. She felt herself slipping into a familiar pattern of self-hatred, which would channel itself into a need to purge and cleanse. She was determined not to succumb to these thoughts, so she started the engine and fished around for her missing phone while she waited for the windscreen to clear.

*

Rula Frears was going to be late home. A big consignment had come into the warehouse and she'd been logging and directing its storage for the past few hours. She'd tried to call her husband but he wasn't picking up, which was unlike him. Maybe he'd gone down to the club for a game, or to the movies. She just wanted to know that everything was alright. Her son seemed so angry and distant yesterday and the thought that he'd not been taking his meds was terrifying. Still, at least she knew they'd been prescribed, and when he next went out on one of his walks, she'd pop into his room and check the bottle. She wasn't supposed to go into his room but forewarned was forearmed.

She started the car, trying home one last time. It rang for a while before jumping to the answer machine. Not bothering to leave another message she set off, only slightly worried.

There were no lights on when Rula arrived home. The door was locked but she could see Alan's car parked outside. She wasn't going to jump to conclusions but her stomach was beginning to churn.

Tiptoeing into the hallway, she glanced at where her son's boots would be, but there were only the two balls of newspaper placed carefully side by side.

With a sigh of relief, she turned on the light and made her way into the kitchen. Strangely, there was no smell of any food having been prepared, and the table and chairs weren't in their usual place.

As she moved forward, her foot slipped alarmingly on the floor, which was wet. Puzzled, she searched around for a source of the flood. Maybe someone had left the freezer door open? She looked around but there was nothing to indicate this had happened. The freezer door was firmly closed.

She walked over to the utility cupboard, where she could see the mop and bucket had been used, as the head was dripping wet. Sighing, she went to find Alan and find out what had been dropped. Surprisingly, he wasn't in the bedroom or in any of the downstairs rooms. Where the hell was he?

She stood at the bottom of the stairs and looked up to the landing. He wouldn't have gone upstairs, would he? 'Alan?' she called anxiously.

Her son had never taken to Alan, despite all the kindness and effort he'd put into making him feel loved. For a moment, she was hit by an overwhelming sense of injustice. Alan had wanted children, but she'd said no after her son had been diagnosed with a schizotypal disorder. If this was the kind of child she produced, then one was sufficient.

Putting her hand wearily on the handrail, she made her way up to her son's bedroom.

She always opened his door with a degree of trepidation. The room had a pungent aroma, which she could only put down to her son's refusal to open the window. A layer of dust covered everything. She'd tackled this years ago but his reaction was so extreme that she determined to let him sit in there and stew in it. Why would anyone want to live like this?

Pulling open his sock drawer, Rula saw his collection of empty pill bottles. He never threw any out and it was with some difficulty that she managed to find a half-empty bottle with the current date on. She did a quick estimate of how many pills there should be left and was pleased to see that he had been taking them. Maybe his current mental state was just a small blip and he'd be back to his version of normality in the next few weeks?

Rula's instinct was to pull up the blind and fling open the window, but she didn't feel robust enough for that sort of confrontation. With a quick visual sweep of the room, she carefully closed the door behind her and descended the stairs.

Grabbing her phone, she called Alan's number. It took her several moments to realise that the ringing she could hear was coming from his mobile. She followed the tone back into the kitchen and spotted his phone on the counter. That wasn't right. Alan didn't go anywhere without his phone in case she needed him.

She felt cold and a little dizzy. Something wasn't right.

She lowered herself onto one of the kitchen chairs, waiting for her son's return.

CHAPTER ELEVEN

The boy was tired. He'd been pushing the man's body for the past twenty minutes and he was getting bored. The shopping trolley was easy to obtain: he'd stolen them before from the local Costco. They just had to be lifted over the barrier next to the far wall and then they could be used to transport whatever he needed, to wherever he needed. Several people had spotted him en route, but none had intervened because the man had been considered drunk, so they averted their gaze and steered clear.

Lifting the man into the trolley was hard work and at the beginning of the ride he'd made little snuffling sounds and groans, which further added to the illusion that he was drunk. The boy had to wait patiently when he arrived at his special place because a man was parking his car and making a noisy phone call, which seemed to be preventing him from going into the building and getting out of his way.

The rain was coming down heavily now and the boy felt large areas of his body becoming damp where the seams of his coat had long ago parted company. He'd had the coat for a long time and his mother always complained that it was the wrong size for him, but the boy liked it and wasn't going to be replacing it any time soon.

Finally the man ran into the building, leaving a clear path between him and the steel door.

Abandoning the trolley by the trashcans, the boy pulled out his screwdriver and carefully removed the lock. He froze, uncertain of what would be waiting for him. What if she was gone, like the dogs? His chest was beginning to feel tight and chilly, but he knew that he had to press on.

As the door opened, he could smell her. Sweet, heavy aromas emanated from the darkness. She was still there – and she was his.

Unable to resist a small peek at her, the boy tiptoed down the stairs. He'd left the door slightly ajar, which let in a minimal strip of light.

Turning on his torch and covering it with his hand, he gazed at the woman. Her face fascinated him. It was ghostly white. Her one open eye was opaque and flattened, and her skin was beginning to take on a mottled appearance. He'd never owned a dead person before and hadn't realised that their skin would change. The dogs' coats had become dull and fallen out in clumps.

He touched her hand gently, feeling the texture of its cold, wet surface. This was the right place for him. He was happy. But he needed to focus. He had more heavy lifting to do and standing gawping at the woman wasn't going to get it done.

Bounding up the steps, he cautiously looked around and then headed over to the cart. What he saw made him feel sick.

The shopping cart was empty.

*

Claddis McAvoy stood in his boxer shorts with his arms wrapped protectively round his flabby chest and stared out into the darkness. He'd turned off the light, hoping that he'd be able to see more, but the rain and lack of street lighting made it nigh on impossible to make anything out.

Pressing his nose against the cold window, he could just make out the area where the trashcans were kept and the entrance to the parking area he shared with his neighbours. It was probably just a couple of raccoons knocking bins over, but he felt jumpy after seeing those dogs.

There was nothing.

He yanked the curtain closed, flipped on the light and hunted for a viable bottle of whisky amongst the piles of newspapers and books that littered his apartment.

There was a feeble knock at his door.

'Yeah?' he called out.

Someone knocked again. Sighing, he grabbed his dressing gown and stood by his front door. 'Who is it?' he asked uncertainly.

'It's Mrs Patel from downstairs,' came the faint reply.

Claddis opened the door. 'It's very late, Mrs Patel. How can I help you?'

'She still isn't back, Mr McAvoy. A detective came, and her car is still there, but she is not.'

'Come in,' he said, ushering her into the apartment. He noted her look of horror as she surveyed the chaos.

'Ignore the mess,' he said with a sweep of his hand. 'Can you remember the name of the detective who spoke to you?'

'Detective Whitefoot. He didn't seem very concerned.'

'I bet he didn't,' snorted Claddis.

Mrs Patel began to wring her hands. 'Veronica wouldn't have just left. Her handbag is still here.'

'I'm not sure how I can help,' he replied.

'You write for the newspaper. Maybe you could ask if anyone has seen or knows anything about her? And,' she hesitated, 'you could go and look for her.'

Claddis opened his mouth and was about to defend his right to leave all such matters to the police when an idea began to form. 'Yes, I could. Leave it with me and I'll look into this. Are you happy to answer some questions for the *Sun*?'

She looked uncertain. 'If it will help.'

'Excellent, well I'm going to get onto this immediately,' he said in a reassuring tone.

'You will go and look for her?'

'Absolutely.'

*

The boy's initial conclusion was that someone had stolen his prize. But, as he thought more logically, he wondered why they hadn't taken the trolley with them. After all the man was heavy – a dead weight. The man had been groaning earlier on – what if he wasn't dead? What if he'd been pretending and had got out and gone to call the police?

This was making him angry.

He began to walk around, looking behind the bins and then the cars. There was no sign of him. How would he get to the man before he got to the police? It was exquisite torment, making his nerves tingle.

Grabbing the handles of the trolley, he began to push it aggressively in the direction he'd come from.

He caught sight of the man within thirty seconds of setting off. He was slumped against a street light, his hand clutching his stomach. The boy wasn't sure whether he was faking the injury; perhaps he was waiting for him to catch up and then he would lay into him?

Cautiously, he began to circle the man, keeping away from the light spill. He could hear moaning. This wasn't right, or fair. He looked around for something to help him. Maybe there'd be a heavy object or something with a sharp edge.

A couple of hundred metres away, he could see a series of cones, indicating that utility works had sectioned off part of the road. Glancing at the man, who still hadn't seen him, he ran over to it. There was nothing but a huge hole filled with rainwater. There were no tools, only a pile of broken paving slabs, ranging in size from fragments of rubble to several feet across.

Deftly, he slid past the barrier and searched for the perfect-sized piece, something that would deliver a sufficient blow without being too unwieldy to grip or too heavy to swing.

It didn't take him long to find the exact piece.

He turned back to the man, who was trying to pull himself to his feet. The boy looked around, gauging how far away the nearest house was and then made his way over. It was then that the man began to scream. It was a high-pitched animal scream, not unlike the noise made by the various cats he'd encountered over the years.

He raised the slab and brought it down onto the man's head. The scream was silenced as the man fell against his feet.

Stepping backwards, the boy raised the slab again and let it fall onto the man's skull. He was about to repeat the action when a man's voice yelled from somewhere above him. 'What the hell are you doing?'

Turning slowly around, he could see a light from a second-floor window and someone peering into the darkness.

'I'm calling the police!' the voice called with less conviction.

Turning away from the light and sheltering the man's body with his, he waited for the inevitable. The window closed and the light disappeared as apathy replaced irritation.

He remained still for a moment or two and then, looping his arms under the dead man's, he dragged the bloodied body towards the edge of the light spill and tipped it into the water-filled hole. He was tired and desperately wanted to get into bed, but he had a job to do before that. He covered the body with broken slabs, turned on his heel and, collecting the trolley, made his way back to his secret place. Whatever else happened tonight, he had to put the screws back into the lock and make sure nobody else could enter.

*

As the clock turned midnight, Claddis McAvoy was well into his stride. The article would be a rounded condemnation of the Toronto PS's lazy approach to dealing with dangerous members of their society.

'*Having ignored the pleas of a neighbour regarding the disappearance of a valued elderly member of their community, the police compounded their apathy by ignoring the advice of one of the country's leading...*'

He scrubbed the last few words and replaced them with '*North America's leading profilers – that a dangerous psychopath was roaming the streets, looking for more than dogs to murder*'. It was classy, provocative and just the sort of story his readership loved.

Sitting back in his chair, he poured himself another well-deserved glass of whisky. He'd get the photography department to knock up some images to add that essential emotive tug.

*

The boy was cold, wet and irritable when he finally made it back into the house. The very last thing he'd expected or wanted was that his mother would be waiting up for him.

'Alan...? Is that you?'

He could hear her getting out of the chair and making her way towards him. Slipping off his boots he ran upstairs and locked the door behind him.

'I've been so worried—'

Her heavy, slow footsteps could be heard climbing the stairs. He knew she wouldn't try to open the door, but he slipped off his bloodied coat, tucked it into the wardrobe and pulled the bedcover over him.

She was standing outside his room. He could hear her raised breathing as she panted from the exertion of climbing the stairs.

'Alan's not here. Have you seen him?'

He listened.

'Honey, did you see him at all earlier?' She made a gentle tapping sound on the door.

'Don't!' he snapped.

But Rula was beyond caring what her son thought. She tried the handle. 'Honey, I need to talk to you.'

He looked at the clock, zoning out her nagging.

Suddenly, she banged on the door sharply: something she very rarely did. 'Open this door! I need to know when you last saw Alan. I think something's happened to him.'

He was getting angry and knew that it was best that she left. 'I haven't seen him,' he spat.

'Not at all?' she asked with her voice lowered.

'No!' he said.

There was a pause and his mother understood that the conversation was at an end. She began to walk slowly down the stairs. Turning off the light, the boy lay on his back and stared at the clock's luminous hands, letting the steady ticking soothe him to sleep. He was happy and warm.

*

Rula Frears stood at the bottom of the stairs and wept. For her missing husband, for her useless son, for all the guilt she carried, but mostly because she believed that all of the horrible things that had happened over the years had been her fault.

Unsure whether she should lock the front door or leave it open just in case Alan came back, she settled on locking it. After all, it was very unlikely that she'd get any sleep now.

Sliding the chain across the door, she turned and saw her son's boots. They were in their usual position but neither ball of newspaper had been placed in either boot. That never happened.

A chill ran down her spine as she stared up at her son's door.

CHAPTER TWELVE

'What's the plan for today?' asked Laurence over the phone.

'I shall be digging until "hell freezes over" to quote Samuelson. And after last night I'm beginning to believe that the freezing process has started,' replied Eleanor. She grabbed the coffee and slid five bucks across the counter. 'But I suspect we won't start until there's a let-up in the weather,' she said, observing a river of rainfall snaking its way along the street.

'Has the thermocouple arrived?' asked Laurence.

'Not yet.'

'Wanna stay with me until it does?' he said cautiously.

She smiled. 'Thanks, but I'm guessing a chill is good for the soul.'

'Offer's there,' he replied, more lightly.

'When are you in? I want to catch up before I head out.'

'Thirty minutes?' he said. 'Traffic's backed up.'

Eleanor was keeping a low profile. She had several missed calls from the dig team, followed by a terse text message enquiring whether, *'she had the time to pop down and help supervise the dig she had organised, or should the team just wait for further instruction?*

Sighing, she prepared to leave her office. She'd hoped that Mo and Laurence would have arrived before she left, but her latest missed call was from Marty, who would be pursuing her any minute now.

She was just pulling on her coat when there was a knock at the door. 'I'm going!' she snarled.

'DI Eleanor Raven?' A man walked in, thrusting his hand towards her. 'I'm Richard Glass from the bonding department. I've been trying to catch you for several days now.'

Eleanor looked at him. He wore heavy-framed, round glasses, which gave the impression of a studious and sincere nature in a marked contrast to his small, widely spaced dark eyes. She imagined his choice of frames might have been either insight on his part or that of a particularly astute optician.

'I have to leave. I'm in the middle of a homicide and a team are waiting for me.'

She grabbed her bag, manoeuvred herself around the table and made for the door, which he stood firmly in front of.

'I understand that you are extremely busy, Detective, but this matter is of extreme urgency.'

'More urgent than the finding of a young woman's body in a public park?' she snapped.

He wavered and looked ready to concede. 'Perhaps not as important as that, but—'

The door was thrust open from the other side, cracking hard into Glass's left shoulder and hip and launching him into the side of the desk.

Marty Samuelson's unexpected arrival rarely elicited such feelings of relief and gratitude from Eleanor, but sliding deftly past both men, she disappeared down the corridor.

*

Laurence stared at Monster and sighed deeply. The photograph did not show him at his best. His eyes were half closed and his tongue was lolling out of the side of his huge snout, diminishing the impact of the gleaming Toronto PS 'Distinguished Service' medal hanging round his neck. He was, concluded Laurence, an idiot.

Apparently not everyone shared this view, as below the image were two similar-sized photographs of police dogs Chance and Zena, and a list of the eighteen officers who wanted a puppy. Newly arrived on the 'Puppy Board' were two ultrasound images of both litters of growing pups. Comments, including 'Cute' and 'Aww', further enraged Laurence. Perhaps it was just as well the bloody dog was going to live with Mags – he'd be well rid of him.

'And where's the proud dad?' asked Timms, leaning against the door frame.

'Monster has gone for a second breakfast in the canteen, with Mo,' snapped Laurence, with slightly more hysteria than the circumstances merited. 'Apparently he needs to keep his strength up.'

Timms smirked. 'Have you found his Kennel Club registration?'

'No!'

'Okay, just asking,' said Timms, opening both his hands in a calming gesture.

'We've got a due date for Chance.' Timms waited for Laurence to show some interest. When none was forthcoming he stood upright. 'End of the month apparently. Going to run it as a raffle.'

'Excellent,' said Laurence, moving past him into his office and closing the door firmly, but not before he caught Timms rolling his eyes.

*

'Raven, are you in the building?' Laurence yelled into his phone.

'No, I'm in the park, looking at mud,' said Eleanor flatly. Despite the improvement in the weather, the excavated area was full of knee-deep rainwater.

'You got a body yet?' he teased.

'I've got a mare's nest!' she snapped.

*

Eleanor stood by the side of the latest hole and watched as it grew larger and muddier. She surveyed the rose garden, despairing that only a third of it had so far been excavated. Her phone made a steady clicking sound as emails and texts arrived from various departments. She dumped Richard Glass's two messages into trash without opening them and read Ruby Delaware's gentle reminder requesting that Eleanor send her some materials. Irritated that she hadn't done this before making her emergency exit, she tapped her phone against her teeth and tried to organise her thought processes.

'Good morning,' said Jacob Hareton quietly. 'Thought you'd like a warm drink.' He handed Eleanor a mug of coffee. 'How's the dig?'

'What are you going to do when we've finished? Can those be saved?' she asked, pointing at the growing mound of rose-bush roots. Jacob had been occupied by the salvage of the roots, wrapping the undamaged plants in hessian.

'Most things can be saved,' he said, smiling. 'It's an opportunity to use the space in a different way. I was thinking we should have fewer roses and create a more natural environment that's bee and bug friendly.' He paused. 'It rather depends on whether you find a body in here.'

'I think you're fairly safe on that score,' she commented dryly.

'I guess if anyone's going to locate a body it'll be you,' he said.

'Why do you say that?' she asked, puzzled.

'I read about you locating the skeleton under the house where that soldier shot his wife.'

'Ah, I haven't really been following the press coverage,' she answered uncomfortably.

'Hmm, maybe you should look at today's *Sun*,' he said cautiously.

'Why today's?' Eleanor asked, beginning to feel the hairs rising on her neck.

'You're still partnered up with Laurence Whitefoot?'

She nodded.

'Maybe you should find a copy.'

*

'Detective Layton, how the hell are you?' asked Mo, settling himself into his armchair and adjusting his headset. 'You improved that golfing handicap?'

Marcus Layton laughed and cleared his throat. 'Work in progress.'

'Just a courtesy call,' noted Mo carefully. 'See how that Roma Joe Greene case of yours is going?'

There was a pause before Layton spoke. 'I was going to call Whitefoot about that today. You worked the case Joe was locked up for?'

Mo leaned forward and grabbed his pen. 'I did.'

Again there was a wait while Layton pondered. 'Did you guys threaten him in any way when you interviewed him?'

'Not that I'm aware of,' answered Mo.

'I got no reason for this guy to suddenly end it. None.'

'You getting pressured to find a reason?' asked Mo, fishing.

'Yeah… I'm about to have a little chat with Roma Joe's mom – fancy accompanying me?'

'Ah, the lovely Betty Greene. I'd be delighted,' said Mo, scribbling a note on his pad.

'I'm on the way into town; how about I pick you up and you can join me? Then you can tell me all about why you needed to talk to our client twenty-four hours before he was found dead.'

Unlike her son, Betty Greene recognised Mo instantly. 'What you want?' she spat, her strong Hungarian accent adding weight to her contempt. 'You are not welcome!'

'Story of my life, Mrs Greene,' Mo replied.

Pinching her lips together, she stood back, allowing the two detectives to enter her trailer. 'Take your shoes off!' she hissed.

Sighing, both men obliged and were led into the lounge. Every seat was covered in thick PVC protectors and it seemed to take Betty several moments before she could reconcile herself to the two men lowering their backsides onto her furniture.

'I know you. Who is he?'

'I'm Detective Marcus Layton and I'm investigating the circumstances of your son's suicide.'

Betty snorted.

'When was the last time you saw your son, Mrs Greene?' asked Layton.

There was a pause while Betty fine-tuned her expression to convey non-compliance.

'Did he seem depressed to you?' persisted Layton.

Betty folded her arms across her chest.

'Did your son mention any enemies in prison or situations that he was finding difficult to manage?' Layton queried.

Betty turned away, shrugging.

Mo lifted his hand and took over the questioning. 'What always interested me about your son's case is why he confessed. He didn't really put up a defence. He just said he did it. Less than an hour into questioning him, he was ready to sign on the dotted line.' Mo lowered his tone and leaned in towards Betty. 'Your son wasn't the type to make life easy for law enforcement. But when I arrested him, he couldn't wait to fess up to the murders. Why?'

Betty said nothing. Her tightly clamped lips and jaw began to pale with the effort to seal her mouth.

Mo continued, 'I saw him the morning before he killed himself. He wanted to see his psychiatrist, not the prison one. Why?'

Betty was becoming angry. Her shoulders were raised and her blinking increased. 'Why couldn't he see him?' she demanded.

'Because your son's requirements aren't high on the taxpayer's shopping list!'

'I want you to leave now,' she said firmly, her body shaking with suppressed rage.

'Joe had spoken to the prison psychiatrist about his mind being cold. Is that something he mentioned to you?' Layton paused, waiting for a response. 'Your son is dead, Mrs Greene, and we are trying to find out why?'

'Joe is dead because *you* kill him! He wouldn't kill himself if you let him see the doctor,' she screamed. Jumping to her feet, she made to lunge at Mo, but Layton stood up and grabbed her upper arms, restraining her.

'Get out of my house,' she spat.

There was a tense silence before Layton gently released Betty's arms and nodded that they would leave.

As they made their way to the door, Mo turned to her. 'You're right, Mrs Greene. What was his doctor's name?'

'You are the *big* detective,' she spat. '*You* find out.'

Mo reached for the door handle, noting Betty's revulsion as he touched the latch.

*

Eleanor's phone rang before she could call Laurence.

'Have you seen today's paper?' he began.

'No, give me the highlights,' she sighed.

'Listen to this: "*Toronto PS negligent in trying to find psychopath, despite warnings from North America's leading profiler that one is loose and active on the streets of Toronto*." I'm named as number one *negligent* asshole.'

'Okay, so?'

'It goes on to insinuate that despite a neighbour complaining that Veronica Sizemore was missing, I've done nothing to locate her. The probable conclusion being that she was abducted and murdered by said Toronto psychopath!'

Eleanor could hear Laurence's inhale as he prepared to vent further outrage and she interrupted quickly. 'So where is she?'

There was a pause.

'I don't know.'

'Hang on, let me get this right. This is the woman who complained that there was a body in the building she lived in. We *didn't* find the decaying corpses of taxpaying members of the public, but on further investigation we *did* find that there was a robust collection of dead dogs there.'

'Yes, but—' began her partner.

'And now she's gone AWOL herself.'

The silence expanded.

'I *told* you not to let this slip. Go and find Veronica Sizemore *and* the dog killer and keep me informed of your progress. Okay?'

'Shall I keep McAvoy in the loop as well?' he added sarcastically.

'If it helps!' she snapped back, disconnecting.

For a moment her irritation with him gave way to a rare surge of guilt. Maybe she should have spent a little more time supporting him and less time just criticising.

*

Instead of dropping Mo back at HQ, Layton had brought him along to interview a former cellmate of Roma Joe's. They waited for Nibs to finish fidgeting and sizing them up before opening the conversation. The prison interview room was hot and stuffy. It smelled rancid.

'So you'd describe yourself as a friend of Roma Joe's then?' offered Layton.

Nibs, aka Jordain Lasky, had shared a cell with Roma Joe for the past three years, but since a change in prison policy had enabled long-term prisoners to have single-cell occupancy, he'd moved to his own room further down the corridor.

'Hmm, yeah. Maybe,' said Nibs without conviction.

'Acquaintance then?' suggested Layton.

Nibs didn't look ready to commit.

'What would you say his mental state was like over the past week,' asked Layton.

Nibs scratched his head.

'Did he seem suicidal to you?' snapped Mo.

'You never know in here,' said Nibs, now on safer ground.

Mo leaned forward. 'You were the last person to talk to Joe, so we really need to know your view of the state of his mental health.'

'I don't know nothing about that,' said Nibs.

'What did he tell you?' asked Mo carefully.

Nibs picked at a fingernail.

Sliding a piece of paper across the desk, Layton tapped a finger against it. 'This is a signed note from the Governor, agreeing that your privileges should receive a little top-up.

Nibs smiled and studied it. 'Ask away.'

Mo nodded. 'What did you talk about?'

'He said he needed to talk to his doctor.'

'What's his name?'

Nibs shrugged. 'He's some guy he used to see about his problems before he got banged up here.'

'His psychiatrist?'

'I guess. This guy got him to thinking he was cold all the time. But after he told him all his problems' – Nibs waved air quotes, 'He felt all warm and cosy.'

There was a pause. 'What the hell does that mean?' asked Layton.

Nibs exhaled and shook his head. 'I dunno but that's what he was saying.'

'What?'

'He *said* if they didn't let him see him, the cold would take him.'

'Those were his exact words?' asked Mo.

Nibs nodded. 'I guess the cold did take him.'

*

For the past twenty minutes Laurence had been trying to get in touch with the two patrol officers he'd left in charge of investigating the hanged dogs. It was, he thought, an exercise in learning that delegation guaranteed a goddamn mess. He was now stuck in traffic and the thought of meeting Claddis McAvoy at his apartment block was sending little shots of irritation through his already dismal mood. He pressed retry on his phone.

'Is that Constable Barns?' asked Laurence, trying to achieve a non-confrontational tone.

'Speaking,' drawled the reply.

'This is Detective Whitefoot – we spoke the other day regarding the progress you'd made on the dog deaths.'

'Yeah, we did,' came the response.

'I'd appreciate you and PC Stamfort meeting me in the next half hour or so.'

'Hmm, well we're a bit tied up with a car theft at the moment.'

'I'm going to make my way over to Veronica Sizemore's apartment and I expect to see you both there.'

Laurence could hear PC Barns making nasal sounds and played his trump card. 'I've just spoken to your commanding officer, who has *assured* me of your complete assistance in this matter.'

There was an icy silence.

'See you in thirty then,' said Laurence, disconnecting. He'd have just enough time to exercise Monster, appease Claddis McAvoy and locate the caretaker before the two PCs arrived.

*

Pulling in next to Veronica Sizemore's tiny Honda, Laurence instinctively put his hand on the engine – it was cold. Monster hopped out of the passenger seat and after a brief sniff set off purposefully in the direction of the boiler-room door. He began to bark loudly as Laurence scrolled through to Claddis McAvoy's mobile number.

'McAvoy speaking,'

'This is Detective Whitefoot,' he said, putting a finger in his left ear to drown out the barking. 'I'm over here conducting further investigations.' Laurence stopped and stared at Monster, who was standing on his back feet scratching energetically at the steel door with his front paws.

'Oh really,' replied Claddis smugly. 'Would that be because—?'

Laurence disconnected and walked hurriedly over to Monster. Clipping the leash onto his collar, he pulled Monster back to the nearby bike rack and fastened him to the structure, then, slipping on a pair of latex gloves, he moved towards the door.

There was no mistaking the heady smell of decomposition.

He examined the lock, noticing the evident damage to the screw heads that had attached the steel plate to the wooden architrave. Each bore signs of having been scratched and dented by a tool.

He slid his penknife under the plate, feeling his stomach churn as it gave slightly under the pressure. Somebody had undone and replaced the screws.

Carefully, Laurence used his penknife to remove them and, switching on his small pocket torch, entered the boiler room for the second time.

He wasn't sure whether seconds or minutes had elapsed before he finally managed to dial his partner. 'I need you,' he heard himself say.

CHAPTER THIRTEEN

Laurence was trying to prioritise his actions but intense pangs of guilt and Monster's unremitting bark were having an adverse effect on his thinking. He'd called Susan Cheung and was now waiting for confirmation of Crime Scene's ETA. Eleanor was on her way and, by his estimation, would be with him in about ten minutes. He could see PCs Stamfort and Barns making their unhurried way over to him from the opposite side of the street. Unlooping Monster and standing in front of the steel door, he waited for their arrival.

The two officers, immediately appreciating the implications of discovering Veronica Sizemore in the same spot as the dead dogs, galvanized themselves into action, cordoning off the area and preparing to receive the numerous teams that supported a murder investigation.

'Is he a serving officer?' asked PC Stamfort, nodding in Monster's direction.

'He's trained,' answered Laurence vaguely.

'I'll have him with me while you secure the scene,' he said helpfully. Taking the leash from Laurence's hand, he leaned towards him. 'It's definitely Miss Sizemore?'

Laurence nodded. 'It's her.'

'Crap,' he said, with feeling.

Laurence caught sight of Claddis McAvoy pulling into his parking space and looking at them with a puzzled expression.

'More crap to come,' said Laurence, lifting his chin towards Claddis, who was hurrying over to them. 'You know who that is?'

'I know him,' snarled Stamfort. 'I'll get rid of him, till you're ready.'

*

Eleanor, spotting Laurence and the two patrol officers, manoeuvred her car across the entrance to the parking area and jumped out. Waving her badge at PC Stamfort, she made her way over towards Laurence. 'Are you sure?' she asked.

He nodded uncomfortably.

'Walk me through,' she said, pulling plastic booties over her shoes and handing spares over to Laurence. Keeping close to the wall, to avoid overstepping any viable shoe prints, she made her way down the steps and into the boiler room.

Laurence opened his mouth but Eleanor put her finger up to silence him.

'Later.'

He nodded uncomfortably.

'What do you see?' she asked him, gazing at the body.

Laurence took his time. 'She's been beaten, and looking at the lack of congestion, I'd say she was probably dead when she was strung up.'

Eleanor nodded and shone her torch at the face. 'How long has she been missing?'

'This is day three,' he answered, feeling his cheeks redden.

'Uh-huh. She looks about three days dead to me. Agree?' she asked.

'Yes.'

'Is there a weapon?'

'I haven't seen one in here.'

'Have you searched the area?'

'Not yet,' he replied.

Eleanor inhaled and counted. 'Perhaps you'd better go and take a quick look around,' she said, her voice sounding tight. 'I'm going to need the photos of the dogs. You took some?'

'On my phone. I'll send them.'

She nodded. 'Who are we going to be looking for?'

'Male. Late teens, early twenties.' He paused. 'Local. Strong and probably white.'

She nodded. 'That's what the stats tell us. Speak to Ruby Delaware, and if this guy's local, then you'd better get those two patrol officers to start running through likely names. Did I just see Claddis McAvoy?'

'Yeah.' He nodded glumly.

'Does he know she's down here yet?'

'A matter of minutes I'm guessing.'

The sound of sirens could be heard in the distance. 'Let's see if we can get rid of him before the circus arrives.'

Claddis McAvoy was in the middle of an animated conversation with PC Stamfort, while his cameraman took photographs of the area. Eleanor set her expression and walked briskly towards them, noticing how Claddis's body language revealed anxiety as he saw her approach.

'DI Raven,' said Claddis, 'you remember Mike, don't you?' He lowered his voice theatrically. 'He took those compromising photos of the – *attack*.' He mimed a punching gesture at his face. 'I'd like to say, for the record, that there is a current restraining order out on DI Raven. She subjected my person to an unprovoked physical assault.'

'Really,' stated PC Stamfort, unimpressed.

Mike took several paces backwards and began to adjust his camera.

Claddis was undeterred by Stamfort's disinterest. 'What's happening here? I must add that it's a sad indictment of the

TPS that you only take action after an article in the *Toronto Sun* draws public attention to your apathy and disorganisation,' he said didactically.

Eleanor was wondering why the sirens had stopped a couple of blocks away. Both journalists' phones began to ring but Claddis was on a roll.

'I, *personally*, am happy to accept an apology, but assaults on the *fourth estate* are never taken lightly,' he said, leaning into Eleanor's personal space.

The intervening months of therapy since she'd repeatedly punched Claddis McAvoy's smug face until he lost consciousness had done little to diminish her desire to do it again.

More sirens could be heard approaching. Mike, the photographer, whispered something to Claddis, who nodded back.

'Never a dull moment!' he sighed, heading over to his car. 'Tell Detective Whitefoot that I'll happily take his call when he's ready to talk to the *Sun* about any progress on finding the psychopath... or poor Miss Sizemore,' he added, jumping into his car, easing it past Eleanor's vehicle and heading off down the street.

'Asshole!' said Stamfort.

Eleanor's phone rang just as the emergency vehicles began to arrive, fortunately from the opposite direction to that just taken by Claddis. 'Yes?'

'Ms Raven? This is Dr Launceston's receptionist. You appear to have missed your appointment slot,' said a pinched voice.

'I've been called out to a homicide,' snapped Eleanor. 'If I get an opportunity to *pop* in, I shall let you know.' She disconnected with relish and walked towards the Crime Scene crew.

*

'This is horribly familiar,' said Manny, Susan Cheung's second officer.

'Hmm,' murmured Laurence. 'You'd better follow me.'

'Dogs again?'

'Little old lady,' responded Laurence glumly.

'*Je*sus!' replied Manny. 'We're on a skeleton crew for the next couple of hours; another call came in at the same time as yours. You the primary on this?'

'Waiting for confirmation, but probably.'

They headed down the stairs to examine the crime scene. Manny looked at the body. 'You've IDed her?'

'Yes, she's Veronica Sizemore and she was reported missing about three days ago.'

Manny turned to him. 'I was *here* three days ago!'

*

Less than half a mile away, Timms and his partner Sarah Wadesky were staring at their own crime scene. Timms was taking his time. Susan Cheung and the technicians stood at a respectful distance, waiting for the go-ahead. He'd seen several hastily covered bodies before, but this was an unusual place to find one.

He looked at the surrounding properties. All fairly basic but well maintained. They appeared to be mainly family dwellings. The hole was overlooked by several windows and the proceedings would have been audible and visible.

He saw Wadesky shake her head in his direction as she opened the gate to interview a second household.

'Ready?' he mouthed to Susan, who nodded and made her way over to begin the laborious process of uncovering the body of Alan Frears.

*

'Run that past me again,' said Wadesky, jotting notes into her book.

The man who stood in front of her didn't bother to hide his irritation. 'I *told* you what I saw.'

'It would be helpful if you could run through it again, for the benefit of my slow handwriting. You heard a noise at about...?'

Sighing heavily, Mr Lambert repeated his version of the previous night's events. 'I heard some guys swearing and yelling at around midnight. They were obviously drunk, as the one guy was on his knees and retching.'

'You saw that?'

'Yeah.'

'How?' she asked.

'Whatd'ya mean? It was dark and they were stood under the street light. So I got a clear look.'

'I'd be grateful if you'd step outside and show me exactly where the two men were standing,' she coaxed.

'Jeez – there!' He pointed his arm in the general direction of one of the street lights.

'Walk me to the spot, sir. Of course, you may prefer to answer my questions at Police HQ?'

He snatched his coat from the rack next to the front door and, after slipping on his boots, yanked open the front door and stomped down the path.

'Here!' he snarled, opening his arms to indicate the area.

Wadesky moved closer to him and looked up at his house. 'Are you sure? Because I can't see your bedroom window from here.'

'Huh?' He looked up at the house and then at the street lighting. It took him a moment or two to reorient himself and move to the next street lamp. 'Guess it was this one. Yeah, this one.'

'Will you stand where you saw the man who was on his knees?'

With a laboured sigh, Mr Lambert positioned himself near to the street light.

'He had his arms wrapped round it and he was yelling.'

'What was he yelling?' asked Wadesky.

Mr Lambert shrugged.

'There must have been something other than just noise that made you open your window and engage.'

'He was calling for help.'

'Why?'

'How the fuck should I know? He was *drunk*!'

'*Was* he is danger?'

'There was another guy that came and helped him.'

'How?'

'Dunno. He came and helped him to stand up.'

'Is it possible that the man who is now lying dead twenty yards away was calling for help because the second guy was going to kill him?'

'Look, I told them I'd call the police if it carried on, but it didn't!'

'But it *did*, Mr Lambert. It did carry on because the guy who called for help needed it. I need a description of the second man.'

'I didn't see his face.'

'Was he tall, short, fat, skinny, Caucasian, black? Did he have an unusual stance? Come on, Mr Lambert, make an effort to redeem yourself!'

'I think he was a white guy and fairly tall.'

'How d'ya know he was tall?'

He thought. 'Dunno... I...' He shook his head and then looked up. 'I don't know if he was tall but the coat he was wearing was too small, like a couple of sizes too small. I could see his wrists... and the shoulders were so tight it made the bottom edge of the coat fan out.'

'What sort of coat was it?' she asked hopefully.

'Like a trench coat. The sort of coats they wore in World War One. You know, old-fashioned; heavy material.'

'Could you make out any of his features?'

He shook his head.

'What about his hair? Short? Curly?'

'Shoulder-length, messy.'

'Anything else?'

'Nothing,' he said, turning towards his house.

'You've been very helpful but we will need you to sit with our forensic artist.'

He opened his mouth to voice a complaint but Wadesky held up a finger. 'A car will collect you in the next thirty minutes. Thank you for your assistance.'

*

'Okay,' said Manny, running a handkerchief around his sweaty face. 'We're just waiting for the ME to arrive and then we can lift her down.'

'Fingerprints?' asked Eleanor.

'Maybe a couple of palm prints,' he answered. 'It's very wet down there and the steel handrail has some smudges. The perp dragged his hand down the rail at one stage, but it's difficult to get a complete. I'm surmising our lady was probably attacked at the top of the steps, fell backwards and was then dragged down the steps by her ankles. There's blood and tissue on most of the steps and some obvious boot prints.'

'When can we see the images?' she asked.

Manny smiled. 'As soon as. We've cleared a safe path down, so keep to the paper and I can show you how he hoisted her up.'

Laurence and Eleanor followed Manny down into the boiler room. A technician was photographing the knot that held the body aloft.

'How did he get her up there?' asked Eleanor.

'I'm pretty sure the rope he used was down here already. The dogs had all been lifted in his arms, then had the rope placed round their necks and the end tied twice round the old heating pipes that run along the ceiling,' said Manny.

Laurence called up the photos on his mobile and pointed this out to her.

'There was about ten feet of unused rope left dangling from the last dog. So, I guess he could have added a couple more, if he'd fancied.'

'You took that rope with you when the dogs were removed?' asked Eleanor.

Manny nodded. 'This piece was left over by the vent.' He pointed to a small, lint-blocked steel vent. 'He placed it under both of her arms, looped one through the other and then, passing both ends over the pipe, he pulled her up, knotted the ends and hooked them under the overflow pipe leading out from the old boiler system.'

'How strong would he need to be?' asked Eleanor.

Manny did a quick mental calculation. 'You could do it at a push; much easier for Whitefoot and me.'

She nodded.

*

Timms looked at what was left of the man's face. 'Think anyone's gonna recognise him?' he asked Wadesky.

'You want me to answer that?' she replied, looking at the body.

His face, or what once constituted his face, was turned towards them; his hands were wrapped around his belly and his legs were tucked into his chest. He looked to Timms as if he'd been rolled into the hole, presumably post-mortem. The water had been mechanically sucked out of the hole and was in the process of being filtered in case there was some overlooked evidence suspended in it.

'He's very pale,' said Timms, hunkering down next to the body. 'Looks to me as if he bled out. Gonna take a bet at him having been stabbed before the final blow to the face.'

'Which would explain why he doesn't seem to have any defence wounds to his hands,' offered Wadesky. 'Where do you want to start?'

Timms sighed. 'Nearest drinking dens. If he did bleed out he'd have left a trail and I want to know where the poor guy came from.'

'It's rained hard,' she said.

'Yeah,' responded Timms. 'But we are clutching at straws.'

*

Eleanor watched as Veronica Sizemore was gently lowered and zipped into a body bag. Looking around the dank little room, she tried to imagine the appeal for the killer. 'You spoke to the caretaker?'

Laurence nodded. 'He says he never comes down here because the new boiler suite is situated inside the building and it's too damp to store anything here.'

'Is he genuine?'

'Pretty sure he's not involved.'

They followed the two morgue assistants as they carefully carried the body up the steps and placed it on a gurney.

'Have you got a list of the tenants?'

'Yeah, no one under the age of thirty-five.'

'Get me the list and check whether anyone has a previous history that we might consider interesting. Whoever did this treasures this space and unless he finds out that we've already removed Miss Sizemore, he's going to come back.'

Suddenly, Laurence looked happier. 'You think that he'll come back?'

'This is his special space and, if we can prevent the story getting out for the next couple of days, we should be able to pick him up. That means keeping Claddis McAvoy out of the picture and setting up a twenty-four-hour watch. Can you organise this? I have to get back to the dig site for the last hour. Choose your spot and keep this under wraps. It hits the paper and you'll lose your advantage. Understand?'

'I hear you.'

'Call Ruby Delaware after you get a list of known animal abusers off the local guys. That's where you start.'

She stared at him. He looked pale and worried. 'You can do this. Run everything past me first and set up your night watch carefully.'

Eleanor's head was throbbing ferociously by the time she made her way up the stairs to her apartment. She'd checked her mailbox for packages but had to settle for a hastily scrawled note from her landlord, which indicated that he'd taken a look and was '*fairly* certain' that she needed a new thermocouple and would order one immediately.

'Eleanor? Is that you?'

'It is.'

Mrs Egerton stood in her doorway, clutching her ancient pug. 'Mr Melgar said your heating wasn't working. Would you like to bathe here?' she asked nervously.

'That's very kind of you, but—' She heard herself rumble out her usual negative response to any unnecessary social interaction and stopped. 'That would be lovely. I'd very much appreciate that.'

'The bath will be run in ten and I'll leave the door unlocked for you.' Mrs Egerton turned, her face illuminated with pleasure, and bustled back into her apartment.

Despite her fatigue, Eleanor felt an uncomfortable sadness as she recognised that the older woman was lonely and isolated, and the very thing that she treasured most, her privacy, was a burden and a fear for most people. She sighed and unlocked her door, trying to recall a time when she had gone out of her way to communicate with her neighbour.

Her apartment was beginning to smell damp and un-lived in.

Catching a glimpse of her exhausted face in the mirror, she grabbed her bathrobe, towels and wash bag. She opened the fridge, pulled out a bottle of wine and, after selecting two glasses and her keys, headed next door.

The bath was deep, boiling hot and filled with rose-scented bubbles. Eleanor was touched to see that her neighbour had placed a pile of towels on the small seat next to the bath.

'Eleanor?' asked Mrs Egerton timorously. 'Have you everything you need?'

Eleanor drew in a deep breath and answered, 'A bit of company after my bath would be nice.'

By the time she'd bathed and listened to the entire meandering life story of Mrs Egerton and her pug, it was heading towards midnight. Eleanor couldn't remember ever having spent that much time making, or rather listening to, small talk. She discovered that if you just made the right facial expressions combined with the odd nod of agreement, people filled in the gaps, just as your presence did.

'Don't be a stranger now,' said Mrs Egerton, closing the door.

Eleanor smiled and took a pace into the corridor, feeling a surge of adrenaline as she saw a shadowed figure leaning against the wall.

'Eleanor?' he asked quietly.

'How long have you been waiting?' she replied, quickly unlocking her door.

'Not so long,' Jacob Hareton said. 'I've brought you a couple of heaters.'

She looked at the three large electric heaters and suspected that he'd made several trips up from his car.

'How'd you get in?' she asked with concern.

'Wow, it's cold in here. Where shall I put them?'

She drew her bathrobe tightly round her and pointed to the living room. Jacob turned on the heaters and a steady warmth began to cut through the cold.

'Who let you in?' she repeated.

'Mr Melgar, your caretaker.'

'Would you like a drink?' she asked carefully.

'That would be spot on,' he replied. 'Wine? Or do I risk arrest for DUI?'

She smiled, grabbed a bottle and left it with him while she pulled on more clothes. When she walked back into the lounge, Jacob was gone. Picking up her glass, she followed the sounds back into her kitchen. He was hunkered down, peering into the boiler.

'Consensus so far is the thermocouple,' she remarked, leaning against the door frame.

Jacob nodded. 'I've got the model details. Leave it with me.'

There was a silence between them as Jacob got to his feet and carefully refitted and closed the front panel. He turned to her and held out his hand. For a moment Eleanor was unsure what he meant by the gesture. Slowly, she reached forward and took it. It was warm but roughened by outdoor work. For the seconds before she released his grasp, a sense of calm settled on her. She was dimly aware that her eyes were closing.

'You need to sleep,' he said gently. 'Listen to your body.'

He smiled, swallowed his last sip of wine and left, closing the door quietly behind him.

*

Laurence was already exhausted, so the thought of sitting in a freezing cold car for the next eight hours wasn't something he relished. However, his spirits were sustained by his strong belief that Eleanor was right and the killer *would* return to the scene of his crime. He could have persuaded Johnson to take a shift but the knowledge that he was personally responsible for Veronica Sizemore's death was weighing heavily. He would stay till 6 a.m., dash back home for a shower, take Monster out for a walk and then make it in for the morning meeting.

He'd cracked a window to prevent the glass from steaming up and enable him to hear any approaching footsteps. Several cars had arrived, parked and disgorged tired tenants, who had tended to head for the opposite entrance to the apartment complex. No one had given a second glance to the boiler room, or made any attempt to head in that direction.

In an effort to keep himself alert, Laurence was binging on max-strength caffeine tablets, which were rewarding him with a pulsing headache.

*

Rula Frears hadn't gone into work until the afternoon. She had never been late before, but having sat up all night wondering where her husband was and, more sinisterly, whether his absence had anything to do with her son, she was incapable of getting into the office before noon.

While she was there all she could focus on was the end of her shift and the receding hope that Alan had made it back home. Her boss said she could leave early and take the next day off if she needed to. Rula was so grateful that she almost told him what was worrying her but, sensibly, she kept her business to herself.

Several scenarios had played through her head, the most likely being that Alan and her son had had a fight and, reaching breaking point, Alan had slunk off for a few days to mull things over. Why she was clinging to this hope was beyond her. Alan had always dealt with her son calmly and had never even raised a hand to him though, God knows, he'd have been justified in doing so over the years. But until she knew more, Rula was sticking to that theory.

*

The boy woke up refreshed and happy. He stretched like a cat, unfolding his long limbs and feeling the cold room lift the heat from his skin. He needed to eat and he was hoping that his mother had left something good for his breakfast.

The clock assured him that she would have gone to work by now, so pulling on trousers and a T-shirt, he made his way cautiously down to the kitchen. Nothing had changed. His mother had tidied everything away and didn't seem to have spotted that he'd been forced to clean up the mess left by the man. All was right with his world.

He felt a strong desire to leave immediately and check that all was well in his secret place, but he needed to wait until sundown for that.

Disappointingly, his mother hadn't left anything out for him. That was unusual, and he suspected that she was angry with him, as was often the case. He shrugged and opened the fridge. He would make himself something to eat; after all, he wasn't supposed to take the pills the doctor gave him on an empty stomach.

*

Rula reached for the phone. The office was empty and no one would be back for at least another forty minutes. She wanted to ask Alan's brother, Jed, if he'd seen him.

As she cradled the phone in her hand and began to tap in his number, she tried to think about how she was going to word this. Jed and Alan had been close once, but after Rula and Alan got married, the brothers' relationship cooled. Jed had suggested that she have her son hospitalised, after assuming that his dog's injuries and subsequent death had been the boy's fault. She hadn't said anything to Alan but he could be in no doubt as to how she felt about that. Slowly, the men stopped meeting up and then the years passed and she had no idea if Jed even lived in Toronto now.

She put the phone back onto its cradle and stared out of the window at the torrential rain. There was no one to call. All of the people they'd been friends with had slowly dropped away, leaving them isolated.

*

The boy arranged the coat on his bed. It was damp and it had a musty aroma rising from it. He didn't mind that. It reminded him of dark private places, where no one but himself would enter. He rubbed at the large stain on the lapel. It was blood and it smeared onto his hand.

He squinted at the coat. It was covered in dark patches but he wasn't worried about drawing attention to himself. People tended to avoid going near him when he was out at night, so having a bloodied coat was only a problem if his mother caught sight of it.

He sighed. He couldn't bring himself not to wear the coat. He had been given another one, but he didn't like it as much as the trench coat, which his mother had found for him in a second-hand clothes store several years ago. She'd been told that a World War One hero had owned it and he'd been so taken with that idea that he'd worn it continuously since, regardless of the weather. There was something magical about the coat having been worn by a man who had murdered other soldiers, and *maybe* even civilians, all those years ago.

He knew his mother would be home in the next thirty minutes, so pulling on his coat and boots, he slipped out of the house into the rain. He had several things to check up on this evening and he was excited.

As the boy approached the spot where he'd left the body of the man, he was shocked to discover that the area had been taped off with 'Police warning tape'. He wasn't sure what had happened. Maybe something else had taken place there?

Ignoring the tape, he bent under it and made his way over to where he'd left the body. The hole was covered in a sort of tent, which was secured with a metal fastening. He fiddled with it for a moment or two and then, using his penknife, split the material open and peered into the hole. There was a small amount of water, but the street light's penetrating glow revealed that the man was gone.

He shook his head with disbelief. What was happening? Maybe the police had taken him?

For a brief moment the idea crossed his mind that maybe he hadn't been dead after all. But that was ridiculous – when he pushed him into the hole he hadn't even had a face! No, there could be no mistaking what had happened. The police had taken the man away and that was that.

Resolved but anxious, the boy stood up, glanced around to make sure he was still unobserved and headed off towards his special place.

The Tauris was parked on the road, between the boy and the entrance to the special place. On any other night he'd have ignored its presence, but his senses were becoming finely tuned to changes in his environment. The car windows were slightly lowered, which didn't make sense in this weather. No one would leave their windows exposed to the rain as the seats would be saturated by the time they came to use it the next day. Why?

He cautiously approached it and saw that the windows were covered in condensation. Someone was inside the car. Again – why?

The car blocked his passage. If he walked past it, he could go and check his space, but alarm bells were ringing. The car shouldn't be there.

He hesitated, feeling an overwhelming physical desire to visit his space *but* whoever was inside that car was looking at it. Maybe the same person who had taken his dogs! Silently, he turned round and headed back home. He needed to think about all of this.

*

As the boy disappeared into the darkness, the curtains of Claddis McAvoy's apartment eased open and he peered at the Tauris. In his opinion, only cops drove a Tauris. He decided to call his friend Kim and see if she'd heard or seen anything that might explain a night vigil.

CHAPTER FOURTEEN

'You look exhausted!' said Dr Launceston, glancing at Eleanor's face.

'In what way?' she asked, checking her watch.

'Tired, bad-tempered and' – he studied her face again – 'put upon.'

'This is not a good time for me to be navel-gazing. I'm juggling three cases at the moment,' replied Eleanor, lowering herself into the chair opposite the grizzled therapist.

'Then this seems to be an excellent time to me!' replied Launceston, rubbing his fingers together slowly. 'You're under increasing pressure from your department and the city to produce results. This level of stress is identical to the stress which left you dangerously confused and self-destructive not so long ago.'

'In what way self-destructive?' speculated Eleanor coldly.

'I've done a little bit of research on you, as I do on all my new patients, and your history reads a little like a suicide note,' he said, indicating a moleskin notebook on his table.

Eleanor opened her mouth and then clamped it shut again. She noted, as he opened the book, only a few pages had been used.

He sighed as he read his notes. 'It seems as though you are a young lady with a taste for dangerous sexual liaisons. The sort of sexual practices that would not only make your position in the Toronto PD untenable but could put you in considerable personal danger.'

Launceston stared at her, letting her make the next move. A familiar tightening of her throat made its unwanted presence felt. She tried to minimise the sound of her swallowing, but she had to make several attempts to clear her throat before she was able to speak.

'It is my right, as a patient, to see the information you hold on me.' Eleanor's voice sounded alien and disconnected to her, as if a different version of herself had taken over the process of damage control.

Launceston smiled, showing irregular, tobacco-stained teeth. 'You are of course entitled to that. I will get those prepared for you immediately. However, a great deal of what you have spoken about in this room, both to Dr Blackmore and myself, has been kept confidential lest it compromise your status as a detective inspector. If you were to request these private records, a copy would have to be registered with our legal team.'

'Are you threatening me?' she asked.

'Of course not! I am trying to protect you,' he replied sincerely.

'From what – or rather *who*?' she asked.

He took a moment or so to answer. 'From yourself.'

Eleanor stared at him for a moment before getting to her feet. 'This is over,' she said, walking to the door. 'For good.'

Eleanor stood in the atrium of the coroner's building and waited for Laurence to arrive. The space was awash with light, despite the wintry scene outside. The floor-to-ceiling windows were an architectural commitment to lifting the gloomy atmosphere attached to the processing of the dead. An overwhelming sense of anger was making her feel twitchy and she tried to pace it out while she waited. The post-mortem on the unidentified man had been scheduled before that of Veronica Sizemore and she saw

Timms slip out of the primary suite and move gingerly along the corridor to where she was waiting.

'You still digging?' he asked.

'Yes,' she said heavily.

'What's the news on Eddie Myles?'

'Got the call this morning. None of the bones taken from Eddie Myles' poop collection were of North American or European origin,' Eleanor replied unhappily. 'It seems all were of a similar racial type – most probably of Afghan origin.'

'So the case goes to the military?' he asked carefully.

'Chief Brocker confirmed that the Armed Forces will be conducting their own investigation into Eddie Myles and the deaths of his wife, Sonny Maitland and Millie Goldsmith.'

'You've spoken to the DA?' Timms asked.

She nodded. 'He's happy for them to investigate and try the case. We should get some sort of summary of their findings, depending on whether the OSA is breeched, which, for their purposes, you can guarantee it will be!' she hissed.

Timms rubbed his forehead. 'Look at it this way, Raven. You can kick and scream about how you think the military will protect their own and cover up, but my experience is that they'll act decisively to uncover who, if anyone, is to blame for Myles' actions.'

'But you won't know whether that's the case because there will be zero transparency to their actions.'

Timms sighed. 'I don't need to know *what* the military is doing. I just need to know that they're doing it.'

'Where's the accountability?' she asked.

The main doors opened and Laurence waved as he handed over his badge to the security guard. He checked his watch and made his way over to them.

'Anything?' Eleanor asked.

He shook his head. 'Nothing. Has your guy been IDed?' he asked Timms.

'They're running the fingerprints through now, but without a face or any tattoos, we're just waiting for a missing guy to get reported.'

'Teeth?' asked Laurence.

'He took one of the blows to the mouth: his jaw's shattered.'

'Weird that it was less than a mile away from ours.'

Timms shrugged. 'Dodgy bit of town,' he added grimly. 'Hoping he's got form but if not, guess we'll have to see if there's any money in the coffers for a facial reconstruction.'

Timms caught sight of Wadesky leaving the post-mortem. 'Okay, looks like we're done. Catch you later.'

'You think I've got time to grab a coffee?' Laurence asked Eleanor.

'You saw no one last night?'

'Nothing!' he answered. 'Back in ten.'

Miranda, the morgue technician, popped her head into the corridor from the second autopsy suite. 'DI Raven?'

Eleanor nodded.

'Dr Hounslow is just about to start your lady's autopsy,' she said in a hushed tone.

'Detectives Raven and Whitefoot, how are you both this morning?' asked Hounslow, without looking up from her notes. Both were fully versed with her working regime and stood in silence as she read. As Chief Medical Examiner for the city, she imposed a rigorous no extraneous noise policy during an autopsy. This, as understood by the initiated, began from the moment she looked at the file.

The external examination, which Hounslow dictated into the overhead microphone, confirmed to the detectives the manner of death as homicide. A series of nine blows from a left-handed hitter had produced numerous fractures and, when Veronica Sizemore's head was opened up, it was found that cerebral haemorrhages had rendered her unconscious, probably from the first blow. In all other aspects she was a healthy 74-year-old woman.

Gently pulling the surgical sheet back over the remains, Hounslow took a moment. 'What can a woman of such advanced years say to someone to provoke such an appalling attack?'

'That's what we're hoping to find out,' said Eleanor, preparing to leave.

'The gentleman I examined before this lady suffered exactly the same type of ferocious attack. Face crushed to pieces.'

Suddenly, Eleanor was listening. 'Fist injuries?'

'No, a paving slab, following a knife attack... Sorry, I wasn't implying the cases were likely to have been committed by the same individual,' she said, removing her plastic apron.

'But there was something that made you see a pattern?' asked Eleanor.

'Crushing someone's features is a very personal attack and not something I see every day, thank goodness. It struck me as... an odd coincidence.'

'Thank you, Dr Hounslow,' said Eleanor, nodding and taking her leave.

'I need a coffee and carbs,' said Laurence with an edge of desperation. 'I'm heading for D'Angelo's – join me?' He headed swiftly through the security barrier before Eleanor could object.

*

Big Al, D'Angelo's proprietor, was in a foul mood. He'd recently been served a warning from the Food Standards Agency for visually declaring that most of his fare was 'low in carbohydrates, sugars and fats', in direct contradiction to the actual contents of his paninis, cakes and granola bars. Big Al's theory that local law enforcement and morgue staff were 'bad for business' had engendered cunning promotional schemes on his part. His attempts to con clientele into buying more food than their waistlines permitted, by labelling produce as 'low cal', had brought swift retribution from indignant dieters and even swifter paperwork threatening closure if he didn't declare honestly.

'Yes,' he snapped.

'Two coffees and' – Laurence's eye wandered over the glass shelves – 'two of those.' He pointed to a pile of large, cream-based pastries.

'These may kill you!' snarled Al, dropping them onto a tray.

'Ok*aay*,' answered Laurence, handing him a twenty.

Eleanor was mulling over possible strategies when Laurence returned to the table. 'Have you got any names of animal abusers off the local guys?'

He nodded. 'Two so far and I've arranged to see both this afternoon.'

'I'll join you – text me details. CCTV?'

'Nothing close,' he answered.

'You've set up tonight's watch?'

'Yup, I'll do six till ten; Johnson's going to do ten till seven.'

She nodded. 'Has McAvoy been in touch?'

'Not yet,' replied Laurence, folding the remains of his first pastry into his mouth.

'Good.' Eleanor stood up. 'We need to box up the Eddie Myles case and start two new boards for Veronica Sizemore and Clarrie Eddow. See you in an hour or so.' Eleanor waved her phone at him.

'Hey,' said Laurence. 'You didn't say how your meeting with the psych went?'

She stared at him for a moment and then went on her way.

'That good, huh?' he muttered to himself.

*

Dr Seb Blackmore had been considerably less reluctant to see her than Eleanor had imagined. He'd suggested that they meet in the nearest LCBO, as he needed to pick up a couple of bottles of wine for the evening and it would look like a chance encounter if anyone saw them. She agreed but thought he watched too much TV. Eleanor grabbed several bottles, to show willing.

'I'm sorry. I don't know what happened—' he began.

'How much of what we discussed about my sex life was repeated to Launceston?'

Seb looked confused. 'Nothing.'

She raised an eyebrow. 'You took notes in all the sessions.'

'I did, but not about that. I'm very circumspect about what goes into an individual's file. It's mainly a list of the techniques used and your responses to it.'

She was becoming irritated. 'You handed the notes over to Launceston.'

'Listen to me.' he lowered his voice. 'I sent my summation in, with my recommendation that you were no longer suffering from any form of PTSD and should be released from the evaluation programme straight away.'

She stared at him.

'I was then asked to hand my notes over to Launceston and told that your department wanted to keep you on the programme, as you'd been showing signs of deterioration. I wasn't privy to what those signs were and they pretty much told me to leave well alone. They also said any appointments with you would be taken up by Launceston. If' – he paused – 'if you are concerned that certain aspects of your life have been documented or verbally transferred to another party, I can absolutely assure you it didn't come from me. You were my patient and what was said or revealed while you were in my care *was* and *is* between us. No one, however senior, is privy to that.' He held her gaze for several seconds.

'Is there any chance that someone could have been listening or recording any of our therapy sessions?'

He shook his head. 'I really don't see how. The rooms are soundproofed, and even if someone had an ear glued to the door, it would have been incredibly difficult to pick anything up.'

'Thank you, Dr Blackmore. Enjoy your evening,' she said, glancing at his basket of wine.

Eleanor sat in her car and thought. Where could Launceston have got his information? She believed Seb Blackmore and, unless his room was bugged, which she couldn't rule out, she doubted that he was the source.

She ran her mind back over the sexual encounters she'd arranged over the years. She hadn't always been discrete, but each meeting was with a stranger that she'd never reconnected with. Eleanor conceded that her torture at the hands of Lee Hughes a year earlier had been the result of carelessness on her part. Maybe that was it – she'd just been lazy. But she'd always changed venue and partner.

It was painful and dangerously thrilling to run back through part of her life she had sworn to herself never to revisit. Then she understood. There was only one other place and person that she'd visited more than once. It made sense that that was where the problem lay.

Eleanor felt a frisson of sexual anticipation as she pulled her car into the dingy, nondescript street downtown. The entrance to La Reine's appeared, to those not in the know, to be little more than a fire exit. There were no handles or means of uninvited entry, apart from a small enamel button bearing a yin/yang symbol, which rang an internal buzzer. Eleanor knew there would be a period of waiting, usually about ten minutes, so that the supplicant could reconsider whether they truly wanted to commit themselves to the therapy provided by La Reine.

By the time the door was finally opened and she was invited in, Eleanor felt that her once urgent need for physical dominance and pain was more muted. It could be almost completely dismissed. She felt strong and self-controlled.

La Reine wore the uniform of her profession, a black, patent-leather catsuit and anonymity. Eleanor knew only that the madam was an academic, lecturing at one of the city universities and that she was, of necessity, discreet in her choice of clientele. Her selection process was determined by personal recommendation and high session prices. But where money and reputations were at stake, there was the opportunity for corruption.

La Reine assessed Eleanor. 'Why are you here?' she asked, with a notable edge to her voice.

'My patronage has become known,' Eleanor said.

La Reine nodded. 'It's unusual but not impossible.'

'Has anyone…?' she began.

'Look,' hissed La Reine, 'if anyone *had* asked questions, they'd have got nothing from me. I am immune to blackmail and I keep my clients' secrets safe. If someone had asked questions, I wouldn't tell you that either. I control information, as well as desires here. As far as you are concerned' – she took a pace towards Eleanor – 'you are my *only* client.'

'Does that go for your other clients?' asked Eleanor.

'There *are* no other clients.'

'You have CCTV?' asked Eleanor.

'No,' said La Reine emphatically.

Eleanor studied the woman's face. A slight saccade of her eyes convinced her. 'You're lying,' she snapped.

For a moment La Reine appeared to struggle with both her immediate response and the sudden shift in status. 'Not inside, but on the street.'

Eleanor lowered her tone. 'Who did you see?'

'No one that wasn't known to me.'

'You know who I am and what I do?'

La Reine nodded.

'As I know you,' Eleanor added quietly.

La Reine appeared to mull over her options. 'There was *no one* watching.'

Eleanor used the back stairs to access her office in an effort to evade detection. A string of texts and increasingly irate phone messages confirmed that Marty Samuelson had been fully informed of her declaration to Dr Launceston that today's session would be her last. She needed more time to work out how, or from whom, he had managed to acquire the information about her past life.

Laurence had cleared and packaged the visual materials on Eddie Myles and left them sandwiched in a manila file, ready to be photocopied. The board had been divided into the two separate murder investigations and photographs of both Veronica Sizemore and Clarrie Eddow had been pinned lopsidedly onto each half, alongside photographs of the boiler room and the dead dogs. Eleanor repositioned both and made a mental note to print out corresponding map references for both women. In Clarrie Eddow's case, despite her reservations, she would get Johnson to locate the map references for all of Toby Adams' victims.

Her phone vibrated, alerting Eleanor that Laurence was waiting for her.

*

Laurence knocked loudly on the door and waited. He counted to three before repeating the process.

A bolt was drawn on the opposite side and the door opened an inch. 'Whatd'ya want?' growled a voice.

'This is Detective Whitefoot and DI Raven of Toronto PS and we'd like to discuss an event that took place several weeks ago.'

'I didn't do it!' bleated the voice.

'Open the door,' snapped Eleanor.

'You need a warrant!' he countered.

'Not to interview you,' she returned. 'Just a loud enough voice to discuss your propensity to set fire to cats so that your neighbours can hear.'

The door was hastily opened and they were ushered into the corridor of the small, dark apartment by what appeared to be a child. At less than five foot two and 100 pounds, he looked incapable of tackling anything larger than a cat.

'I ain't touched one of them bastards!' he spat, extracting a cigarette from behind his ear and lighting it with his right hand. 'It was youthful pranks.'

'No, you've been convicted on three counts of cruelty to animals. Less prank and more lifestyle choice, I'm guessing,' said Laurence.

'Huh?'

'We're investigating the torture of six dogs. Your name was put forward as a likely candidate.'

'I like dogs!' he protested. 'And when was this because I've been away for a few months.'

'Where?' asked Laurence.

'Montreal, staying with my brother. I got back last night.' Registering their dubious expressions, he spoke more forcefully. 'I can prove it!'

*

'Check it out,' said Eleanor, when they got back into the car. 'He's right handed and he doesn't look physically capable of the attacks but *always* follow up. Who's next?'

Laurence passed her the file. 'Two more. Both live with mom and have been diagnosed as having some sort of psychotic condition. Info's on the back seat.'

Eleanor reached behind the passenger seat, noting that there were several letters with a solicitor's stamp, which had been scrunched and flung there. Seeing the notebook, she picked it up and flipped through the handwritten pages until she came to the right name. 'Okay, no official record but several interviews regarding attacks on dogs… cats and a horse! Any details of what he did to the animals?'

'No charges brought and, as he was a minor, nothing kept on him,' answered Laurence, checking his satnav.

'Exclusion from school and now unemployed and living at home,' she read. 'Let's see what he has to say.'

*

The boy heard the knocking from his room. It was determined and extremely unusual. No one knocked for long because he never answered.

He waited for several minutes after it finished and then slunk down to the hallway, where he noticed that a piece of card had been pushed through the letter box. Suspecting that the intruder was waiting for him, he left it a good forty-five minutes before approaching the note and reading it. It didn't make any sense to him, and he was forced to read it several times. DI Eleanor Raven wanted to speak to him urgently. Nowhere did it say why. Why would a detective want to talk to him?

*

Eleanor's efforts to avoid her boss by taking a significant detour back to her office had not worked out.

'Stay where you are!' shouted Marty Samuelson. 'If you move I will have you arrested.'

Eleanor let out a sigh and turned to face him.

'What are you doing, Whitefoot?' he asked, pointing a finger at him.

'Leaving, sir. I'm due on surveillance,' said Laurence quickly.

'Well, it's going to be a lonely vigil because DI Raven is staying here to talk to me.'

'I'll get my bag,' she said flatly.

'Not unaccompanied you won't. In fact, we'll have the meeting in your office. I'm armed and extremely irritable, so no sudden escape moves on your part, Raven.'

'Hi, Kim,' Eleanor said, on opening the door to her office and seeing the office cleaner.

'I need to have a chat with DI Raven; have you finished in here?' Marty asked Kim, taking Mo's comfy chair.

'I'll take the bins out and bring 'em back when you've finished,' she said, closing the door quietly behind her.

'Right, tell me why you've quit the psych programme, despite our deep mutual understanding that you needed to continue and bring things to a natural close.'

Eleanor stared at him. 'There's a limit to the amount of interference I can cope with.'

'No, there isn't!' hissed Marty. 'Have I not explained in minute detail that unless you get cleared from the support programme, the Chief will question whether you're able to function as a DI in this unit?'

'I'm not going to expose every detail of my personal life to some asshole I don't trust.'

'Have you spoken to the bonding guy?'

'No!'

'Jeez, if you'd just—'

'What? Cooperate?' She stood up and grabbed her bag and coat. 'You should be protecting me from this, not asking me to bend over. I'm *not* going back to therapy; I'm getting on with my job.' She slammed the door behind her.

*

Marty sat back in Mo's chair and loosened his tie. There was a knock on the door. 'What?' he bellowed.

'It's just me,' said Kim quietly. 'Can I leave the bins?'

*

When Johnson arrived at ten, Laurence redirected him to park to the left of the dumpsters; Laurence believed there would be less chance of being spotted.

It had been an unproductive evening so far. There had been a similar pattern to the evening before – very few residents used the back entrance to the building. Once parked, they would head towards the main entrance.

Johnson, Laurence noted, was considerably more organised than he had been, packing coffee, sandwiches and a blanket. Leaving clear instructions to arrest anyone seen trying to get into the old boiler room, Laurence climbed into his car and headed back home.

*

The boy arrived after midnight, determined to access his secret place. He was pleased to see that everything had returned to normal. There were no cars parked suspiciously and he had a clear line of sight to the place, but he still wanted to take his time.

*

Johnson didn't mind surveillance. It was quiet and purposeful. No one gave you a hard time, or questioned you. It was peaceful, and he had no problem staying focussed.

He'd been watching and listening for the past couple of hours when he saw a figure creeping cautiously around the side of the building and moving towards the door. His senses were on full alert, and he held his breath as he watched the man stop in front of the door, pull something out from his pocket and begin to prod around the door frame. Johnson flicked on his full headlights and jumped out of the car, drawing his weapon.

'This is the police. Show me your hands!' he yelled, walking quickly towards the figure.

The man spun round and put his hands in front of his eyes to cover the glare. 'What the hell!'

'Show me your hands!' yelled Johnson, moving rapidly towards him and cuffing his right hand. 'I'm arresting you on suspicion of murder.'

'Are you insane?'

'What's your name?'

'Claddis McAvoy! I live here.'

The boy, watching from the corner of the building, was astonished. He'd crept forward so he wouldn't miss what was being said. That was why the police were watching. They knew that someone had stolen the dogs and they'd come to find out who'd done it. He hunkered down behind the dumpsters, where he could spy on the unfolding drama.

'You idiot!' bellowed Claddis. 'I'm investigating the crime you couldn't be bothered to! This is going to be all over the papers tomorrow and your badge will be—' His outrage disappeared into the back seat of Johnson's car, as the door was slammed shut.

*

The boy waited for some minutes before he felt confident enough to approach his special place. Unscrewing the lock from the architrave, he checked that no one was watching and then made his way down into the old boiler room. What he saw made him feel violated and angry. What belonged to him had been taken, but this time he knew exactly who had it.

CHAPTER FIFTEEN

'Say that again,' snapped Eleanor into her phone, trying to disentangle herself from mounds of blankets.

'Johnson arrested a guy as he tried to access the boiler room. He's going to process him,' said Laurence, trying to contain his relief.

'You're heading in?' she asked, grabbing items of clothing.

'I'm setting off now. Meet you there.'

'Did he give a name?' She heard Laurence turn the engine over and accelerate away.

'No. See you there.' He disconnected.

Eleanor glanced around her room. The low wattage electric heaters only really made an impact if she shrank her living space, moving out of the bedroom and into the living area. The result was the sense that she was living under siege conditions and it was taking its toll.

Staring at the messy heap of blankets she'd been using to ward off the cold, Eleanor decided that she wouldn't tolerate this any longer.

Police HQ had a very different vibe during the night shift. Civilians who were being processed tended to be more emotional, more injured, more outraged and inevitably more intoxicated than the day-shift clientele. The atmosphere felt dangerous and visceral, but this held no fears for Eleanor. She ran up the stairs to her office, meeting Laurence en route.

'Johnson's in Interview One. Let's go.'

'What do we know?' Eleanor asked, keeping up with him.

'Johnson arrested a guy who was using a penknife to open the door to the boiler room.'

'What else did he have on him?'

'Nothing but the penknife.'

They reached the bottom of the stairs and Eleanor grabbed his arm. 'Rein in your judgment.'

Laurence turned to look at her.

'Just because it's a convenient answer to the problem doesn't make it the right one.'

He inhaled and nodded. 'I hear you,' he said, knocking on the door to Interview One and stepping inside.

Claddis McAvoy was leaning back in his chair, arms folded and jaw tightly clamped, when they entered the room. It took a moment for Laurence to work out the full implication of what had happened. Eleanor watched with interest as her partner's back stiffened and then relaxed as he planned his approach.

'Mr McAvoy, could you explain to us the reason why you were caught breaking into a crime scene?'

Claddis was torn. His desire to maintain a haughty and uncommunicative demeanour was conflicting with his desire to inform the three officers present just what assholes they were.

'This is what I think,' Claddis said smugly. 'You messed up big time! You failed to follow up on Veronica Sizemore's disappearance, even though Dr Delaware *warned* you that the dog killing was indicative that some really dangerous guy was on the loose. The same maniac grabbed her and hung her from the ceiling, after beating her to death. You *failed* to protect a member of the public and I'm gonna make sure that the people of Toronto know it too.'

'As I see it,' Laurence said calmly, 'you barged your way into an active police investigation and, as a result, may have prevented us from catching the guy who did this. Will you be putting that into your article?'

'That's crap,' spat Claddis. 'You ignored Miss Sizemore's complaint, which resulted in her murder!'

'How'd you know Miss Sizemore had been murdered?' asked Eleanor.

Claddis was silent for a moment before answering. 'I guessed.'

'No, you didn't.' Eleanor leaned closer to him, scrutinising his face. 'You've got a source here, haven't you?'

Claddis struggled to neutralise his expression.

'Officer or civilian?' she asked with growing anger.

She let him stew for a couple of seconds before moving her chair closer.

'Cops don't like you, McAvoy. You criticise them openly, so I'm guessing it's more likely a civilian worker, someone who has access to documents or – offices.'

Claddis blinked.

'You've just cost her her job. How'd you feel?'

'Look, there's no—' he began defensively.

'I will make sure she knows that you betrayed her *personally* and all the other sources you've nurtured over the years will know that too. There will be no more 'heads-ups' for you, Claddis; no more titbits and no more lead-writer status.'

She stood up and opened the door.

'Wait!' he said.

She turned to look at him.

'We could work on this together.'

She shook her head and walked out.

'Raven!' he squawked, struggling to get to his feet.

Laurence stood up menacingly.

'Whoa, okay, okay!' said Claddis, making an appeasing gesture with his hands. 'I can help you.'

Eleanor turned back, maintaining a neutral expression.

'I won't publish anything *unless* it helps find the killer.'

'You have zero integrity,' she snapped.

Claddis was too thick-skinned to take offense. 'I've helped you in the past,' he wheedled. 'I ran a false story and helped you to catch Lee Hughes.'

The silence extended.

'I can work with you and Detective Whitefoot, to both of our advantage,' he coaxed.

'I need to think about this, Claddis,' Eleanor said, making eye contact with Laurence and Johnson, who took their cue, stood up and left the room with her, closing the door behind them.

'You think he's trustworthy?' whispered Laurence.

'Not at all, but we need as much control over this as possible.'

'Who's the "she"?' Laurence asked.

'No idea, just took a shot. Most likely one of the office support staff and the highest percentage are female employees,' Eleanor replied. 'Leave that to me.'

'Have I messed up?' asked Johnson.

'Don't sweat it. It may be to our advantage,' Eleanor said. 'Leave him for an hour or so and then take him home.'

Johnson nodded and left.

'Let's get Ruby Delaware to give us a profile and work on how we can use the media to pull this guy out of the haystack.'

*

The boy had walked home quickly after discovering the identity of the thief. He had a clear mental picture of the man and needed to learn what his name was and where he lived. That was stage one in the complex plan that was unravelling in his mind. He wanted both her and his dogs back, and now that he had a clear idea of who was to blame, he would be able to retrieve them and make sure that he never lost any precious things again.

How does someone go about locating a person that they don't know the name or address of? But it was slowly beginning to dawn on him that he had, in fact, seen the man before, but where?

*

Mo was tired and grumpy when he finally made it out of bed that morning. He felt himself shrinking, physically *and* emotionally as the gastric band worked its magic. Every punch seemed to take so much longer to roll with, and every time he thought about dead colleagues, dead dogs and murdered old ladies he felt heavy and miserable. Maybe it was time to quit? Worry about his golf handicap, rather than taking on the pain of the world.

He put his tie on and noted that his shirt collar was way too large now; he'd have to ask Minnie to get him a size below.

He looked at himself in the mirror and saw an old man. 'Minnie! I look old today,' he yelled at the bathroom door.

'You *are* old,' she replied.

'I'm gonna quit. Play golf and fix the garden. Whatd'ya say?' he asked, pulling on his jacket and reaching for his phone.

'Sounds good. We can spend more time together and mind the grandkids.'

There was a pause.

'Maybe a few more weeks?'

He heard her laugh. 'Perhaps the job you *think* is aging you is actually keeping you young.'

He smiled.

'Make today count,' she said firmly.

He repeated Minnie's mantra to himself as he made his way down to where Detective Marcus Layton was waiting. Glancing at the heavy skies, he closed the gate behind him and headed for the car.

*

Wadesky was steadily working her way through the statements and general information they'd managed to acquire on the John Doe, whilst trying not to be distracted by her partner's noisy phone conversation with Forensics.

'You're sure?' asked Timms, not bothering to hide his frustration. 'Okay – No, not yet – I will.' He disconnected and rubbed his shoulders.

'Fingerprints?' asked Wadesky, inputting data into the MISPER site.

'AFIS has completed its first run and there are no matches,' he said, rocking back in his chair. 'What have we got?'

Wadesky sighed and grabbed the post-mortem and forensic findings. 'Clothing indicates strong likelihood of Torontonian resident – he was wearing generic mid-range garments available in three chain stores across the city. Age range is forty-five to sixty. Muscle tone indicates manual labour, but there's no distinguishing wear pattern, which would narrow the field. Slightly underweight, which may indicate disease or recent illness. Only surgical intervention was an appendectomy but certainly not recent, and a healed fracture to his wrist and elbow.'

'Tox screen?'

'Still a week or so off that, but blood alcohol was zero. Hmm…' She scanned the pages. 'Oh, only thing of interest is that our John Doe had been sitting or placed on a grid of some description.'

Timms raised an eyebrow and put out his hand for the photograph. He studied the image, which showed a distinct bloodied outline of a centimetre-squared pattern on both the shirt and trousers. Adjusting his glasses, he peered at the pattern. 'Hmm…' He pulled his lips together as he scrutinised the image.

'Ideas?'

'Metal chair?' Wadesky offered.

Timms shook his head and reached for his magnifying glass. 'It looks like two sheets of metal, soldered together. His backside the only place with the imprint?'

Wadesky handed him another image. 'There's a small amount on the base of his shirt, which is why I thought a chair.'

'I've seen this before. Years ago!' Timms stood up and paced, his eyes flicking blindly, as he sorted through mental images. He stood still and smiled. 'It's a shopping trolley.'

Wadesky looked at the photograph again. 'You're right!'

'Thought I'd seen it before. Whoever killed our John Doe pushed him around in a shopping trolley.'

'Have you any idea how many stores use them?' Wadesky said.

Timms waved a hand dismissively. 'It's a lead and we've worked with less. Get Forensics to see if they can narrow it down to a particular supplier and then we do a radius from the point of find.'

Wadesky nodded and reached for the phone. 'Where will you be?'

'The boss says no to reconstruction but I'm going to charm Ryerson into doing it for free,' he answered confidently.

Wadesky raised an eyebrow and smiled. 'Honey, if anyone could charm the birds outta the trees, it's you.'

Timms grabbed his coat and nodded. 'Absolutely.'

*

Eleanor stood by the latest hole and stared at the skies. The rain had begun an hour earlier but was being held at bay by a series of tarpaulins stretched over the pits. She needed some time to manage her thought processes and had made a point of avoiding Jacob Hareton. She let her mind drift and tried not to let her belief that the military had little intention of investigating whoever was responsible for Eddie Myles' violent behaviour overwhelm her thinking. She had to put that to rest, at least for the time being, while she supported Laurence through the Sizemore case.

She closed her eyes. Why would any murderer use the same place twice, particularly as it had already been located and cleared by the police? It didn't make any sense. Even the most deranged of killers had a sense of self-preservation. So what did that leave them with: a killer with extreme confidence or someone whose thinking didn't come close to the average person's?

He'd visited the bodies after decomposition set in, which was unusual. Toby Adams kept hold of his murder victims, but he'd preserved them, much like an embalmer would, and as soon as the bodies began to putrefy he got rid of them. Not many untrained people could stand the stench or visual impact of autolysis. It triggered an atavistic response in a normal person, who would experience revulsion. That meant either the killer was trained, or that they didn't experience what 'normal' people did.

'I'm calling it a day,' said the CSO responsible for the dig. 'Weather's too bad. You okay with that?'

Eleanor kept a neutral expression as she nodded her agreement.

'We're a good two-thirds in now,' he sighed. 'I'm guessing if we can get a three-day run of dry weather, we'll have it excavated by the weekend. You got plans to dig anywhere else if there's a nil find?'

'No plans. We'll finish here and then I'll go back to interview Toby Adams.'

Wiping the mud from his face, he nodded. 'I'll call you tomorrow.'

'Thanks. You want help clearing?' she offered.

'You're good,' he replied, waving her off.

*

Mo adjusted the passenger seat and turned down the heating on his side of the car, while Layton edged calmly through the traffic.

'Who told you?' asked Mo.

'Prison psychologist. A *very* nice lady called Elsa Begum,' said Layton appreciatively. 'She was very concerned about Roma Joe's mental health, in particular some of the crazy ideas he seemed to have picked up from his psychiatrist.'

'Like what?' asked Mo curiously.

Layton sighed. 'Joe was convinced that his mind was essentially a freezer, which only became warm enough to survive in when something good happened.'

'Hippy-dippy but not too outrageous.'

'I agree – but that wasn't the problem. The problem was the nature of the "good things".' Layton waved air quotes as they waited for the lights to change.

'Go on,' said Mo.

'Well, one good thing was murdering those women.'

Mo turned to Layton and stared in disbelief. 'What?'

'Joe said that the doctor made a point of emphasising that the more women he murdered, the better the place his head would be in.'

'That can't have been right. No professional would have said that. Joe misinterpreted that, surely?'

Layton nodded. 'You'd think so but Roma Joe was pretty stuck on this idea, so much so that Elsa called up this doctor and challenged him.'

'And?'

'He was pretty defensive and admitted to trying some radical new techniques on Roma Joe's psyche but denied ever having said that Joe had carte blanche on dismembering prostitutes.'

'So what was the outcome?' asked Mo.

'Well, lovely Elsa's speciality is behaviour analysis or something, which means she's trained in knowing whether people are lying or not.'

'She thought the psychiatrist was lying?'

'No, she couldn't tell but she believed Roma Joe was telling the truth,' said Layton thoughtfully.

'So what's this psychiatrist's name?'

'Blackmore... Dr Seb Blackmore.'

*

Timms had handed Dr Grenson the file and was now waiting, with increasing irritation, as the academic tutted and shook his head. The pungent smell of formaldehyde and the gloomy interior of Ryerson's forensic anthropology department reminded him of a spinster aunt who had a penchant for taxidermy. It wasn't a fond memory.

'In a case like this, it would take us months, multiples of months, to forensically reconstruct a face this badly damaged,' said Grenson, wafting the photographs around in disbelief. 'I'd have to sacrifice a post-doctoral student for the duration: a situation I absolutely cannot agree to.'

Timms cleared his throat, giving himself an extra couple of seconds to adjust his tone. 'This man was murdered a couple of days ago. We need to have him identified as soon as possible.'

'I'm *sure* you do, but this is an academic institution and our mandate does not include propping up a financially challenged public body!'

'So you're happy to spend millions on giving a face to some Stone Age asshole you yanked out of a cave but not to some poor bastard whose tax payments keep you in sandals and vegan cheese!' bellowed Timms.

Grenson thrust forward his chest and ratcheted up the volume. 'We receive money from the taxpayer based on our mandate which does not include freebies for the police! Perhaps you could see Detective Timms out, Rachel.'

Rachel Gilbey nodded and followed Timms as he stormed out.

'Detective?' she called.

'Yes!' Timms snapped. 'Sorry,' he said, opening both hands.

'Perhaps I might help? My partner is a surgical resident who specialises in tissue reconstruction. If you can grant access to the body, she can reconstruct the face, without using the skull. It's faster than using the forensic programmes.'

'Give me his details. Sounds good, thanks,' said Timms.

Rachel smiled. '*She's* called Caroline and I'll get her to contact you today.'

*

'Gentlemen, how can I help you?' asked Dr Launceston as he ushered Mo and Layton into his office. 'My secretary has informed me of the death of Joe Greene by his own hand.'

'It's Dr Blackmore we need to talk to,' said Layton.

'Unfortunately that's not possible – he's in Vancouver for the next couple of days. Although Dr Blackmore was Mr Greene's primary psychiatric counsellor, I have some knowledge of both the treatment and the patient and will assist you as much as I can.'

'So you've treated Joe Greene yourself?'

Launceston hesitated. 'I saw him for his initial assessment, following his recommendation from the probationary services.' He glanced at the notes in front of him. 'That was in September 2008, following a short prison sentence. Having evaluated Greene, I passed the case on to Dr Blackmore, who seemed more than qualified to treat him.'

'Are you surprised by him taking his own life?' asked Layton.

'Not really,' replied Launceston.

'Is it something you may have discussed with him previously?'

'Gentlemen, you don't really imagine that I am going to talk to you about a patient that I haven't had any contact with for several years without a subpoena? Mr Greene's sessions here were confidential and, as such, are protected under the laws of privilege. Do you have a subpoena?' he asked politely.

'We have a belief that Dr Blackmore's therapy sessions with Joe weren't of a conventional nature,' said Layton.

Launceston smiled. 'All members of my team tailor their sessions to the needs of each individual client. It appears, looking at our results, to be a successful strategy.'

'How did Dr Blackmore's approach to Joe Greene differ from any other patient?' Layton asked.

Professor Launceston put his hands together and sighed.

'We're not looking for personal details, Professor, just trying to get a sense of why he took his own life?'

'Mr Greene, according to our files, hasn't been treated here by us since July 2009. Surely you'll find it more productive to speak to his current practitioner?' suggested Launceston.

'We have,' said Layton. 'She seems to think that Dr Blackmore had been indoctrinating Joe with strange beliefs.'

'Such as?' asked Launceston, puzzled.

'Persuading him that killing prostitutes might make him feel a little better about himself.'

Launceston looked at him with raised eyebrows. 'I think you may have to clarify that for me.'

'Dr Elsa Begum said that Blackmore's treatment of Greene made him believe that the more women he murdered, the better place his head would be in.'

'I can't begin to explain how ridiculous a concept that is,' said Launceston.

'It appears that on the evening before his death he called this office from the prison and left a message.'

'Then you'll have a recording of it,' said Launceston, leaning back in his seat.

'We have,' agreed Layton. 'It's a little confusing.'

'Really?'

'Joe's put through to Dr Blackmore's office by your secretary and, from what we can tell, his answer machine fails to kick in

The prison's recording has Joe banging on about how he needs to speak to his doctor and, after leaving his message, Joe disconnects.'

'What's strange about that?' asked Launceston, confused.

'The line is live until Joe puts down the receiver. For three minutes he talks but there's no response from anyone.'

'Which means what exactly?' said Launceston, unable to hide his confusion.

'Either Dr Blackmore's machine failed to run a message warning he wasn't there and carried on recording Joe's message, or someone was on the line listening to him,' said Layton slowly.

Launceston smiled. 'Seb Blackmore has not collected his messages as he's away on conference. Although we all uphold patient confidentiality, our practice always clocks incoming messages, in case there's a problem that needs immediate attention. It's my duty as lead physician to monitor calls for absent colleagues and I can *assure* you that there were no messages left for Dr Blackmore on his answer machine. Now…' said Launceston, standing up, 'I'm afraid I have a patient scheduled. It's been a pleasure talking to you both.'

Layton stood up and held out his hand. 'Thank you for taking the time to speak to us, Professor.'

Mo and Layton were ushered out of the room and into the reception area. Mo waited for Launceston's door to close before speaking to the receptionist. 'Dr Launceston has just informed us that Mr Joe Greene telephoned on the twenty-seventh. Did you take the call?'

The receptionist pursed her lips and opened a large black notebook to the right of her computer. She ran a finger down a list and stopped. 'Yes, he called at 4.46 p.m. and I transferred the call through to Dr Blackmore's extension.'

Layton nodded. 'Thanks for your help.'

*

'Whatd'ya think?' asked Layton as he turned the engine over. 'We just wasting our time?'

Mo rubbed his chin. 'I dunno: maybe. But something doesn't smell right. How about we go listen to that last testament of Roma Joe Greene. There may be something we've missed.'

Mo and Layton had listened to the tape three times now and felt they were getting no place fast. The quality of the recording was poor, and background prison noise obscured any subtleties.

The two detectives sipped coffee and listened to the entire phone call made by Roma Joe to Dr Blackmore one more time. After asking the receptionist to *'get the doc 'cos it's an emergency,'* Roma Joe listened to her briefly explain that the doctor was unavailable and that he could leave a message; he made several impatient interjections as she spoke. There was a ten-second gap where Joe asked if she was '*still there?*' before she assured him that she was *'connecting him now'*.

'Doc?... You there?' Silence. *'I really need to talk to you! Cops came in today and started talking about them bitches... Pick up the goddamn phone: this is really important.'*

A sound, which they agreed was probably a sob from Roma Joe, made the next phrase difficult to interpret. A further sniffing sound and Joe began again.

'It's getting colder, doc and I ain't fighting it so good. The faces keep coming in and telling me I'm gonna die.'

'So he's saying literally that he's going to kill himself?' asked Layton, pausing the tape.

Mo shook his head. 'Yeah, maybe.'

Layton pressed the play button again. There was a pause before Roma Joe started speaking once more. *'You said that as long as I keep the flame in my head, the faces would go away, but they're back and it's so goddamn cold here! … I really need to talk to you. I gotta tell you what I'm thinking, so you can stop them chasing me.'*

A dull thumping sound, followed by a groan, filled the next thirty seconds.

'I think that's him hitting his head,' said Mo.

'Call them and tell 'em you need to see me… I need to talk this through… Doc?'

There was the sound of the receiver being replaced and three seconds of tone. Layton scratched his head and pressed the pause button. 'You any the wiser?'

'Not at all. Give it to the Data department. Maybe they can clear it up a bit.'

*

The boy lay in his bed and stared at the clock. He was agitated and confused. The answer he was searching for was in his head, but he couldn't dislodge it from its hiding place. He needed to know why he thought he knew the man who had been arrested for stealing his prizes.

It wasn't as if he had a huge repertoire of faces to call on. Since being prevented from attending school, he very rarely saw anyone apart from the police officers and his doctor. But it was worrying him that he couldn't place where he'd seen the man before. He had a vague sense that it was something to do with rain but couldn't take the link any further than that.

There was movement below him. It was his mother, but they weren't really on speaking terms. She seemed angry and distant whenever she spoke to him and now she didn't appear to be observing mealtimes. Yesterday, she hadn't prepared any food for him and the nagging pain in his belly had forced him to seek his own meal. He didn't understand what was happening and, after shouting at her, had gone up to his room and locked the door.

*

Rula Frears sat in the kitchen and held the phone tightly between her palms. She'd recharged the battery, keeping tabs on the messages that were coming in for Alan. There had been several from his old workmates, asking why he hadn't turned up for the annual social and hoping he was alright. Her rational self knew that something awful had happened to Alan and that the person most likely to know about it was her son. But emotionally she couldn't bear to accuse her son of doing something to her husband. What if the answer was yes? What was she going to do then, call the police? She'd be left with nothing and no one, just the spoken knowledge that he had pushed Alan into either leaving – or worse.

Rula wasn't eating, going to work or keeping herself clean, and she was beginning to doubt her own sanity. What was she doing? Nothing! That's all she'd ever done. Left him to get on with what he wanted because peace was easier than screaming and hatred. She had to confront her son but not now. She was too exhausted and upset.

Tomorrow she would ask him about Alan and find out the truth.

CHAPTER SIXTEEN

Eleanor took the stairs two at a time, weaving between startled civilians and fellow officers. Flying past the team room, she caught a glimpse of Timms, a copy of the *Toronto Sun* raised in his left hand, gesturing a thumbs up with his right. She didn't need to record the expression on his face.

Shutting the door firmly behind her, she flung her coat onto the chair and looked at Mo and Laurence. 'Anything rolled down yet?' she asked breathlessly.

'Any minute now,' scowled Mo, hanging up his coat.

'I should have expected as much,' began Laurence.

Eleanor turned to look at him in disbelief. 'You mean you *didn't* anticipate that Claddis McAvoy would stitch you up?' Even Mo raised his eyebrows.

'McAvoy's job is to write stories that sell papers. We provided him with one. I hoped we could come to some agreement which would minimise its effect on the case, but that didn't happen. So now we turn it to our advantage.'

'How?' said Laurence shrilly. 'Look at the headline! He jabbed his finger on the front page of the *Toronto Sun*, where the bold, inch-high leader read: *'TPS RESPONSIBLE FOR MURDER OF CONCERNED RESIDENT'*. Beneath the headline were photographs of a smiling Veronica Sizemore and the now bereft dog-owner, holding his *'Beloved spaniel, Benji'*.

The next paragraph proclaimed that: *'The notorious dog killer, whom Dr Ruby Delaware was so adamant should have been TPS's primary concern, has begun to murder people… even leaving Veronica Sizemore's body in the same boiler room where the dogs had been found several days earlier.*' Detective Laurence Whitefoot, described as a '*novice who was unqualified to handle even his own dog*', had been paired in this '*saga of incompetence*' with DI Eleanor Raven, who '*had been issued with a restraining order after attacking and badly injuring the* Toronto Sun'*s lead writer*'.

This message was further boosted by two photographs taken the previous year, one showing Eleanor punching the unconscious face of Claddis McAvoy and the other of Laurence, both arms wrapped tightly around Eleanor as he dragged her off.

Mo grimaced as he read the message on his mobile. 'Samuelson is on the move. Stand clear.'

Knowing her boss's propensity for explosive entrances, Eleanor moved away from the door. They all fell silent as the sound of thumping feet moved towards them.

Surprisingly, there was a polite knock before Richard Glass popped his head into the room. 'Ah, Detective. Is now a good time?'

'Why not?' Eleanor sighed. She was trapped and the inevitability of her suspension seemed inescapable and, at that moment strangely welcome. Mo and Laurence took their cue and left the room.

Glass made himself comfortable and withdrew a file from his briefcase.

'Now, what I have to discuss with you is a matter of some delicacy.'

'No doubt,' she added tartly. 'That's a lot of investigating.' She pointed to the bulging file, which was now sitting between them

Glass looked puzzled. 'I don't really investigate. As I said before I work for the bonding company.'

'You're Internal Affairs.'

'Yes, but not in an investigative capacity. I'm a civilian appointee.'

'I'm confused. Why are you here?' she asked.

'Because...' He lowered his voice. 'You were badly injured during the apprehension of a suspect last year.'

Eleanor scowled. 'And I've been receiving appropriate support from the Serving Officer's Psychiatric Assist Programme since returning to work.'

'Yes. Dr Blackmore has informed me that you have completed the programme to both of your satisfaction and are no longer receiving treatment. Which means that I need to discuss the terms and conditions of your insurance policy.'

'What insurance policy?' she asked, bewildered.

'This is the departmental policy you took out when you joined the Toronto PS twelve years ago and pay into as part of your superannuation deductions.' He placed a sheet in front of her. 'It has been confirmed by the medical agents who treated you that you were technically killed by Lee Hughes during the assault.'

Eleanor felt her throat tighten and her heart begin to pound.

'The terms of your serving officer's insurance policy decrees that your loss of life guarantees its complete financial realisation.'

'But I'm not dead,' she said weakly.

'That's immaterial to the policy... But not, of course, to yourself or your family,' he added swiftly. 'It takes a long time to gather the necessary proof and then process it, but I am pleased to let you know that you will receive this amount.' He slid several sheets of paper towards her. 'It's not going to obliterate what you went through,' he said carefully. 'But it does enable you to make decisions about your future in a less... constricted way.'

Eleanor shook her head as she saw the six figures.

'There's a small amount of administration that needs completing but, if you're happy for me to proceed, I will try to process this as fast as humanly possible. I have also included the new policy documents, as you are entitled to further coverage if you continue as a serving officer.'

There was a long pause.

'Thank you,' she said quietly.

Indicating where she should sign, Glass gathered his paperwork and let himself out.

*

Rula Frears sat at the kitchen table and reread the newspapers. She didn't bother with the national press; if there was any information to be gleaned it would, most likely, appear in a Toronto paper.

There had been a couple of suspicious deaths since the evening that Alan disappeared, but none of them seemed a likely match, which was of considerable relief to her. The first was a teenager, mowed down by a truck as he ran across the expressway, then an unnamed man who had been found badly injured after falling into a hole, but the *Toronto Sun* stated that he was young and drunk. Today's paper was all about an elderly woman who appeared to have been murdered by the police. Rula was confused as to how the police were responsible, but as the story definitely wasn't about Alan, she ignored it.

The boy was making his way down to the kitchen. She was finding it hard to speak to him at the moment – every time she tried to rise above her suspicions she ended up snapping at him, or walking away.

'Morning, honey,' she said quietly.

Her son stood in the doorway and looked at her. 'Can I eat?' he asked.

She felt awful. Why was she punishing him on account of her suspicions? He had done nothing wrong. Alan had left them, probably because he needed a break. Her son was difficult and would tax the patience of a saint, but he was *her* son and she loved him.

'Would you like some breakfast, honey?' she asked him.

He nodded. 'I thought you were angry with me?' he said, scowling.

'I'm just scared. I miss Alan.'

'I'm hungry,' he repeated.

'Sit down and I'll make you something nice.'

He sat down, keeping a weather eye on her. 'I didn't do anything!'

'I know. I'm sorry,' she heard herself say. 'It'll be alright.'

*

His mother began to take items out of the fridge and arrange them, while he pushed the newspaper away so he could eat. Instantly, he recognised the photographs on the front of the paper.

He pulled it back towards him and unfolded it. There was a photograph of the man he'd been trying to place. He read the name 'Claddis McAvoy' and remembered exactly where he'd seen him before. He was the man who'd sat in his car making a noisy phone call on the evening he'd waited to visit his prize. When he'd finished the call, he'd headed over to where all the other people had entered the building. Maybe that's where he lived?

Below the photograph of Claddis McAvoy was a photograph of the woman and one of his dogs. He felt a sudden rush of anger, which made him throw the paper on the floor.

'What's the matter?' asked his mother. She bent over and retrieved the paper, looking at the page her son was reading. 'Is this making you angry?'

He knew he shouldn't say anything else, in case she began to work out his plans. So he nodded cautiously.

'That's okay, honey. It makes me angry too.'

*

Rula stole glances at her son as she finished setting out his breakfast. Maybe he was finally beginning to develop a sense of empathy? Being upset by an article about the murder of an elderly lady was something that he'd resolutely failed to respond to before. She felt herself smile. Perhaps things were changing in his head.

*

Eleanor sat silently at her desk and tried to put the information into context. Before she could really get to grips with it, the door opened and Laurence walked in with Dr Ruby Delaware, whose pink cheeks mirrored her scarf and beret.

'I am mortified!' she began. 'Everything that's been reported by the *Toronto Sun* is a lie.'

Eleanor opened her mouth but Ruby was in full flight. 'I have never spoken to that man – Claddis McAvoy – never even met him! So how is he able to quote me? Do I need legal protection? Can I issue a rebuttal?'

'Please take a seat and hopefully we can advise you,' said Eleanor, pulling out a chair for her. 'You've never officially spoken to Claddis McAvoy?' she asked.

'I've never even met him,' shrieked Ruby, outraged.

'Who else have you spoken to, about your thoughts on—' Eleanor began.

'No one, other than here in your office. And what's more concerning is that McAvoy quoted me verbatim.'

Laurence glanced at Eleanor.

'You suspect it may have been someone in the room?' Eleano asked carefully.

Ruby shook her head. 'I don't want to leap to any conclusion particularly as officers were involved. However, it was reported by *someone*.'

Eleanor paused momentarily. 'I'll get onto this immediatel and let you know. Have you had time to put together a profil on Veronica Sizemore's killer?'

Ruby nodded and placed a file on the table. 'It is my belie that Miss Sizemore's murder resulted from an escalation after th dogs were discovered and removed.'

'So you're convinced it's the same killer?' asked Laurence.

'Absolutely! No doubt in my mind and exactly what I feared would happen.' Ruby pinched her lips together and gave Laurence a hard stare. 'I'm suspecting that some evidence was left and this hasn't matched any on record yet?'

Eleanor nodded.

'It's because this is just the beginning for him. He's probably very young, most likely under twenty-five, and hasn't acquired the skills that will keep him safe and hidden. But he *will* acquire them. If you don't catch him before he learns how to hide, he may never be stopped. He's making mistakes, which is to your advantage.'

'How does he think?' asked Eleanor.

'Like no mind you've ever visited before. He's as exciting as Toby Adams, in that he sees every event through the eyes of a narcissist. He has no empathy or thoughts for any other beings. He sees people as being less than animals destined to serve the meat industry, but has, up to this point, been aware that they fight back and have the potential to destroy him. He's just found out they can't. He's inviolate and will continue to kill people on a whim, on a phrase, on an opportunity.'

'Surely he must have been tagged before? Someone must know he's dangerous?' said Laurence, rubbing his forehead.

'Oh, he'll be known to the authorities, but you'll have to try and sift through hundreds of targeted youths in order to narrow the field. I'm happy to help with that process.'

Eleanor thought for a moment. 'Is someone protecting him?'

'I would imagine so. He's unlikely to be able to function in a work environment like Toby Adams, so probably a close relative looks after him.'

Eleanor leaned back in her chair and stretched out her leg. A familiar, dull ache was settling into her scar tissue and turning back her mental state.

'Right,' she announced, sloughing off the sensation. 'We'll send over some profiles and tag any that look promising.'

'Of course,' said Ruby, standing up and rearranging her scarf. 'I look forward to hearing from you on the matter of walls with ears.'

Laurence opened the door for her and watched her leave.

'Who was the guy in here earlier?' he asked.

'I've not had a response from either of those two calls in Leslieville,' she said, ignoring his question.

'Want me to pop over?'

'Yes, let's track them down and get Johnson onto looking for likely candidates.'

'He's going through CCTV footage with Wadesky at the moment.'

'Then let's start the ball rolling ourselves. I'll get onto Child Protection Services and Young Offenders. Maybe Mo's free?'

Laurence grabbed his coat.

'Who's covering the boiler room?' she asked.

He checked his phone. 'PC Mari Steel from downtown.'

'Give me her number.'

Mo popped his head round the door. 'So what did that guy want?'

Eleanor sighed. 'He came to reward me for being murdered by Lee Hughes.'

'In what way rewarded?' asked Mo uncertainly.

'Not the way I expected,' she said quietly.

'You're not in trouble are you?' asked Mo. 'Because I can—'

'I'm good,' she said, smiling. 'You still working with Layton?'

'We're waiting for a tape to be cleaned up. You need me?'

'Wanna help spot a psychopath?'

'Ha! You betcha.' He reached for the outline left by Ruby Delaware.

*

Laurence was running late. He should have collected Monster earlier from 'Doggie Daycare', a small, privately run kennel situated on a side street near Kensington Market, but it had been a busy day. He still needed to check on the two missed calls in Leslieville and catch up with the surveillance team before getting back to the office. There was, as always, nowhere to park by the market, so he was forced to tuck the car into a private parking lot and hope for the best.

Deirdre's expression hardened as he entered reception. 'Mr Whitefoot, you're late!'

'I am. It's been a chaotic day and—' he began, but Deirdre wasn't in the mood. She opened a large ledger on the desk and swivelled it round, stabbing her finger against the entry titled 'Monster'.

'You booked Monster in for a four-hour session, but according to our calculations he's been here for seven!' She held his gaze. 'This is not acceptable, Mr Whitefoot. We have allocated spaces and any changes have to be notified well in advance.'

'I'm sorry,' snapped Laurence. 'I'm in the middle of a difficult case.'

'You do possess a mobile phone, don't you? It wouldn't be unreasonable for you to call us and indicate that you were having trouble making the scheduled time, would it?'

'No, it wouldn't!' he agreed irritably.

'But you didn't,' replied Deirdre with equal irritation. 'Which is why we are removing your dog from our list.'

'What?' snarled Laurence.

Setting her jaw, Deirdre leaned across the counter and lowered her voice. 'You will have to find alternative arrangements.'

He could see the parking ticket tucked underneath his windscreen wiper and flapping energetically in the wind before he reached his car. He yanked open the passenger seat for Monster and, slamming the door shut, snatched the ticket, balled it and flung it in the back seat. Monster, sensing increased tension, remained silent for the journey, staring resolutely ahead as Laurence muttered through his frustration.

*

Rula Frears nervously opened the door. She didn't know the man standing there but suspected who he was and why he'd come.

'Mrs Frears?' Laurence asked, reaching for his badge. 'I'm Detective Laurence Whitefoot. May I come in?'

Rula could feel her head beginning to spin. She nodded and held open the door for him. He stepped inside, wiping his wet feet on the mat.

Noting the change in her demeanour, he put his hand on her arm to steady her. 'Are you alright? Perhaps you'd prefer to sit down?'

She shook her head. 'Just tell me.'

'I was wondering if your son was in? I'd like to ask him a couple of questions.'

'What about?' she gasped.

'Is he in, Mrs Frears?'

'Yes. I'll call him,' she said, trying to control her anxiety. 'Perhaps you'd like to wait in here.'

'Of course,' he replied.

Rula showed Laurence into the kitchen and offered him a seat. 'I'll go and call him.'

She ran up the stairs and knocked on her son's door frantically. 'Honey?' she whispered. 'A detective's here and he wants to speak to you.'

The boy, who was watching the clock, snapped back, 'I don't want to talk to him.'

'Honey, you *have* to and he's in the kitchen. What does he want to speak to you about?' She listened for a response. 'Please open the door.'

'Tell him I haven't done anything.'

'You'll have to tell him that yourself. He won't go until you come down.'

He made a slamming noise from behind the door and then opened it. 'I don't want to see him,' he hissed.

'Well, he wants to speak to you,' Rula said emphatically. 'Are you coming down, or shall I send him up?'

Her son's thunderous expression was her cue to leave.

Walking downstairs, she misjudged the steps and had to snatch at the handrail to prevent herself from falling.

'He's on his way,' Rula said nervously. 'Can you tell me why you want to speak to him?'

The boy appeared in the doorway and stared aggressively at Laurence. 'What do you want?' he asked.

*

Laurence stood up and neutralised his expression before his shock could become visible.

'Are you Nathan Bridgewater?' Laurence asked.

He noted the boy was almost as tall as him and reasonably robust. His hair was dark, shoulder length and tangled, his eyes and expression completely dead. The boy might have been attractive if it wasn't for the massive damage to his cheek and nose. Laurence surmised that the injuries had, most likely, been sustained in childhood, as the skin grafting was tight and paper-thin over his left cheek, eye and what remained of his nose. His left eye drooped significantly where the muscle had been removed.

'Yes,' he snapped.

'I'd like to ask you a couple of questions. Would you prefer to answer them here or down at the station?'

'I don't want to answer any questions.'

'Okay,' said Laurence, taking out his notebook. 'We can start here, and if you find yourself unable to cooperate, we will do this officially at the station. Would you prefer to sit down?'

The boy looked at him, maintaining a brooding silence.

'Several days ago,' Laurence began, 'six dogs were found in the basement of an apartment building in Leslieville. They had all been beaten and then hung from a rope.'

'I didn't do it!'

'But you have a history of abusing dogs, don't you?'

Rula had eased herself into the kitchen.

The boy stared at Laurence.

'You've had several complaints made against you concerning your aggressive treatment of animals.'

'That's not true,' spluttered Rula. 'Nathan's scared of dogs! And he has good reason to be,' she said, looking pointedly at his face

'You have been cautioned by the police on three occasions after complaints were made. Did you kill those dogs, Nathan?'

'No,' he hissed.

'He rarely leaves the house. He's afraid of people. He feels safe inside, with me,' Rula replied, her voice shaking.

'The body of an elderly lady was found there after the dog were removed. What do you know about that?'

'He read about it in the paper and was very upset!' she screeched.

Laurence stayed focussed on the boy's reactions. 'I need to know your whereabouts for the past week.'

'I can confirm that he's been here every night with me,' Rula said angrily.

'*Can* you confirm that?' asked Laurence. 'Can you say that while you were asleep, your son didn't leave the house at all?'

'I'm a very light sleeper and I *would* know.'

Laurence sighed. 'Maybe Nathan should confirm this himself?'

'I never left the house,' said the boy deliberately. 'Not once.'

Laurence scrutinised the young man in front of him. His pale skin and dark eyes were unreadable.

'I think my son's answered all of your questions now,' said Rula, opening the kitchen door for him.

Laurence nodded, picked up his coat and left.

*

Eleanor sat in Mo's armchair, watching the rain's erratic pattern as it hammered against the windowpane. It was barely six in the evening and all natural light had been replaced by the bleached glare of surrounding office lights.

She was waiting and ruminating on the day. Marty still hadn't caught up with her, which made her feel uneasy. Surely there were few hands left for him to play. Without her voluntary attendance at Dr Launceston's request, he'd be forced to consider her insubordination as a disciplinary matter.

After discovering that the spare part needed to repair her boiler was no longer manufactured, she dreaded going back to her apartment. Her landlord had promised a new system would be installed over the next week, but now that winter was setting in there was a long waiting list for approved plumbers.

She stretched out her leg and was considering abandoning her plan and getting back to work when a light tap on the door and the sound of it opening made her wait. The light was switched on and, after a few seconds, she heard what she had hoped to: the steady click of a mobile phone taking photographs.

'Kim?' she asked as she stood up and stared at the office cleaner.

Kim let out an involuntary shriek and dropped her phone. 'Christ, what the hell are you doing?'

Eleanor bent down and retrieved the phone. Kim put out her hand nervously. 'Thank you!'

Eleanor turned the phone around in her hand. 'Is this for Claddis McAvoy?' she asked, swiping the phone's surface and examining the snapshot of the murder board.

'I was just making a call,' stammered Kim.

'No, you weren't,' said Eleanor calmly. 'You were supplying classified information to a journalist.'

'Of course I wasn't.' She laughed nervously. 'I was making a *call*.'

Eleanor held the phone up and pointed at the screen. 'You signed a legally binding contract, which prevents you from discussing anything overheard, seen or surmised while you work in this building. How long have you been supplying information to McAvoy?'

'I didn't,' Kim whined. 'I've never done anything…'

'Stop lying,' said Eleanor firmly. 'How long have you been taking photographs, listening to and reporting on conversations and passing this information on to journalists?'

Kim shook her head, allowing it to drop on to her chest. 'Am I going to lose my job?' she asked timorously.

Eleanor shook her head in disbelief. 'Your job is the least of your concerns.'

'I only did it a few times and I never gave him anything really important. Honest!'

'Collect your things, Kim. Your supervisor is expecting us down in her office.'

Eleanor felt uncharacteristically miserable about getting Kim sacked. This was a new and unwelcome emotion for her. In an effort to slough it off she decided to pay a visit to the cause of the problem.

'What the hell?' came the voice from behind the door, responding to the sudden, loud bang. Eleanor gave him a second or two to look through the spyhole and then began hammering on the door again. 'I'm not letting *you* in!' he yelped.

'Open the door, Claddis!' she said loudly, noting that sounds were coming from the other apartments now. 'Your neighbours are getting upset!'

She thumped the door again, pushing it when she heard the bolt draw back.

'You can't just bully your way into—'

'Too late to call your lawyer, Claddis. Man up!' said Eleanor as she secured the door behind him. 'I'm here to talk.'

She headed into his living room, pushed a pile of papers onto the floor and sat down on his sofa. 'Kim will no longer be able to supply you with titbits, as she is no longer employed by TPS.' she said firmly.

Claddis perched cautiously on the edge of the table and shrugged. 'Why should that concern me?'

Eleanor raised her eyebrows. 'She's an unskilled worker who now has no references. I doubt she's going to find it easy to pick up another job.'

'Not my concern,' he replied.

'You understand that she may be prosecuted for supplying you with sensitive material?'

He sighed. '*Again*, not my problem. If you and Whitefoot had taken the hand of friendship when it was offered to you, we could have made this relationship work for both of us.'

'I want to know what else Kim told you about ongoing cases?'

Claddis shook his head. 'No can do, Raven. These are mistrustful times.'

Eleanor stared at him, aware that her hands were balling into fists.

Making a conscious effort to relax her emotions, she stood up. In an unlikely burst of speed, Claddis lunged towards the door, opening it wide and ushering her out.

'You understand there will be consequences for this,' she said quietly.

'Good evening, Detective Raven,' he replied.

She waited for a moment or so, then turned and walked towards the stairs.

CHAPTER SEVENTEEN

When he arose, the boy was pleased to discover that his mother had returned to work. That she may have been doing something else was beyond both his imagination and his interest. His breakfast had been left on the table, ready for him. All he had to do was pour on the milk and boil a kettle. This was a good sign. Whatever was making her angry had stopped and everything was back to normal.

There was a note left by his bowl reminding him that he had a doctor's appointment in the afternoon and she would collect him. He wasn't really registering events so far in the future at this moment, because today's plans were preoccupying him. Today, he was going to find and confront the man who had stolen his things and demand their return. He knew the man's name and where he lived.

It seemed to him that the likeliest scenario was that Claddis McAvoy had stolen both the dogs *and* the woman, and was keeping them in his apartment, which was the building where he'd discovered his secret place. Knowing the man's name would make it easy for the boy to locate him, as the mailboxes located in the entrance of the building would identify the man's apartment number. Another reason, he considered, for not owning a name.

He ate his breakfast and then stood up and walked away from the table. His rule about not leaving the house before dark wouldn't be too much of a compromise, as the sky was thunderous.

Daylight was barely illuminating the umbrella-hidden people who braved the downpour. He would be anonymous.

He enjoyed the route to his private place. It was familiar and always made him feel warmer inside. He remembered the room he and his mother had lived in before moving in with the man. It was safe. No one ever came and talked about him there, or suggested that he was a bad person, but best of all, he and his mother had been alone. She had stayed in the room with him, making him meals and never forcing him to go outside. Their apartment had been directly opposite the main entrance, and when he'd stepped out of their front door, it had only taken him moments to run around the building and hide in the special place.

He moved cautiously round to the entrance, pressing in the memorised four-number key code and pushing the long steel handle that released the door. There was no one in the small lobby which he was grateful for, and he took his time examining the piles of junk mail that were left abandoned on the shelf below the mailboxes.

It took him less than a minute to locate the apartment number of Claddis McAvoy, and only two more to run up the stairs to the first floor and find it. He put his head against the door and listened. He could make out a man's voice talking in the background. At first he thought he might have been speaking to another person, but by the long silences between the sentences he surmised he was talking on the phone.

The talking stopped and the boy knocked quietly. There was a small glass spyhole in the door, which the boy covered with his hand.

He knocked again, more loudly this time and heard, 'Yeah Who is it?' shouted from inside the apartment. The boy said nothing, knocking again.

*

Claddis McAvoy was going to be late for work. He'd forwarded his story last night and had an editorial meeting scheduled for 11 a.m. He wasn't going to make it, but then he regularly missed set meetings.

He grabbed his coat and laptop and approached the door, suspecting that it would be Mrs Patel, but being more cautious after Eleanor Raven's nasty surprise visit, he peered through the spyhole.

'You're leaning against the glass!' said Claddis, irritated. 'Move your hand.'

His mobile phone rang. He dropped his eye to the screen; seeing it was Mike Curtis, his photographer, he answered. 'Yeah?'

*

Unsure of what to do now, the boy dropped his hand and stood well to the right of the door. Generally, if he was patient, good things happened.

*

'I'll be there in the next thirty minutes,' concluded Claddis, disconnecting and reaching for the door handle. He checked the spyhole, which revealed nothing but an empty corridor. Whoever it was had left while he'd taken the call.

Pulling on his coat, he gave the visitor an extra minute or so to depart and then, picking up his laptop bag and checking he had his keys, Claddis McAvoy opened the door.

*

Timms stood in the corner of the autopsy suite and waited for all the glad-handing to cease. Dr Hounslow had initially been reluctant for someone to come into her kingdom and start reassembling body parts, until she recognised the name 'Caroline Isherwood'. She was, apparently, some Big Kahuna in the medical world.

Most of the conversation had involved words that didn't seem to have sufficient vowels, and Timms was beginning to feel the need to ask everyone to step it up a gear. However, good sense prevailed and he waited while the two women discussed the price of tea, or whatever their conversation was about.

Just before he lost the will to live, Hounslow departed to conduct an autopsy, leaving them with what could only be described as a tray of offal. The most unconvincing part of this 'highly technical exercise' was the polystyrene head, usually seen in wig-shop windows, which had been placed on the steel cutting table, next to the pared remains of his John Doe.

'What is that?' Timms asked, with an edge to his voice. 'I thought this was going to be a reconstruction?'

'This,' replied Caroline, pointing to the polystyrene head, 'is going to act as a support for our gentleman's face.'

Timms stared at her. 'Really?'

Caroline lifted the largest piece of flesh and offered it up to the model head. 'It's a little hard to imagine at the moment but this flap of skin, once it's cleaned and stitched, will be attached to the support.'

'By support, you mean that plastic head?' asked Timms.

'I do. The polystyrene has no discernible features; it's just a basic skull shape and takes surgical pins. It won't dry the flesh out either, which is important for maintaining a true form.'

'How long's this gonna take, Doc?' sighed Timms.

'If you'd prefer to go get breakfast, I can call you when I'm done,' she said tartly.

Timms waved a dismissive hand. 'I need to know that some one's gonna recognise this poor bastard when you've finished.'

She looked at the unconvincing collection of bloodied tissue on the tray before answering. 'I believe they will,' she said confidently

Timms checked the morgue clock and watched as the surgeon examined her tray of fine-threaded needles, surgical pins and scalpels, and began.

Despite his initial scepticism, Timms was astonished by the process and the subsequent result. The facial tissue, which had been pulverized by the paving slab, was carefully reassembled, stitched together and pinned onto the polystyrene support. Gradually, a recognisable face appeared. There were some areas of the man's forehead which hadn't been salvageable, but what sat on the steel gurney was definitely a face.

'That's incredible,' said Timms, shaking his head.

'It gives you a sense of what he probably looked like,' said Caroline, swabbing the left eye. 'I'm sure your forensic team can enhance the photographs. Give him a bit of colour.'

Timms nodded. 'Good work, Doc.'

'My pleasure. Let me know if he gets identified.'

'You betcha.'

*

Claddis McAvoy tried to focus on the shape that loomed over him, but something was wrong. He seemed to be lying on the floor, rather than standing. What wasn't clear was *why* he was on the floor.

The sound of heavy breathing and groaning was coming from somewhere behind him and it filled him with alarm. Was he hurt? Who was standing above him?

He tried to touch his face but his hand kept missing. His fingers seemed to be in contact with something wet and hot, but it wasn't registering as his own face.

Claddis began to understand that he was making the groaning sound himself. A sudden tide of pain rose in his right temple and surged across his cheekbone, settling into his eye. He'd been hit and the likely source of his injury was standing over him and talking.

The pain ebbed as a sudden release of adrenaline cleared his thought processes and enabled him to speak.

'W-Who the hell are you?' he stammered through a metallic cough. He listened carefully but couldn't make out what the figure was saying. It sounded like 'dogs'. That made his stomach churn. The word dogs was bad: *really* bad. 'What?'

'You have *my* dogs and *my* old woman. I want them back!' said the angry voice.

This was insane.

'I don't have any dogs,' he managed as he calculated the damage he'd sustained. His right eye was closed and his left hadn't managed to focus properly yet. 'Do you *see* any dogs in here?'

A glimmer of hope made its improbable way into the absurd conversation as the figure appeared to look around him. He didn't have any dogs in the apartment and once the madman had worked this out, maybe he'd leave.

'They're hidden. I want them!' the figure shouted.

Hope drained away as Claddis tried to clear sufficient brain space to process a response. He was in trouble and desperately needed to get help. For Christ's sake, there was an officer standing outside.

Clarity.

The journalist heaved his breakfast over his legs as the identity and desires of the figure became obvious. This was the psychopath that everyone was looking for. He'd plastered this maniac's MO over the paper and now the reality was here, demanding an impossible and insane scenario – that he hand over the murdered body of Veronica Sizemore and the dogs he'd slaughtered.

'I don't have your dogs. The police have them… Detective Eleanor Raven has them: all of them. I can take you to her.

She'll give them back to you, I promise.' He could hear his voice becoming increasingly shrill. 'I saw her take them. The dogs and – the old woman. Eleanor Raven put them in a van and took them with her.'

The silence was a good sign. The maniac was listening, lapping it all up. All he had to do was talk him into going to Homicide and asking for the missing bodies. Perfect.

'I *know* where they are. You can just ask Raven and she'll hand them over.'

Claddis felt he was making progress. Then another wave of nausea hit and he began to vomit again. The vomiting increased the pressure on his right eye. He groaned as he swallowed blood. 'Need help,' he pleaded.

*

The boy looked at the creature on the floor and began to feel angry. He needed to think. Maybe the man was right. He didn't have his treasures but the detective he named had. It was beginning to make sense now. Eleanor Raven had left him a note demanding that he get in touch with her. He'd ignored it but perhaps she was trying to tell him that she had his dogs and the woman. The journalist didn't have the treasures, but he did know who'd stolen them. Eleanor Raven had them and he knew now where he had go to get them back.

'I'm not going to the police house,' said the boy stubbornly.

'No, no, you don't need to. I know where she lives. I can tell you where. Just help me and I'll get my book,' he managed.

'What book?'

*

Claddis was going to die if he didn't get help. 'Promise me you'll leave me alone!'

'What book?' repeated the boy, kicking at the man's leg to make him focus.

'It's there!' Claddis sobbed, pointing at the desktop. 'Oh God, just take it and go!'

He needed to get to the door and call for help. If he could make it to the door, someone would see him and call an ambulance.

He tried to move but none of his limbs were responding to instructions. He was becoming paralysed.

A sudden flash of terror freed his vocal chords and he began to scream a long, high-pitched scream.

*

The boy had picked up the contact book and was just leaving as the wall of sound hit him. Instantly, he felt an overwhelming rage build in him.

Turning on his heels, he ran at the large, shrill object and began to kick at it, swinging his leg back then letting it fly at the bloodied face: it didn't take long before the noise ceased.

As he ran out of energy, a warmth spread through his mind and body, calming him. He stood back, surveyed the mess and then slipped out of the apartment, along the corridor and down the stairs. Taking the fire exit, he stepped out into the rain, avoiding the side of the building that exposed him to anyone watching the old boiler room.

*

Opening the door to the office, Eleanor was greeted enthusiastically by Monster. He'd been lounging in Mo's armchair and had filled the room with a methanous fug. Flinging the window open, she tried to establish why she was sharing her workspace with this smelly creature. A yellow note pasted to her desk stated that Laurence had yet to secure adequate day-care arrangements for Monster and would be bringing him in until further notice.

Eleanor sighed and stared at Monster, who was beginning to whine.

'Wow, is he ill?' asked Mo as he cautiously entered.

'Inappropriately self-fed, I suspect,' Eleanor replied, pointing at the empty food wrappers strewn across the floor.

'Jeez,' said Mo, opening the door widely to allow a through draught. 'Have you seen Samuelson yet?'

'Not yet,' she answered.

'Bad news travels fast. Hold on to that thought. I've narrowed down the list by half so far,' said Mo, arranging the files into two piles.

'Me too. Let's see how many match. Dr Delaware gave me a prioritised list.'

As Eleanor began to look through the material, Mo set up the coffee machine.

'I've got to go meet up with Layton in thirty. Forensics have cleared up that tape.'

Eleanor looked at him with confusion.

'The recording of Roma Joe's last conversation with his psychiatrist,' Mo replied, selecting cups. 'Not sure it's going to clarify anything but I'd love to have something to poke at the pompous asshole.'

'Which asshole?' said Eleanor distractedly as she checked through the profiles.

'According to the prison shrink, Roma Joe's earlier shrink had been telling him that his mind was a freezer and unless he did things that would warm him, he'd stay in the ninth circle of hell, or something like it.'

Eleanor focussed her attention on Mo, who was on a roll.

'But the best thing was, this guy tells him that the good thing, the *thing* that will turn up the heat in his chilly brain, is killing women.'

'Mo,' she said firmly. 'What's the name of the psychiatrist?'

'He's called Blackmore.'

'Seb Blackmore was Roma Joe's therapist?' she asked, surprised.

'Yeah, Blackmore's still at a conference in Vancouver, so we spoke to Dr Launceston, who's head of the practice. He checked Blackmore's messages every day and claims there never was a message from Roma Joe, but the line was *live*, no sound of an answer machine kicking in, just Joe talking about the cold coming for him. It's not like Launceston committed any crime, but why would he lie? Why say you didn't pick up the phone when you did?'

'I know Launceston,' she said slowly. 'He's the psychiatrist that took over from Dr Blackmore and insisted I wasn't psychologically ready to leave the Serving Officers Psychiatric Assist Programme.'

'*What*?' said Mo, astonished.

'He lied about Dr Blackmore's recommendation that I'd finished the programme satisfactorily.'

'You sure?'

'I've spoken to Blackmore, who assured me he'd put it in writing, and Richard Glass, the bonding guy, confirmed this.'

There was silence as Mo thought about the implications. 'You interested in hearing that tape?'

'Very much so,' she replied.

'Doc? – You there?' Silence. *'I really need to talk to ya! Cops came in today and started talking about them bitches.'*

'Okay, now listen to the enhanced version,' said Danny the sound technician, adjusting the sound quality. There was a palpable clicking noise during the silence between Roma Joe's *'You there?'* and his next phrase.

'That,' said Danny, 'is the sound of the recipient's answer machine being turned on manually.'

'So, Launceston was there and listened to the message?'

'I can't say who was listening but the breathing, hang on – Danny isolated a skein of sound and played it through the headphones – 'is that of a male, probably a smoker, or someone with a chest condition. There!' She replayed the sound. 'The breathing has a wet, congested sound on the exhalation.'

'I hear that,' said Mo.

'The breathing is consistent until after the speaker says the phrase "*really important*" and then it speeds up slightly. Once background noise is removed, you can make out what he's saying.' She ran the sound, which was unmistakable.

'Rapture? What does he mean by that?' asked Layton. 'You think he's referring to the religious thing?'

'Isn't that when Christians are pulled up into heaven… Or something?' speculated Mo.

'It's not the subject speaking,' said Danny. 'That's another voice: the person on the end of the line, which is why it's hard to hear. He just whispers the word rapture.'

'Could you clean it up any further?' asked Layton.

'Maybe,' Danny said carefully. 'That's not admissible in court though, even if we could match it. One word's not enough.'

'So Launceston, or whoever, whispers the word rapture and Roma Joe kills himself?'

Mo shrugged. 'It's not enough… Surely?'

'Maybe if the word is linked to an instruction,' suggested Eleanor.

'Explain,' said Layton.

'Sometimes,' she said quietly, 'a word, particularly an unusual word that rarely, if ever, pops into a normal conversation, can be used to signify or instruct.'

Mo shifted uncomfortably in his seat.

'Rapture may be an instruction.'

'Hang on, I'm not getting this,' said Layton.

'The word could be an instruction for Roma Joe to kill himself,' she said.

'How the hell do you persuade someone to act on a word?' replied Layton, unconvinced.

'You implant it into a patient's subconscious during therapy. Possibly when they're being hypnotised or medicated,' she explained.

'You know this is something that happens?' Layton asked quietly.

Eleanor looked at him for a moment. 'Can you play Joe's response?' she asked.

Danny nodded and they readjusted their headphones.

'*It's getting colder, Doc and I ain't fighting it so good. The faces keep coming in and I'm gonna die.*'

'Is that a statement of intent?' Layton asked.

'Well he's dead, so I guess,' responded Mo.

Mo waved Layton off and then hurriedly stepped into Eleanor's car. 'We any the wiser? There's still nothing we could shake at a judge.'

Eleanor pulled into the traffic and headed back to the office. She was silent, ruminating. Mo watched the traffic.

*

Wadesky picked up the call at 3.51 p.m., exactly four minutes after the paramedics entered Claddis McAvoy's apartment complex. Mike Curtis, a friend and colleague of Claddis, had called for help after entering the apartment of the deceased. The paramedics, after checking for signs of life, had called Homicide. There was no doubt in their minds that Claddis McAvoy had been the victim of a violent assault.

Timms made his own way over to the crime scene, having just delivered the photographs of the reconstructed head to Susan Cheung. Parking next to the ambulance, he looked around slowly.

This was a down-at-heel neighbourhood. There was little in the way of garden space and few signs that the area was nurtured by its inhabitants. Why did Claddis live here? Surely he was on a decent wage from the *Sun* and could have moved into a more salubrious part of the city?

Sighing, Timms headed over to the main entrance, noting the absence of any monitoring equipment and identifying that the entrance was via a key code. A patrol officer greeted him.

'Check everyone coming in and don't let anyone touch the door,' he instructed the officer.

'I'm PC Steele, sir. I was on surveillance duty today,' she said, her cheeks colouring.

'Whatd'ya see?' asked Timms through pursed lips.

'Nothing,' she offered. 'I couldn't see this aspect of the building as I was watching the old boiler room.' She pointed helpfully to the rear of the building.

'Everyone sees something,' he said, with a growing edge. 'I don't care about what you didn't see. I want to know what you did. Start thinking.'

PC Mari Steele nodded enthusiastically. 'I will, sir.'

'Where are they?'

'Room 116. Take the stairs and turn right.'

The paramedics and Mike Curtis were standing in the corridor talking quietly when Timms arrived and entered the apartment. Wadesky was hunkered down next to the body. 'Jeez, he's a mess,' said Timms.

'Surely is,' said Wadesky. 'Looks like someone got real mad.'

'Maybe the sword, or likely the boot in this case, was mightier,' said Timms mirthlessly.

'You think this could be linked to the case Raven's working on?' she asked.

'Wouldn't be surprised.'

'Want me to go and talk to the neighbours while you get a sense of the place?' she offered.

Timms nodded slowly. This was how they liked to work a scene. Wadesky would get an initial impression and then go and talk to witnesses and neighbours, while he got a sense of the place.

He looked around him, noting the mountainous piles of newspapers towering above the general chaos.

*

After dismissing the two paramedics, Wadesky began her information-gathering with Mike Curtis. He'd been waiting for Claddis in the car park and, knowing that they were late for the editorial meeting, he'd decided to go upstairs and goose the writer into action.

'Why'd you collect him: he had his own car?' she asked.

'The meeting was going to be a discussion about the handling of the Veronica Sizemore murder and recent concerns from the readership.'

'Concerns about what?'

'Public safety, how the police were handling the case… you know the sort of thing. Managers wanted to know about follow up. I'd been asked to pick up Claddis, in case he didn't show which was a likely event.'

'You were friends?' she asked.

'I worked with him,' he answered vaguely.

'Was he concerned about anything or anyone?'

'Yeah, he thought Detective Raven was out to get him,' he said. 'But then again, he pissed a lot of people off,' he continued shrugging.

Before she could ask any further questions, a patrol officer entered the corridor, accompanied by a man wearing stained grey overalls. 'This is Mr Addison; he's the building supervisor. He'd like to talk to you.'

'Perhaps you'd wait in the lobby for a few minutes?' she asked Mike.

'He been murdered?' asked Addison with a resigned air.

'Mr McAvoy is deceased, yes. Have you seen anyone in or around the building who wasn't a resident, either today, or over the past few days?'

'Yeah I guess, but no one that looked like they were gonna kill anyone,' he mused.

'Has there been anything unusual that's happened recently?'

'Well, we've had six dead dogs and a resident murdered and strung up in the old boiler room. That's pretty unusual!' He leaned in to her and lowered his voice.

'Is someone working their way through the residents here? You know, like a mafia hit?' His eyes widened at the thought. 'It's gotta be the same person, hasn't it? I mean this isn't a violent city – there can't be that many people that live here and kill people, can there?'

'Have any of the residents complained about seeing anyone unusual over the past few days?'

He thought for a moment. 'Yeah, I got a message from 118, but then she calls me twice a day with some goddamn problem, so I wasn't going to come running up to deal with some woman knocking on a door too loudly, am I?' He looked at Wadesky, as if challenging her to disagree.

'What was the message?' she asked.

'That some woman with fair hair was banging on the door and demanding that McAvoy let her in. He yelled at her that she wasn't coming in and then she threatened to kill him.'

Wadesky raised an eyebrow. 'She's sure of that?'

The caretaker sighed. 'Look, I didn't get any other complaints about that and I saw Mr McAvoy leave the next day, so she obviously didn't—' He furrowed his brow and lowered his voice. 'But he is dead now, isn't he?'

'What's the lady's name?'

'Miss Devlin. She'll be in.'

'Thank you. I'll let you know when we're finished.'

Wadesky barely had the opportunity to lower her hand before the door was snatched open by Miss Devlin. Small, grey-haired with a lemon-sucked expression, she began her diatribe.

Wadesky held up a hand. 'Miss Devlin, it might be more productive if I ask the questions and then—'

'But you don't understand. It *must* have been the woman that murdered him. In fact' – she paused theatrically – 'I *know* who the murderer is!'

Miss Devlin arched her eyebrows and waited for a suitably dramatic response from Wadesky.

'You do?' Wadesky asked flatly.

Miss Devlin nodded and disappeared back into her lair leaving Wadesky in the doorway, exposed to a tart waft of cat piss. Wadesky hadn't sufficient time to rearrange her features before Miss Devlin reappeared and thrust a newspaper into her hand.

'That's her!' She stabbed a finger at a black-and-white imag on the lead story.

Wadesky took the paper and shook her head. 'Are you *absolutel* sure this was the woman you saw banging on the door?'

Miss Devlin lowered the corners of her lips. 'Of course I'm sure.' She stabbed a finger at the name below the image. 'D Eleanor Raven. That's her!'

CHAPTER EIGHTEEN

Eleanor had just finished confirming her appointment time when Laurence burst through the door. Judging by his angry expression, she supposed the negotiations with Mags hadn't leaned in his favour. He slumped into his chair, rubbing Monster's head vigorously.

'So why won't you just remortgage?' asked Eleanor.

'I just *can't*,' Laurence moaned.

'Everyone can remortgage. You've got a steady income and haven't defaulted.' He was silent. 'Oh, I see. It might be worth talking to Timms as he's—'

'I'm *not* talking to Timms!'

'It was just a suggestion... What about Monster?' she asked cautiously.

'He's going back to Mags... He's not really mine,' said Laurence quietly. 'She picked him up from the shelter and named him. I just... bitched about him.'

'Then why don't you let him go?' she asked.

Laurence shook his head and gazed at the unremitting rain. 'I need him,' he said quietly.

'Look, there are puppies on the way. Maybe you could have one?' Eleanor was fighting the impulse to stop talking. She was well out of her comfort zone and wasn't sure whether she was helping or hindering his coming to terms with what had to happen. 'Have you offered Mags one of the puppies?'

He shook his head. 'We didn't get that far. I was feeling hemmed in.'

'Wasn't it supposed to be a negotiation meeting?'

'It was and I didn't!' he snapped. 'I'm sorry,' he said. 'You're right. I need to stop clinging to the past. I can rent somewhere; get a pup…' His voice trailed off. 'A new start. It'll be good.'

She looked at him and nodded. 'Did you catch up with Nathan Bridgewater?'

'I did,' Laurence replied, pouring himself a coffee. '*Really* weird kid. Refused to confirm his whereabouts, but mom swore he was in. He's got a hideous injury to his face. A dog bite, I'm guessing.'

'Dog bite? What makes you think that?' asked Eleanor, pulling his file out.

'His mom implied that was the reason why he was scared of dogs.'

'You believe mom's alibi? Because he's down on everyone's list.'

'She said she was a light sleeper and she'd have known if he'd left the house in the night.'

'I don't want to dismiss him. If he's ticking the boxes, I'm interested. I'll drop in today and see him. Who else have we got? Dr Delaware has got it down to eleven red flags and three ambers.'

Her phone rang. 'It's Timms.'

Eleanor observed Laurence watching with interest as her face hardened.

'On our way,' she said heavily.

Laurence raised an eyebrow. 'What and where?'

'Claddis McAvoy's been murdered in his apartment.'

Eleanor and Laurence arrived just as Dr Hounslow was finishing her *in situ* examination of the body. The Forensic team were waiting for their cue to enter, allowing Eleanor only a few moments before the next stage of the proceedings began.

'What happened?' she asked.

'No witnesses located as yet,' replied Timms. 'He opened the door to his attacker, who, by the looks of it, hit him hard, continuing the assault as he lay on the ground.'

Timms glanced around the room. 'Hard to know if it'd been ransacked or whether the guy just lived like this.' He looked closely at Eleanor.

'I was here the other night and it looked very similar,' Eleanor said.

'Why were you here?' Timms probed.

'I wanted to tell him we'd sacked Kim for leaking information to the *Sun* in the hope that he'd defend her, and then let me know what else he was going to publish. I got neither from him.'

Timms sighed. 'Did you threaten him while you were here?'

Eleanor looked at him carefully. 'I hammered on the door, aware that his neighbours would hear and he'd be more likely to let me in if they were disturbed. There were no threats.'

'You didn't mention that you intended to kill him?' asked Timms.

'No, I didn't,' she said firmly.

Timms nodded. 'Okay.'

'Has someone implied that I threatened him?' she asked.

Timms nodded.

'He's been deceased for approximately two hours,' Hounslow stated. 'I will confirm that and the cause of death after the autopsy. However, I will say that the gentleman sustained the majority of his injuries to the right side of his face.'

'A left-handed assault?' asked Eleanor.

'These injuries are beginning to look disturbingly familiar,' she said to both Eleanor and Timms.

There was a pause.

'Thanks, Doc.'

*

The boy had taken a less pedestrianised route back home, which had kept him safe from prying eyes but saturated his boots and coat with mud. At some point he was going to have to ask his mother to wash the coat, as even he recognised that the increasing blood spatter was likely to provoke interest and questions.

Sitting in his room, he read through the contact book Claddis McAvoy had given him. It felt wonderful to have been given something so private and personal. He didn't recognise any of the names, apart from Detective Eleanor Raven's, but knew they had been important to the dead person, which made them desirable.

He liked the man's handwriting. It was spidery, and his As and Ds were difficult to tell apart.

He picked up his pen and tried to copy the jerks and loops of the handwriting. This must have made him feel happy, as he failed to notice the clock's movement, and when his mother knocked at his door, it was already 4 p.m.

'Honey?' She tapped again. 'We need to go for your doctor's appointment.'

He felt a sweep of irritation. 'I don't want to see him,' he snapped.

'But you're making so much progress at the moment. I think it's important that you go.'

'No.'

He returned to practising the handwriting, as he was beginning to feel that he actually understood the man. When he curled the letters, a sense of otherness crept into him. He didn't want to stop.

'Honey,' she said more forcefully. 'You have to attend these sessions and I'm not going until you leave your room and come downstairs.'

The boy felt a pulsing anger. Why wouldn't she shut up and leave him alone? He was happy and she was spoiling everything.

For a brief moment, a sense that she was the enemy began to overwhelm him. Maybe he should kill her and then he could go about life peacefully, without being nagged or disturbed, but then who would look after him? He had no idea how to cook or how to clean his clothes.

'Listen!' she shrieked. 'If you don't go and see the doctor, he'll make the authorities come round and take you away. Is that what you want to happen?'

The boy considered this.

'You know what he said to the school board – that as long as you were under his care you'd be safe.'

Hiding the contact book under his sheet, he stood up, opened the door and stared at her.

'Sweetie, you look tired,' she observed. 'Would you like me to make you something to eat in the car?'

He shook his head.

'Come on then, or we'll be late.'

The doctor seemed pleased to see him. He swept his hand towards the chair and smiled. 'How are you feeling today?' he asked solicitously.

The boy stared at him. 'I don't want to be here,' he replied flatly.

'Why not?' said the doctor, leaning towards him. 'Do you feel so much better that you no longer need the people who care about you?'

The boy narrowed his eyes. 'I don't need to talk anymore.'

'But you do,' said the psychiatrist quietly. 'Without me the police will come and lock you in a small room.'

'No, they won't!' snarled the boy. 'I haven't done anything wrong.'

'But you *have* done things that people don't like, haven't you?'

The boy turned away, but the doctor snapped his fingers. 'Look at me. Unless I am here to protect you, the police will be forced to lock you away. They don't understand why you do the things you do. Only I understand that.'

The doctor let the silence lengthen but it had little effect on his patient. 'Let's go to the quiet place, in your head, shall we?'

'No, I don't want you to be there,' replied the boy, sinking further into the chair and folding his arms tightly around his chest

'You still like the sound that the clock makes, don't you?' The doctor gently pushed the arm of the metronome, letting its heavy tick fill the room. The boy immediately felt his body relax and his limbs grow heavy.

The silence, punctuated only by the leaden tick, grew.

*

'Listen to the sound of time passing,' said the doctor, studying his patient's face. 'Only my voice can be heard above the sound of the clock. Only mine.'

The boy's eyes were unfocussed, his body sluggish and still.

'You are falling into a deeper sleep as you listen to the clock' beat.' The doctor lengthened the metronome's beat. 'You are deeply asleep, listening to the only sound in the room: my voice.

The doctor looked dispassionately at the creature lolling in his chair. 'You are walking into your mind, Nathan. Walking down a long corridor that is beginning to get cold. Do you feel the cold Look at the walls of your mind. They are covered in ice, and the pain of the cold is biting into you.'

The boy's breathing began to change. It became a shallow and unproductive pant. The hairs on his arms were beginning to rise and his skin puckered as the perception of cold activated his unconscious senses.

'You are bitterly cold. Nothing will alleviate that pain. Only my voice can enter the space and warm you.'

The boy's teeth were beginning to chatter. He was waiting in pain for the doctor to make things bearable again.

'What makes you warm?' asked the doctor. 'What fills your cold room with heat?'

The boy's lips twitched. He was trying to speak but his clamped jaw muscles were too tight.

'You have to tell me what it is that makes the cold retreat?'

'Dead things,' stuttered the boy. 'The dead things make me warm.'

The doctor stared at him.

'The room is getting warmer now and you feel better.'

He watched as the boy's body relaxed and regained its colour.

'Listen to me very carefully. One day soon, you will have to become a dead thing yourself. You won't have to worry about when, or how, because you will know instinctively how to become dead. I will tell you when you need to do this. You will hear my voice and it will say the word redemption and you will kill yourself. This is important. Do you understand what I am asking you to do?'

'Yes,' he replied quietly.

'What is the word you'll hear me say?' the doctor asked gently.

'Redemption,' the boy repeated.

'Good boy,' said the doctor, relaxing. 'Now, you're going to tell me about what you have been doing since our last talk.'

*

Rula sat in the car and chewed at the edge of one nail. She flung the newspaper onto the passenger seat. There was still no mention of a body turning up that could have been Alan. She was beginning to feel certain that there'd been a row and he'd gone off for a couple of days. It had been longer than she'd anticipated, but maybe he just needed the time to work things out?

Rula felt hurt that he'd not bothered to let her know that he was alright but she would forgive him. He was a good man and even a saint needed time to sort out his feelings. She was patient. All was going to be well.

A movement to her left caught her attention. Her son followed the doctor out of the back entrance. He looked tired but relaxed. Pulling up her hood, she stepped out of the car and hurried over to them.

'Mrs Frears. How are you? Your boy's been very open and helpful this session. I feel we're really making progress now. I'm sure you've noticed how much better he is at home?'

'Yes – yes, I suppose I have,' she answered unconvincingly.

'That's wonderful. We'll have him back into the midst of society in a matter of weeks.'

'Will we?' she asked, bewildered. 'I'm not sure that he's ready—'

'Nonsense,' the doctor replied. 'Nathan's an integral part of our society and I'm here to make sure he succeeds at living within it. See you same time next week,' he added, opening the back door.

'Can I?' she began, but the door had closed behind him.

'I'm cold,' said the boy. 'I want to go home.'

'Of course,' she answered, gazing at the door. 'Let's get you back into the warm.'

*

There was to be a twenty-four-hour watch on Claddis McAvoy's apartment complex. Having established that the likeliest point of entry for the killer was through the main doors, the key code was changed and the occupants informed. No one had seen any non-residents enter the building and none of the residents had drawn any real suspicion. Most were elderly, or had alibis for the time when the murder took place.

Both Timms and Eleanor believed that the murders of Veronica Sizemore and Claddis McAvoy had been committed by the same man. Three youths had been seen loitering around the car park on the night before Claddis was killed. A tip-off from a local handyman identified them as local lads, with a history of petty crime and nuisance-making. All were alibied.

'What are we left with?' asked Timms, stretching his shoulders and loosening his tie. The crime scene officers had processed the apartment and departed, leaving Timms to check through Claddis's laptop and notebooks, looking for a suspect's name.

'If he used the key code to access the building, someone had to have informed him what the number was,' said Eleanor. She turned to Wadesky. 'Did the building manager indicate how long that code had been in usage?'

Wadesky nodded and checked her notes. 'Since 2003. I'm making up a list of everyone who had knowledge of the code. It's pretty long, as most elderly residents had family members who visited regularly. I'm running those names through the database as they come in – so far no bells ringing.'

'All it would take is someone looking over your shoulder as you key it in,' suggested Laurence.

'What about previous residents?' Eleanor asked. 'Our guy is pretty comfortable there – maybe he's lived in the block before?'

'I've got a printout of everyone who lived there from September 2009 – that's when the records were computerised. From 1970, which is when the apartments were constructed, all data on residents was kept in ledgers. These are being tracked down now.'

'Let's get those ASAP,' said Eleanor, glancing out of the window and seeing the media teams for the local television stations and newspapers staking their spots on the forecourt. It looked as if the building were under siege.

Wadesky had drawn the short straw, which meant she was to run the gauntlet of journalists and photographers at the front entrance to Claddis McAvoy's apartment, while Timms, along with Eleanor and Laurence, sneaked out of the back. There wouldn't be a clear run from the back stairs, as journalists tended to anticipate the likely machinations of Toronto PS, but the combination of Timms' personality and fewer numbers gave him some chance of getting back to the office before midnight.

Wadesky barged through the scrum, trying not to let any individual questions penetrate her consciousness. Key words and phrases, such as her name, 'Claddis McAvoy' and 'Detective Raven' lit up neuronal pathways as she tried not to use her elbows to make progress towards the entrance.

'Detective Wadesky! Can you confirm that Claddis McAvoy was murdered by a member of the Toronto PS?'

Wadesky knew better than to engage but the question threw her. 'What?'

She saw the journalist thrust his microphone closer to her face; the sound of camera clicks heightened the tension. Wadesky inhaled. 'What you're suggesting is—' She saw the glint in his eye as she provided copy. 'Excuse me,' she said, moving assertively towards her car.

*

The note pinned to Eleanor's office door was uncompromising and succinct. She was expected to go directly to Marty Samuelson's office on arrival. For a luxurious moment, she considered ignoring the command, but the use of block capitals and three exclamation marks deemed this unwise.

Marty looked irritable and exhausted. 'Why has it been my misfortune to have taken three separate calls today, all referring to yourself? And' – he held up his hand – 'why have all of these calls involved me having to defend you?'

'What am I supposed to have done?' she asked flatly.

'Well, let's start with the *Toronto Sun*'s belief that you threatened to kill Claddis McAvoy the evening before he was found murdered?'

'I didn't threaten, but I was there,' she added. 'It's hearsay.'

Marty stared at her. 'You have refused to continue with your compulsory meetings with Dr Launceston, despite—'

Eleanor cut him off. 'I've thought better of that decision and I have an appointment with him tomorrow morning. The earliest I could arrange.'

Marty leaned back in his chair and grimaced. 'I don't buy that!'

'It's true – you can contact them tomorrow to confirm it. The final call, sir?'

There was a pause. 'Chief Brocker is concerned that you're dropping the ball.'

Eleanor's throat tightened and she adjusted her position. 'In what way?'

Marty rubbed his forehead. 'There's a third of an acre of park still untouched, with no recommence date set.'

'The weather's too bad to—'

Marty put up a warning hand. 'You've made no relationship with the military over on Base Borden, which has left us without any knowledge of what's happening regarding the Eddie Myles murder. And *yes*, I understand that the DA has advised us that there is to be no police investigation – hear me out!'

Eleanor clamped her mouth firmly shut.

'You and Whitefoot had a responsibility to open a channel of communication between us and them. *You*, being the more diplomatic and visually appealing, should have achieved this. Don't bother citing political and gender correctness to me on this because it would be a screen to mask your apathy. Finally, why didn't Whitefoot follow up on the dead dogs story? You wear the promotions; you could have prevented the murder of an elderly lady who pleaded with the police to help her. And now we have a dead journalist in the same apartment complex. It reads culpable negligence to the Chief and, more importantly, to the Toronto public.'

Silence.

'I agree,' Eleanor said simply. 'That's how it reads to me too.'

Marty snarled and leaned closer to her. 'Don't think about doing the noble thing and handing over your badge, Raven. You are the architect of this mess and *you* will be bringing me results within the next forty-eight hours. Are we on the same page?'

Eleanor stood up. 'We are.'

Marty pointed a finger at her. 'You don't get to walk away from this, Raven. I want information, results and less time spent justifying your existence to Chief Brocker. Understand?'

'Understood,' she replied.

The downstairs lights were out when Eleanor arrived at the small house. It had occurred to her that the address was less than three miles from the apartment complex, which made it more important that she evaluated the youth.

The paperwork on him had been filled with patchy, unsupported accusations that he had an antipathy towards animals and people, and it had been suspected, though not proved, that he'd been responsible for numerous acts of cruelty. A psychological evaluation at his school had underlined his narcissistic nature and inability to empathise with any other living thing. He was deemed too fragile and uncontrollable to be let loose in a social situation: therefore further observation and a regime of appropriate medication and mentoring had been recommended.

She had knocked and rung the doorbell, but neither had been heeded, so Eleanor peered through the letter box. There was little to see due to the gloom, but she could hear the muted tones of a radio playing somewhere downstairs. The house, although part of a terrace, was open to the left and Eleanor followed it around to the back of the property, noting that there was nothing in the garden to indicate that a family ever used the space.

The back door had a frosted-glass window, which revealed a shape moving inside. Eleanor knocked loudly on the door. 'This is Detective Inspector Raven of the Toronto Police Service. Please open the door.'

The figure inside froze. Eleanor hammered on the door again. She heard the bolt being drawn and a middle-aged woman opened the door.

'What's wrong with the front door?' asked Rula Frears.

'It's apparently out of your hearing range,' replied Eleanor. 'I'd like to speak to your son.'

'You can't just—' Rula began.

'I absolutely can,' replied Eleanor. 'I'd be grateful if you could go and fetch him.'

'Stay there,' snapped Rula, closing the door.

Eleanor waited until she disappeared before reopening the door and walking into the house. She could hear the woman's heavy, slow progress up the stairs and made the most of the few minutes she had before she returned. The small room appeared to be some sort of utility area, with a washing machine and outdoor clothing hanging up on coat hooks. Running her hands over them to check whether they were damp, she noticed that there was a bone-dry male coat and a damp female jacket. A pair of men's shoes, which she checked as a size twelve, were neatly placed on a rubber mat next to a pair of women's size seven-and-a-half trainers, which had been worn earlier.

She could hear the sound of footfalls on the stairs above her head. Sliding her hands into the coat pockets she found a set of car keys in the men's coat.

'What are you doing?' asked Rula angrily.

'Waiting,' said Eleanor coldly.

Rula stood back and ushered the boy into the room.

'Are you Nathan Bridgewater?' asked Eleanor.

'He is,' snapped Rula.

'I'm sure your son is capable of answering questions for himself,' said Eleanor, studying the belligerent youth in front of her.

'I'm DI Eleanor Raven and I'd like to ask you a few questions.'

He was immediately more attentive. 'Raven,' he repeated.

'I left you a card a couple of days ago, asking you to get in touch.'

He shrugged.

'My colleague Detective Whitefoot and myself are investigating the murder of a Miss Veronica Sizemore; we wondered if you could help us with our enquiries?'

'I told the other detective that Nathan stays in the house, except for when I accompany him to appointments,' said Rula with resentment. 'My son's a good boy; he doesn't hurt anyone.'

'He has a history of hurting dogs, Mrs Frears,' said Eleanor, watching for a response. 'That's why your face is injured, isn't it?'

She could see Rula Frears' face flush with anger.

'You were bitten by a dog you were trying to hurt.'

'I don't hurt dogs or people,' said the boy. 'I don't leave the house.'

'Is your father in?' asked Eleanor.

'I don't have a father,' he hissed.

Eleanor glanced at the coat hanging from the peg. 'Do you drive, Nathan?'

'No,' he growled.

'Are you left-handed?' she added.

'I use both of my hands,' he answered, thrusting both hands forward aggressively. 'I don't want to talk to you anymore.'

'I think you'd better leave now,' said Rula, her lips pursed. 'Nathan has answered your questions helpfully and I have assured you that he hasn't left the house at night.'

Eleanor let the silence settle. People had a tendency to fill in the gaps, but the body's social skills were beyond the norm, and his mother had herself under control now.

'Thank you. You've both been very helpful,' said Eleanor. 'Shall I leave through the front?'

Rula stepped forward and opened the back door for her.

CHAPTER NINETEEN

Eleanor woke early, after an erratic night's sleep. It was freezing cold in the room, and the condensation on the inside of the glass had formed a rib of ice on the sill. She turned on two of the electric heaters; the third had a tendency to knock out the aged power switch in the apartment.

Still wrapped in her duvet, she boiled the kettle to wash and determined to get home earlier that evening, so she could accept her neighbour's offer for her to bathe there. She felt unfocussed and angry. Maybe the sessions spent tamping down her anger in the psychiatrist's chair had left her a better person but a worse police officer. The accusations levelled at her by Marty were just: she hadn't formed a workable relationship with the military and had effectively handed over the case to them without a struggle. She'd let Laurence mess up the handling of the dead dogs case and, as a result, two people had been murdered. What was the matter with her? She was psychologically adjusted and it was a disaster. It was time to reset her clock.

'Come in,' said Dr Launceston, holding the door open for her.

Eleanor followed him into his therapy room and settled herself into the chair.

He looked at her, the corners of his lips twitching.

'You seem pleased,' she said icily. 'A little smug, even.'

'Certainly not smug,' he responded. 'Perhaps I'm just pleasec that you've realised I'm not the enemy, and that I have your bes interests at heart.'

'I wouldn't say that was a conclusion I'd reached.'

He smiled and put his fingertips together. 'How are we goin to work together if you are antagonistic towards me? A little bi of suspicion is natural, but without trust we won't make an progress.'

Eleanor adjusted her position. 'What progress have you ir mind for me?'

He took his time in answering her. 'You are a complex anc dangerous creature, Eleanor Raven. And I believe that you recent psychiatric treatment here has resulted in the normalisin and dilution of your unique and essential nature. For all of you previous faults, addictions and dysfunctional personality traits you *were* an achiever.'

'What does that *mean*?' she said irritably.

'You are letting things run away from you. Cases and situ ations which you would have instinctively understood in th past have drifted away from you. You are socially redeemed bu flavourless – without merit. You,' he said with a flourish, 'hav been defused.'

Eleanor cleared her throat and stared at him.

'That's why you're here, isn't it? You want rearming.' He hel up a finger. 'No, there's a second reason too, I'm guessing. Yo believe that I am, in some vague and incalculable way, responsib for the death of Joe Greene, which is how you've justified you appearance here. You are pretending that you're investigatin me, so you don't have to ask me to replace the recently sanitise Eleanor Raven with the self-loathing, dangerously unpredictab version of yourself that managed to get crimes solved and avengec Isn't that right?' he said, leaning back into his chair.

'You *don't* know me,' she said.

His mouth twisted slightly in concession. 'Maybe not, but I know a great deal more than you'd imagine.'

'Dr Blackmore assured me that he didn't share any of the details of my therapy sessions with you,' she stated. 'I believe him. So how do you know what was said between us?'

He smiled.

'You listened in on the sessions, didn't you?' snapped Eleanor, feeling her anger intensify. 'How?'

He smiled. 'Small, discreet devices, strategically positioned. The sessions were deliciously vanilla. Give Blackmore his due, he could reduce Genghis Khan to a Stepford wife, given sufficient time.' He chuckled. 'But what good is that? I will go further and say, what good are you?'

He scrutinised her for a moment or two. 'You no longer have a place in your world, do you? You've played at being the noble version of yourself, found it lacking and now want to be re-engineered back to the Eleanor Raven that arranged for strangers to tie her up and sexually humiliate her. All as a dubious penance for allowing a little school chum to be sodomised and strangled all those years ago.'

'Is that how you treated Joe Greene? By convincing him he needed to retain and indulge his violent streak?'

'I convinced Joe Greene of *nothing*. As you know, he wasn't my patient. He was beyond any conversation or medication known to psychiatry. In fact, when Joe confessed he was murdering prostitutes *I* persuaded him to hand himself over to the police and to believe that he'd be safer in their hands. I'm sure you've already checked that he wasn't caught but handed himself in?'

'You said he wasn't your patient; who did he confess to? Or did you listen to those sessions as well?'

Launceston lowered his voice. 'Joe Greene was removed from society. Does it matter by what *means* if it saved lives?'

Eleanor was silent.

'I'm not here to judge, Eleanor. I'm here to listen, observe anc remedy, if possible.'

'I don't believe that,' she said. 'I think you choose your patient very carefully.' She leaned towards him. 'You're playing a gam with the predators, not the prey.'

'You work Homicide, not bike crime. Isn't that the same thing?

She shook her head. 'I want to neutralise the predators; yo want to control them.'

He laughed. 'You think I'm playing with serial killers anc maniacs?'

Eleanor nodded. 'Yes. I do.'

'What does that tell us about *you*, Detective?'

'You wrote a letter to TPS contradicting Dr Blackmore's recom mendation that I had completed the Serving Officers Psychiatri Assist Programme,' she said tightly.

'If I was wrong and you are happy with your new anodyn self, then walk out of the room and I will send a second lette affirming that you are cured. *But*, having learned the consequence of this reprogramming of your personality, if you would prefe to be the guilt-ridden but effective officer you were before, sta and let me work my magic on you.'

'Is it magic or manipulation?' she asked.

'It will be a little of both,' he said gently.

Eleanor looked at the door but didn't move. Launceston le the silence hang.

'How do you propose to reprogram me?'

'You need to relax a little more, to begin with,' he said quietl reaching over to start the metronome's steady, dull tick.

Eleanor stood on the rocky bank and looked at the lake. It w an endless sweep of greys, indistinguishable from the skylin The water was sluggish and oily, beginning to form into an ic sheet which would freeze the shoreline. She glanced at her bare legs and feet, wondering why she hadn't worn shoes or a coat.

'Are you cold?' asked a voice from somewhere close by.

Wrapping her arms protectively round her chest, Eleanor looked around. The lakeside had seemed empty, but when she focussed her eyes, she could see coloured lights, twinkling dimly, some way off.

'The fairground,' she heard herself say. 'It's closed.'

'It's open to you,' coaxed the voice. 'Don't be afraid. You need to ride the ghost train.'

'I don't want to go in there anymore,' she said fearfully and turned back to face the lake, but it was gone, replaced by the gaping maw of the ghost train.

'He's waiting inside for you. Without you, he can't complete his vision.'

A figure was emerging from the darkness. She knew who it was. It was Lee Hughes and he'd come to kill her.

'There is no explanation for the living, if we don't create the dead,' Hughes said.

She looked at the canvas backdrop, alive with writhing, tortured figures. She could see an image of herself clawing her way through the bodies of the dead – *her* dead.

Hughes reached out his hand towards her, sliding it around her throat. She grasped at it, trying to loosen its hold. 'I don't die here!' she screamed.

His face was close to hers. 'You're wrong. You're not looking at the signs.'

Darkness.

Someone was speaking to her from across the lake. What the voice said wasn't important, because she was dead.

'Are you listening to me, Eleanor? You have to wake up now.'

She lay silently on the rocky shoreline, feeling the cold water envelop her. She didn't want to wake up, but her alarm clock was ringing. The distant voice was counting down from ten.

'Ellie?' said Caleb.

She opened her eyes and looked at her childhood friend. She couldn't visualise him as a living boy any longer. He only existed as the cadaver she'd found under the trash bags all those years ago.

'Don't leave us,' he whispered.

'Three… Two… One.'

Eleanor felt emotionally drained as she made her way to her car. Her limbs were heavy and uncoordinated, and she banged her thigh against the driver's door as she lowered herself into the seat. Suppressing the urge to swear, she grabbed her phone and dialled. As she started the engine and cleared the windscreen, the answer machine delivered its invitation to leave a message.

'Sergeant Morton, this is DI Eleanor Raven speaking.'

*

Johnson had been staring at video feed for the past twenty-four hours and it was beginning to take its toll on his eyesight and concentration levels. Just as he determined that the only way to get through the remaining fifteen hours of blurry security tapes was to have another strong cup of coffee, he hit gold. He re-ran the tape, trying to enhance the poor quality by adjusting the contrast. The security tape had been provided by an enthusiastic Costco manager, who had yet to make any impact on the common and expensive problem of shopping-trolley theft.

A solitary male, wearing what looked like a trench coat, appeared to the right of the camera, selected a trolley and began pushing it to the left of the camera, which led directly to an area of shrubby plants, a low wall and ultimately to the street. Having taken a freeze-frame of the figure, Johnson began to search through the gathered material to see if any further progress of the man and the shopping trolley had been captured.

It took him another two hours to locate a second sighting. The footage came from a camera that had been placed by a pedestrian crossing, 300 yards from the intersection. It wasn't a high-traffic area, but there had been a cyclist injured there a year earlier and it was deemed appropriate that a camera was placed there to monitor movement. The same man was visible in the corner of the frame, enabling Johnson to place the suspect 300 yards away from the John Doe murder scene.

*

'That's it?' muttered Timms, disappointed.

'Look, these two frames prove firstly that you were right, and hat a trolley was stolen from this store' – Johnson pointed to he map – 'and was pushed towards the roadworks where the body was found.'

Timms grunted. 'Play it again.' They watched the tape for a second time.

'Stop! See that!'

Johnson rolled the tape back and restarted.

'There's something in the trolley. Can you enhance it? That,' aid Timms, tapping the screen, 'is our John Doe.'

Is that our John Doe?' asked Wadesky, closing the office door behind her.

'That is he,' said Timms, leaning back in his chair and looking t the forensic photograph he'd pinned to the murder board. The original surgical reconstruction had been toned and airbrushed by the technicians.

'Caroline did an amazing job,' noted Wadesky, peering at the enhanced photograph. 'Are the papers going to run it?'

'This evening's main three will all carry it.'

'Think he'll be recognised?' she asked, slipping off her we boots and taking the seat next to her partner.

Timms examined the face. 'He looks pretty identifiable to me Let's hope his family are regular readers.'

He pushed over several photographs and repositione the map so she could see the landmarks. 'Johnson's runnin through the rest of the security material, to see if we can spo our trolley thief.'

'That's not going to get a recognition,' she said, examinin the photographs.

Timms shrugged. 'The coat might.'

She nodded. 'Maybe. Have we got a timeline?'

'These two cameras are positioned within eight to ten minute average walking pace of each other. The second clocks the gu pushing the trolley twenty-four minutes after stealing the trolle So he either has to lift or persuade John Doe to get into the trolle just off-screen of the Costco camera, *or* he takes the trolley bac to where the initial attack happened.'

'If our John Doe *was* attacked,' Wadesky butted in, 'he coul have just been too drunk or stoned to—'

Timms shook his head. 'Got the tox screen back an hour ag No alcohol or detectable recreational drugs in his system. So th guy was sober when he was dumped into the trolley. *However*, h did have fairly high levels of Toprol in his system, which is use for treating high blood pressure. Now, as the autopsy showed litt heart damage, the doc reckons he could have been taking it f migraine relief.'

'Okay, that's something. I'll email the local prescribers in th area,' Wadesky said, noting it on her pad.

'If he was attacked at either his house, or somewhere local to the Costco, it means that there was only a possible fourteen to sixteen minutes before he shows up at the second camera.'

'Show me,' she said, looking at the map.

Timms put his finger on a pencilled line that ran in a circle around the Costco.

'Now that's the sort of area I like to canvas,' Wadesky said, miling. 'How many patrol officers do I get?' She looked at Timms' expression. 'Oh man, tell me I get two!'

Timms held up one finger.

'That *sucks!*'

'But what doesn't suck is that I'll be pounding the pavements with you for the next' – Timms checked his watch – 'next two hours.'

*

Eleanor stared at what was left of the rose garden. A single muddy arpaulin covered the area due to be exhumed when weather permitted. She had spoken to the dig coordinator, who assured her that the forecast predicted sufficient improvement by the start of the new week. Rain lashed her uncovered face as she arranged her thoughts.

'Have you been here long?' asked Jacob, approaching her autiously.

She glanced at him and shook her head.

Jacob stared at the mud, letting the silence settle between them.

'She's here,' said Eleanor quietly.

'Instinct?' he asked.

She looked at his profile.

'You were convinced she wasn't. What changed your mind?' he said slowly.

'I did.'

He nodded his understanding.

'Would you trust me with your spare key?' asked Jacob gently

Eleanor looked surprised. 'I don't—'

'I've managed to locate a thermocouple and I could pop in when I've finished and see if I can get things working? So you can have some heat.'

Eleanor felt strangely conflicted. Handing over a key to her apartment to someone other than Mo wasn't a concept she'd considered before. 'Yes, of course. You're sure you don't mind?' she heard herself answer.

He smiled. 'It would be my pleasure.'

Eleanor extracted her car keys from her shoulder bag and unclipped the two keys to the building and her apartment. 'There's coffee and…' Her voice trailed off.

Jacob watched her expectantly.

'I'm not sure when I'll get in,' she said uncomfortably.

'I'll lock up when I'm done.'

'Thank you,' she said.

He bowed his head, turned and walked in the direction of his office. Eleanor surprised herself by watching him as he walked away.

Her phone rang, breaking her reverie.

'Detective Eleanor Raven?'

'Speaking.'

'It's Sergeant Robert Morton from Base Borden here.'

Eleanor held her breath.

'I got your message regarding the name of the psychiatrist that treated Lieutenant Myles,' he sighed. 'As you already know the TPS case is no longer active, but I can assure you that there is a full military investigation underway, which means that the sharing of information is no longer possible, as I'm sure you are aware,' said Sergeant Morton.

'I understand that completely, but in the course of our investigations regarding a civilian incident, we've had the name of th psychiatrist mentioned. I need a heads-up from you that we're not going to be compromising each other's cases.'

There was a significant pause as Sergeant Morton worked through his conflicts.

'Look,' Eleanor said, trying not to sound as if she was baiting, 'if TPS begin to openly investigate Dr Launceston, it will make access to his records and person much more difficult for your team.'

'I'm not sure what you want from me?' said Sergeant Morton.

'I'm offering you the integrity of my department. I won't start the lesser investigation until you've conducted yours.'

The silence held.

'I'd appreciate that,' said Sergeant Morton before disconnecting.

*

Laurence and Mo had just wrapped up their fifth visit of the day, and they both needed a break. 'I need a coffee with two sugars and three Advil before I interview any more assholes,' said Mo with a grimace.

'I hear you,' said Laurence, pulling into the Tim Hortons' drive-through and ordering. 'What are your thoughts so far?'

'My thoughts are that we should have more straight-jackets available for certain members of the public. That last guy has my vote,' Mo snarled.

'You've said that about everyone we've seen so far.'

Mo looked at him, astonished. 'I have?'

'Yup. Though I agree. He was a new level of asshole *and* he's a left-hander. Let's see if his feeble alibi holds water.'

'How many more?' asked Mo, sipping his coffee.

'Six,' sighed Laurence, tearing off a corner of his doughnut and giving it to Monster, who was sitting in the back seat.

'I thought that was bad for him,' said Mo.

'It is, but his digestion is no longer my responsibility. He's going back to Mags on Friday.'

'She didn't accept your puppy offer?' Mo asked.

Laurence shrugged.

'You didn't offer? Why not?'

'Next on our list of animal-abusing potential killers is John Maynor, aged twenty-one, who has a penchant for shooting dogs with an air rifle.'

'Jeez, can't wait. Onwards,' directed Mo.

*

The boy was excited. He wasn't technically minded and in trying to find exactly where the apartment was located, he'd had to resort to using his mother's crumpled street map, which had been gathering dust under the coffee table in their lounge. Using his thumb as a guide, he estimated the distance from his house to Eleanor Raven's apartment to be approximately six miles. That would take a lot of walking but it wasn't beyond him. There was a bus service that would reduce the trip considerably, but he had only used public transport a few times due to his intense dislike of being looked at by people. However, if he started walking in the next few hours, he might cover the distance.

He'd been in a lather of planning since learning where Eleanor Raven lived. He wasn't entirely convinced that she would have the dogs or his old woman in her apartment, but Claddis McAvoy was pretty certain that she had them. Of course, there would be hurdles along the way, but he'd thought these through.

He had a plan and it was excellent.

*

Eleanor was late getting back to HQ, but she was pleased to see Andy Harrison talking to a woman in her mid-thirties who was wearing theatre scrubs under a huge padded jacket.

'You must be Mags Lindhoff?' said Eleanor, holding out her hand.

Mags nodded.

'I'm Eleanor Raven, Laurence's partner.'

'I'm really pleased to meet you,' she said enthusiastically.

Eleanor walked Mags back towards their office, slowing next to Timms' puppy board.

'Oh wow!' said Mags. 'I didn't know he'd received a medal?' She looked with disbelief at Monster.

'He's a valued member of the department… and Laurence loves him.'

'He does?' she replied with more incredulity. '*Really*?' She studied the scan images. 'I didn't think Laurie liked Monster at all. Are these the puppies?'

'Those are the two litters due' – Eleanor quickly checked the dates next to the two scans – 'next week for Chance's litter and three days after that for the second.'

She watched as Mags examined the scan photos. 'Aww.'

'Detective Timms is having to run it as a lottery, there are so many officers wanting one.'

'Oh,' said Mags quietly as she ran down the list of names. 'Laurie has put his name down.'

Mags settled herself into Laurence's chair and glanced at the coffee machine. 'You mentioned on the phone that you had a proposition?' she said, smiling.

CHAPTER TWENTY

Jacob pulled into the private parking lot attached to Eleanor'
apartment complex and glanced around. He couldn't see her ca
but wasn't particularly surprised by that – she was in the middl
of several cases and he suspected he'd have the boiler up an
running before she arrived back from work. He'd briefly toye
with the idea of dragging out the job in order to catch her comin
in, but he valued privacy and determined that a warm apartmen
and a tank full of hot water was probably a better gift than hi
presence after a long day.

Humming, he collected his tools from the back of his Jee
and made his way to the entrance. The first key opened th
main complex door and he made a point of waiting till it close
and locked before heading up the stairs to the second floor. H
knocked first, just in case, and then opened the door and le
himself in.

It was cold and smelled damp. He flipped on the light
placed his toolbox in the kitchen next to the boiler and bega
to switch on the heaters in an effort to get the place warmed u
a little. Unfortunately, the third heater tripped the mains switc
and plunged him into darkness. Jacob searched his pockets fo
his phone, so he could illuminate the room, but found only h
Jeep key. The phone was probably still in the car, as was his torc

Unsure of exactly where the mains switch was located, or whe
he'd placed the keys to Eleanor's apartment, he decided to gra
his torch from the car before he knocked over anything valuabl

Sighing, he made his way cautiously, running his hand along he wall until he came to the door. He flipped back the latch so hat the door wouldn't close on him, jogged down the steps and, fter repeating the process at the main entrance, ran to the Jeep.

*

The boy, who'd been hunkered down in a small alcove adjacent o the entrance, couldn't believe his luck. The man who'd recently merged, propping the door open, had his back to him as he ummaged for something in his car.

In a matter of seconds, the boy slid through the open entrance nd, spotting a small arrowed sign bearing apartment numbers, nade his way upstairs.

The door to Eleanor Raven's apartment was slightly ajar. With a gentle push it swung open. It was dark and cold in there. He inhaled deeply, trying to catch a smell of her, but there was othing. There was neither movement, nor a sign that anyone vas at home. So why was the door unlocked? Perhaps she was in here waiting for him?

For the briefest of moments he considered backing off and iding somewhere in the building to figure out what was hap- ening, but the open door was too good an opportunity to miss. With a quick look around, he cautiously entered the apartment nd, sliding his hand along the wall, followed it for ten feet or o until it opened up into a larger room.

He thought he could hear someone making their way up the ncarpeted stairs. Unsure as to whether this was someone about o enter the apartment, he felt around to get his bearings. There vas a sofa, or a bed with a duvet-like covering to his right. Pulling he cover over his head, he wedged himself into a corner, sinking s low as he could behind the armrest.

*

Jacob shone the torch around the kitchen area but couldn't se
anything resembling a fuse box. It was most likely concealed inside
cupboard, so he began to investigate those at head height. He sighed
maybe it wasn't in the kitchen at all. It was unlikely to be in the bas
cupboards, but systematic coverage was the only way he'd find it.

Lowering himself, he shone the torch into what appeared t
be a pan store and, seeing nothing, reached for the second. H
heard the footfall a split second before he felt the blow to hi
back. The pain travelled through his shoulder and into his ches

Before Jacob could speculate on what was happening, hi
instinct for self-preservation kicked in. Grasping the edge c
the worktop with one hand and gripping the torch tightly wit
the other, he spun round and lashed out. On impact, the torch
connectors were dislodged and the light extinguished.

*

The boy, confused by the sudden reversal, kicked out hard, onl
to find his leg snatched and yanked, toppling him backwarc
against the sink unit. Outraged and angry, he began to kick a
hard as he could, but now that the figure had turned round
was apparent that it wasn't Eleanor Raven, but a man.

*

Jacob tried to stand, but whatever had hit his shoulder ha
punctured his lung. It didn't matter how hard he gulped in a
– nothing was going in. He put his weight behind the torch an
rammed it into the attacker's face, pushing against the scream

*

The boy felt the skin on his face tear and one of his incisors sna
backwards. In a flurry of rage, he pulled the knife out from th
man's shoulder and began to push it into the side of his throa
There was a desperate flailing from the man, his hands grabbi

and twisting the boy's grip. The knife made a clattering sound against the tiled flooring and then it disappeared from reach.

'You hurt me!' screamed the boy, pushing at the figure, but there was no reply. The man lay face down on the floor. He was damp and still.

Pulling himself upright, the boy felt around for the knife, but it was gone. He leaned against the counter to try and catch his breath; he felt betrayed and hurt. All he'd wanted was to find his dogs and the old woman, but this person, who shouldn't have even been in the apartment, had attacked him. What was he going to do now? He was alone in a dark and unknown place without anyone to look after him. He wanted his mother. Why wasn't she here?

He felt a dangerous indignation stirring in him. She was never there when he needed her and she didn't seem to care one jot about his well-being. He hated her. There was only one reason for her being alive and that was to make sure he was happy, and he definitely wasn't that.

*

Wadesky and Timms stood next to the store manager in the parking lot. It was bitterly cold and the rain was beginning to turn to snow. The wind had died down, which indicated that more bad weather was on the way.

'If I get a heads-up from the public, I'll send one of the floor-workers out to locate it and bring it back. Sometimes they're in too difficult a spot to be got, or it's not ours but another store's, and then we send in a local guy who has a hoist. You see *we're* responsible for any injuries to the general public who fall over or crash their car into one of our trolleys. I've been trying to get ours updated to the self-locking type, but they're expensive and there's a waiting list to have the strips embedded in the entrance and exits. So we just keep on monitoring our losses and hoping we get them back. These trolleys can cost up to 200 bucks each!'

Timms nodded. 'How many are missing at the moment?'

'Three, but we had a notification yesterday that one was blocking someone's garage over on Hind Street. So we've brought it back.'

'Has it been put back with the other trolleys?' asked Timms.

The manager looked at him with surprise. 'I imagine so. They get a clean and check over and then we put them back.'

'Hind Street is two blocks from here,' said Wadesky, showing Timms the map on her phone.

'Who collected and cleaned the trolley?'

The manager's forehead creased. 'Bill, I guess. He's our maintenance guy.'

'Call him,' said Timms. 'I want to speak to him.'

The manager dialled and waited. 'Hey, Bill, I've got a detective that wants to speak to you about that trolley on Hind Street.'

Timms made an impatient gesture for the mobile phone to be passed to him. 'Detective Timms of TPS here. The trolley you collected yesterday – has it been cleaned?'

'Not yet. It's got some damage to the front wheel, so I've left it in the delivery bay until the part comes on Saturday.'

The trolley had been parked next to several broken plastic chairs, which were also awaiting repair. Timms and Wadesky pulled on latex gloves, much to the interest of Bill and the store manager.

'You've not wiped or cleaned this in any way?' asked Wadesky.

Bill shook his head. 'Just walked it back.'

Timms pointed out the blood-stained material trapped between the child seat and the main frame and then the splash marks on the plastic wheel coverings. Wadesky stepped away and called for forensic support.

'Right, we're going to have to have this trolley processed,' said Timms, reaching into his coat pocket. 'Do you recognise anyone in these photographs?' he said, passing them to the two men.

'Jeez, is this guy dead?' Bill asked, pointing to the facial reconstruction.

Timms nodded.

Bill lowered his voice and pointed to the trolley. 'You think this has something to do with him?'

'There's a possibility that his body was moved in it. So we're going to need a set of your fingerprints, for exclusion.'

Bill nodded. 'Sure.'

'I've seen this guy before,' said the store manager, holding up the photograph of John Doe. 'He shops here.'

'Know anything about him? Like who he comes in with, where he lives?' asked Timms hopefully.

'No. Just think I've seen him in here before.'

Wadesky parked the car opposite the garage indicated by Bill and stared at the street. 'We're half a mile from the Costco and one-and-a-half miles from the body dump,' she noted.

Timms nodded slowly.

'You're getting that cosy feeling?'

Timms smiled. 'Uh-huh.'

'Wanna separate?' she asked.

'No, let's do this together. You ask the meaningfuls and I'll watch. I'm guessing our perp didn't turn back on himself, so let's start here and head east.'

'This is what I don't get,' said Wadesky as they crossed over to the garage. 'Why didn't he leave the trolley where he dumped the body? Because pushing an empty shopping trolley draws attention to you.'

'Not if you're homeless. Aspirational real estate!'

'Or if you have something else in the trolley?' suggested Wadesky, knocking on the door, which was opened by an obviously inebriated middle-aged man.

'Yeah,' he said, swaying slightly.

'I'm Detective Sarah Wadesky. You reported to the loca Costco that a supermarket trolley had been abandoned outsid your garage.'

'Yeah!' said the man suspiciously. 'They came and got it.'

'Any idea who may have left it?' asked Wadesky.

'No way.'

Timms and Wadesky looked at him.

'I mean who does that sort of thing?' he offered.

'Did you touch the trolley at all?'

The man narrowed his eyes. 'You mean fingerprints? No way

'Okay, thanks,' said Wadesky.

'Hey, it's great you guys take this crap seriously,' he said, fis pumping.

Timms sighed. 'It's gonna be a long evening.'

'Sure you don't want to divide and conquer?' asked Wadesk checking her watch. 'I'll take the odd numbers, you the even?'

Timms nodded and headed towards the next building an knocked loudly. The door opened cautiously.

'Yes?' answered Rula Frears quietly. Her face was ashen an her breathing shallow.

'Ma'am, are you okay?' asked Timms.

She nodded.

'I'm Detective Timms of the TPS and I'm investigating—'

'He's not in,' she said hurriedly.

'Who isn't?' asked Timms with interest. 'May I come insid ma'am? You're losing your heat with the door open.'

She shook her head. 'I'd prefer you not to.'

'We're investigating the murder of a gentleman whose boc was found a couple of miles from here. You said *he* wasn't in; wh are you referring to?'

She shook her head. 'I'm sorry. I thought you wanted to spea to my son.'

'What's his name?' Timms asked, flipping to a new page in his notebook.

'Nathan,' she answered reluctantly.

Timms raised his eyebrows. 'Nathan?'

'Nathan Bridgewater,' she replied, watching him carefully as he wrote the name down.

'And you are?' asked Timms.

'The papers said he was a young man.'

'Sorry, ma'am?'

'The man that was killed.'

'They were wrong,' said Timms carefully. 'The man murdered was in his late forties to early sixties. I have a photograph.'

'I've seen it in the *Sun!*' she answered too loudly. 'I'm sorry, it's very upsetting. We think it's safe here, but it isn't.' Her voice trailed away.

'I didn't catch your name,' said Timms.

'Rula Frears,' she said quietly.

'Is there something you wish to discuss with either myself or my female colleague?' asked Timms.

She shook her head. 'No, nothing. I just feel a little worried.'

'When is your son going to be back?'

She looked alarmed. 'He's back tomorrow. Yes, tomorrow.'

'A shopping trolley was abandoned three doors down from your house. Can you recollect seeing anyone pushing one?'

She shook her head. 'Why?'

'It may be connected to the murder investigation.'

'In what *way* connected?' she asked anxiously.

'The victim may have been transported in it.'

Rula made a gasping sound. 'That's horrible.'

Timms nodded and handed her his card. 'Just in case you think of anything you want to talk to us about.'

She nodded and closed the door.

Timms stood on the pavement and looked critically at th
house. He reached for his phone. 'Johnson? Pull up the detail
on a Nathan Bridgewater, will you? Lives at the following…'

*

Rula walked unsteadily back into the kitchen, where she sat dow
and stared again at the image of her dead husband on page tw
of the evening paper.

*

Eleanor was exhausted by the time she pulled into her parkin
space. She felt immediate irritation as she spotted Jacob's jee
parked near the entrance and had to remind herself that he wa
there to fix her heating.

Scowling, she gathered her bags, locked the car and heade
towards the building. Pushing open the door to her apartmen
she was puzzled as to why it was cold and dark inside. She flippe
the light switch: nothing.

'Jacob?' she asked quietly. Maybe he couldn't hear her?

She had a small torch attached to her key ring, which allowe
her to make her way into the kitchen, open the cupboard do
and check the mains box. For a moment she wondered if the
was a safety reason why the power was off, but as the apartme
was empty and cold and there was no sign of Jacob, she decide
to risk turning it back on.

It took her several seconds to process the scene in front
her. Jacob's body lay face down between the counter and t
sink. The bloody tear in his shirt and neck determined h
next move.

Unholstering her Glock and scanning the room, Elean
checked for a pulse. Before she could call for assistance, protoc
demanded that she secure the area.

Despite the compact dimensions of her apartment, it seemed to take an age to check each corner and determine there was no one there.

Keeping her weapon to hand, she called for backup and waited, whispering gently to Jacob.

*

The boy was cold, angry and exhausted by the time he made it back home. He slumped onto the stool in the hallway and unfastened his boots laboriously.

'Where have you been?' asked his mother, emerging quietly from the kitchen.

He ignored her.

'I've made you some supper,' she said, her voice weirdly strained.

He pushed the balls of newspaper into his damp boots and lined them neatly against the wall.

'What happened to your face?' She moved closer to him, making him feel cornered.

'Nothing!' he snapped.

She stared at him with an expression he couldn't fathom. 'Come and eat your supper.'

'My mouth hurts,' he whined.

'I see that. Did someone hit you?' she asked, peering at his bloodied, swollen lip.

'No.'

'It's soup – your favourite. It will be easy to eat.' She gently steered him into the kitchen, poured a bowlful from the pan and sat across from him. 'Have it all.'

He scowled at her but ate the soup anyway.

*

Once he'd finished, Rula watched him head up to his room. 'Goodnight,' she said quietly.

Left alone in the kitchen she put the bowl into the sink, washed it and placed it to dry.

CHAPTER TWENTY-ONE

It was 2.30 a.m. and Rula Frears knew that if she left it any longer she'd be incapable of carrying out what had to be done.

She pushed off the bedcovers and stood up. The room felt cold and empty, and for a moment she had to sit herself down and pick up the newspaper in order to remind herself that there were no choices left. The print was beginning to blur where she'd worried the text, but the images had taken on a clarity and narrative beyond their reproduction. The reconstructed face of her missing husband, with his closed eyes and obvious surgical scars, was far more potent than the artist's impression.

There were errors there: his skin was too heavy and the pale eyes lacked the sparkle that had made him so easy to love. She wasn't interested in the 'as he'd been in life' photograph – that was an obscenity to her. Her focus was on *why* his face had been so damaged that they'd been forced to call in a surgeon in order to identify him. What had her son done to him?

It was undeniably him. You couldn't identify him directly from the two still photographs taken as he pushed the trolley, *unless* you recognised that coat. That bloody coat!

She felt a weight pressing on her chest and forehead. *Her son* – the son that Alan had taken on and loved – had destroyed him. The only sane thing in her world was gone, and she was angry. Everything had become clear now: the wet floor, the police visits, his refusal to explain Alan's disappearance.

Her hatred was palpable to her: it had a sacred quality. As if the Old Testament God of her childhood had decreed, through

a tablet of stone, that the creature she had bought into this worl
was hers to remove.

Rula quietly opened his bedroom door and listened. Her son wa
breathing heavily, not the usual irregular snort of his nightmare
laden dreams but a deep, bullish rasp.

She opened the door, walked in and hesitantly switched o
the lamp. She thought that when she saw him there would be
maternal surge. Perhaps she'd see the child in him and rage agains
the violence she was about to perform – but there was nothin
She could no longer see the boy – just the man.

Rula looked at his swollen lip and the bloodied cut that ra
around his jaw and wondered what awful things he'd done t
deserve it. Maybe he'd been tormenting dogs; that wouldn't hav
surprised her.

She sighed deeply and tried, in the spirit of fairness, to fin
something about him that she could still love.

Looking around the room, she saw his coat. It was soakin
wet and had been dropped onto the floor. Touching it carefull
she noticed the profusion of bloodstains on the collar, sleeves an
front. Some were hardened and had matted the fibres into rigidit
Some were still red, smearing her fingers as she examined it. Th
was her husband's blood. He'd killed Alan and then, stealing
trolley from the store, he'd taken his body and dumped him i
a pit by the side of the road, as if he were trash.

She didn't want her son to be alive any longer. He'd bee
given to her as some sort of punishment and now she was goi
to end that.

She moved towards him, knowing that the sleeping table
she'd dissolved into his soup would allow him to sleep throu
the distress of his ending and then take him into the silence
eternity. She closed her eyes and listened for an inner voice th

vould signal she was either right in her actions, or at least not ılone – but there was nothing.

*

Raven!' bellowed Timms from the corridor. 'Get in here.'

Flinging her coat onto the chair, she sprinted into his office ınd was greeted by Marty Samuelson.

'How are you feeling?' Marty asked as Timms arranged papers ›n the table.

She paused momentarily before answering, unsure of how she ctually felt. 'Angry,' she concluded.

'How angry?' he asked, his eyes narrowed.

'The right amount,' she offered, taking a chair.

'Okay,' said Timms. 'We've got a print and palm match off he knife.'

'Whose?'

Timms shook his head. 'Don't know but this is going to blow our mind. It matches one of the three viables we took off the hopping trolley.'

'I don't understand.'

'Join the club.' Timms beckoned her over to the murder board ositioned behind his chair. 'Forensics analysed the prints off the nife and found that whoever stabbed Jacob had left partials in hree other crime scenes.'

'Three? And he's not on AFIS?' she asked, astonished.

'Nope, but the palm print has been matched to those taken from ıe Veronica Sizemore crime scene. There were also a couple of partials ıat had an eighty per cent chance of being from the same person.'

Laurence, Monster and Wadesky arrived, shaking off wet coats nd filling the room with a damp exhaustion. They acknowledged Iarty's presence.

'What are the other two?' asked Eleanor, nodding brusquely › her colleagues.

'I'm just telling Raven about the print results,' said Timms.

'*Which* other two crime scenes?' asked Eleanor with growin
tension.

Timms raised an eyebrow. 'One from a worktop in Claddi
McAvoy's apartment and the final one from the shopping trolle
used to transport the body of our John Doe to his resting plac
as I said.'

'This means that your cases are linked to ours?' asked Laurenc
'So we're looking for the same killer?'

Timms nodded. 'And because Raven was targeted by him, rath
than the rest of us, we need to know what she knows that we don't

He turned to look at her, but before she could open her mout
Johnson walked in.

'Printed off two copies, as you both wanted info on the sam
guy.' He handed a stapled sheet to Eleanor. 'Nathan Bridgewate
aged sixteen.'

*

Rula knew that the quantity of barbiturates she'd fed to her son we
more than likely sufficient to kill him without further interventio
but that seemed cowardly in her mind. As if this would someho
make a case for her lack of involvement when she wanted to b
fully culpable. She'd made this monster, so she'd destroy it.

Taking a last, emotionless look at him, Rula placed the pillo
over his face and leaned her weight onto it.

Several minutes passed. A part of her hoped that he'd put u
some form of struggle, but there was nothing, just a slight liftir
of the chest and a series of muscular twitches.

She pressed her forearm under his nostrils, hearing th
cartilage snap and feeling his face sag. Sitting back and releasi
the pressure, she was surprised to find her forehead sweaty wi
the effort.

Cautiously, she lifted the pillow from her son's face and looked at him. A trickle of blood had run from his nose and gathered in the corner of his swollen mouth, creating an eerie contrast with his pale skin. Thankfully, his eyes were still closed. She wondered if she'd cry, but she felt strangely elated, as if everything had finally fallen into place.

Rula stood up and opened her son's drawer, feeling for the bottle of pills that his doctor had prescribed. There were at least twenty left in the bottle and, reaching for the glass of water next to his bed, she calmly swallowed them all.

*

'Let's go get him,' said Eleanor, standing up.

Timms held up a warning hand. 'Let's just make sure we're on solid ground before we gather the posse.'

'Seconded,' said Marty.

Eleanor sighed and nodded her agreement, but remained standing.

Timms spread the information in front of him. 'Bridgewater is the surname on his birth certificate – it's his mother's maiden name. His mother marries Alan Frears in 2008 but the boy isn't legally adopted by Frears.'

'Are we thinking that Alan Frears may be our John Doe?' asked Wadesky.

'Can you call up his details?' Timms asked Johnson.

'Absolutely,' replied Johnson.

'He *also* lived in Claddis McAvoy's apartment building until he was nine, which would explain how he knew the key code, and why he used the old boiler room,' noted Laurence.

'He left partial prints at each of the murder scenes, which have now been identified and linked through the multiple prints taken from the knife in Raven's apartment.'

'Why doesn't he appear on the animal abusers list?' asked Eleanor.

Timms threw down his pen. 'Unless he's tried and found guilty, his prints and past history are all supposition.'

'Let's not waste time bitching about the system. What else have we got?' snapped Marty.

Johnson turned his laptop round so they could all see Alan Frears' driving licence. Timms held the forensic image next to the screen.

'Bring him in,' snarled Marty.

Wadesky and Laurence took their position by the back door of the Frears' house, while Timms and Eleanor entered through the front. It had been calculated that the safest arrest strategy would be to enter quietly and extract Nathan before he had a chance to prepare.

The door was opened with a lock pick and bolt cutter, and Eleanor made her way carefully into the house.

Various low-wattage lamps gave them sufficient light to manoeuvre with, and after the downstairs rooms were secured and the door was unlocked for Wadesky and Laurence, they made their way upstairs. Eleanor, her Glock levelled at chest height, led the way up the stairs, stopping outside the first door and listening. Signalling Timms her intention, she opened the door.

It took her several moments to process the scene in front of her. Rula Frears sat next to her son, barely registering their presence. Eleanor stepped forward and checked the boy's carotid pulse. He was cool to the touch and possessed no discernible beat.

Timms followed her into the room.

'Mrs Frears, are you responsible for the death of your son?' Eleanor asked.

Rula Frears nodded. 'He killed Alan.' She turned to Timms, vho was calling for emergency response. 'You can't bring him ack!'

'Mrs Frears, what have you taken?' questioned Eleanor, extracting the bottle from her fingers.

'Nothing!' Rula hissed angrily. 'They're nothing. I *should* be lead.'

Eleanor read the label and immediately recognised the mplications.

t was five in the morning by the time the scene had been processed nd Rula Frears had been taken to a local hospital for observation. leanor sat in her car and rested her head against the window, rying to make sense of the past few hours.

Her phone rang.

'Hey, Mo, any news?' she asked wearily.

'Jacob's out of surgery and in ITC. Prognosis is good but he's ot going to be brought round for at least twenty-four hours. innie's up and waiting for you. She says she's baking breakfast nd will run you a bath. I'll see you there.'

Eleanor had been so preoccupied with the momentum of vents that's she'd forgotten that access to her apartment would e barred.

'Thanks.'

A steady barrage of snow hit the windscreen of her car, forcing er to start the engine in an effort to warm the interior and clear e windscreen. Eleanor knew that she should wait for the call at would confirm what she believed, but would it make any al difference? The architect of this mayhem would never be unished because there was nothing you could pin on him. He ad manipulated the thoughts, behaviour and actions of Eddie lyles, Roma Joe Greene and Nathan Bridgewater. Would they

have proceeded with their massacres if he hadn't been involve
in their lives? Maybe – maybe not. That was supposition and sh
worked with truths, which was why, as she stopped at the junctio
ahead of her, she turned right, rather than left.

It took her thirty minutes to locate Dr Launceston's house.
occupied the highest point on the maple-lined street. A testamen
to his arrogance, the building exuded a sense of primacy wit
no overt security measures. A wrought-iron gate opened onto
red-brick path that led directly to the front door.

For a moment Eleanor wavered. What was she hoping t
achieve by confronting Launceston on his home territory? Sh
knew he wouldn't confess to having any culpability, nor had sh
any evidence that would enable her to arrest him. It was, sh
thought, an exercise in futility.

She placed her finger on the doorbell and listened to th
unremitting alarm echoing within the house.

Several minutes passed before she heard Launceston on th
other side of the door. Rather than opening it immediately, h
pulled back the curtain in an adjoining room, shaking his hea
as he recognised her. Keeping her finger on the bell, she waite
until the front door was unlocked before releasing the pressur

'What do you want, Raven?' he snapped, pulling his dressin
gown tightly against the cold air.

'I'd like to discuss a problem,' she replied, pushing past hi
into the hallway.

'There are plenty of daytime appointments,' he said irritab

'I'm sure there are. But this won't wait. Where shall we talk
she asked, looking around at the beautiful elm panels and th
series of framed photographs, mainly of Launceston himse
'Your office?'

'That door.' He gestured to the left.

'Is there anyone else in the house?' she asked.

A glimmer of uncertainty crossed his features. 'No, I live alone.'

Eleanor opened the door and ushered him towards it. He tared grimly at her for a moment before walking into his office nd seating himself. 'What do you want?' he said.

'Did you send Nathan Bridgewater to kill me?' she asked.

'Well, not to any great effect apparently,' he said, smiling. 'No, f course not. He's not a robot and has never mentioned that he nows you. So why are you here?'

'I want to know *why*?' she said, making herself comfortable n the proffered armchair.

'Isn't that what we all want?' he replied, reaching for a pack f cigarettes on his desk.

Eleanor nodded. 'He's dead.'

'By your hand?' Launceston asked, with interest.

'No, his mother's.'

'I hadn't considered that as a possibility. Rula Frears as judge nd executioner.' He inhaled deeply, lifting his head back to blow he smoke away from Eleanor.

'Nathan murdered her husband. But I imagine this isn't news o you – after all, you were his confessor and confidante,' said leanor quietly.

'I have some small knowledge of the workings of his mind ut none regarding his actions.'

'Bullshit! You knew exactly what he, Eddie Myles and Roma e Greene were doing, because you were their puppet master,' ie said angrily. 'You encouraged them to explore and indulge ieir darkest thoughts. Maybe you even planted those thoughts ı their minds!'

Launceston's expression hardened. 'Have you any proof nderlying these accusations?'

'We can hear you talking to Joe Greene on the recording. We now that the antipsychotic meds you prescribed to Nathan Frears were sugar pills, and that you were aware that Eddie Myles wa eating body parts but decided not to warn his military supervisors

Launceston leaned towards her. 'I *meant* the sort of proof tha will stand up in court.' The silence between them lengthenec 'I thought not.'

'Why'd you do it?' she demanded. 'You knew what they wer capable of. You had an intimate knowledge of their though processes and how they might behave.' She felt an overwhelmin anger rising in her. 'Did Eddie Myles explain what he was goin to do to his wife? Or did you go as far as suggesting he kill her

Launceston looked steadily at Eleanor, making no attempt t comment or contradict her.

'You convinced them that their minds were frozen space filled with demons that could only be exorcised if they indulge their violent natures. Which is why we have a growing pile (dead bystanders.'

'Nonsense,' he replied. 'You have no proof that I intende this, or was even capable of achieving it.'

'You tried the same manipulation on me,' she answere coldly.

Launceston shook his head. 'I did nothing of the sort. On Seb Blackmore had expunged your sense of guilt for Caleb's dea and the fear of being murdered from your memory, there w nothing left to motivate you. I taught you to fear your past agai so you could carry on as a detective.' He looked at her criticall 'Perhaps you are here to kill me then?' He leaned towards her. ' would be a rather blunt way of proving your theory.'

'You're right. I've nothing that will stand up in court, or eve get ten minutes of the DA's time. What I have got is the beli that you selected patients with damaged minds and turned the into the very thing you were meant to deactivate. I just do know *why*,' she said, with feeling.

'You think I have the ability to do that?' he sneered. 'You don't just crawl into someone else's mind and set the dials to a favourable outcome. There are too many variables.'

'Variables? You're supposed to explain that there are ethical concerns. That your oath to do no harm is the mantra you practise by, not give me an explanation of the difficulties.'

'What you are suggesting,' he said patiently, 'is just not correct. I have treated my patients to the best of my abilities.'

'You've played God with their minds,' she said calmly.

There was a long pause as Launceston seemed to mull over his options. Eleanor shifted her position in the chair, trying not to break his reverie or lose the moment. Finally Launceston lifted his head and focussed on her. He smiled.

'The human mind, Eleanor, is possibly the most complex thing in the whole universe. It is exquisite, and I have dedicated my entire adult life to studying and working with it. But what was I tasked with? Listening, exploring and then turning the abnormal into the socially acceptable, just as Seb Blackmore has with you. But look at what we've lost. So many unique minds, disapproved of, despaired of, but *ultimately* it is those minds – your own mind among them' – he raised his finger, as if lecturing – 'that have moved our society forward. Without insanity there's nothing but the status quo. We need fear or progress and creativity will be lost.'

'You're wrong.' Eleanor stood up, shaking her head. 'Nothing noble or good comes out of butchery or terror. I intend to make sure that you're called to account.'

Launceston extinguished his cigarette and stood up. 'I think it's time for you to leave now.'

Eleanor remained silent.

He opened his mouth, but she held up her hand and lowered her voice. 'You have *no one* other than yourself in the house?'

'No one,' he snapped. 'It's time—'

'Stay in here,' she hissed. 'We're not alone.'

The faint sound of breaking glass put her on the alert. Drawing her weapon, she slipped out of the drawing room and headed in the direction of the noise. The corridor, illuminated by one lamp, tapered into darkness as it branched towards several other rooms. For the briefest of moments there was a flicker of light visible under one of the doors.

Releasing the safety on the Glock, Eleanor took an adversarial position to the right of the door handle. Holding her breath and listening carefully, she thought she could hear movements inside. Slowly, she twisted the door handle and, feeling the latch release its tension, let the door swing open several inches.

The room was dark and had the unmistakable odour of food preparation. It was considerably cooler inside, which indicated that an external door had been opened.

Knowing the light in the corridor wasn't to her advantage, she pushed the door open entirely and felt for the light switch with her left hand. From where she stood, she could see that a door, presumably leading to the garden, was closed, but the floor around it showed a series of wet footsteps. She had to act.

'This is the Toronto PS. I am an armed officer. Raise your hands!'

There was no movement or sound so she entered the room quickly, her weapon raised. Two figures, clad entirely in black combat attire, rushed at her with incredible speed from both sides. Eleanor felt her hands twisted, her weapon taken and her feet knocked from beneath her.

As she fell, a hand pressed her neck and head into the floor and an immense weight pushed into her back. The kitchen light was extinguished and she felt a hand checking for concealed weapons. There was little doubt in her mind as to who used these tactics and why they were there.

'This isn't right,' she managed, despite her jaw being practically mmoveable.

A minute passed. She could hear purposeful movements around her. Suddenly, she was lifted to her feet and dragged into he corridor and pushed against the wall.

'Don't do this!' she said, trying to calculate how many Special orces operatives were in the house. 'This *isn't* right,' she hissed t the man holding her.

A second figure appeared at her shoulder. He leaned into er and spoke steadily. 'You're going to leave now and maintain ilence. Are you listening carefully?'

Eleanor tried to reposition herself, to no avail. 'You have no uthority to—' she began.

'There is no negotiation here. You will maintain silence or you on't leave.' He lowered his voice. 'Do you understand what I'm aying, Raven?'

Eleanor opened her mouth, but before she could speak, the oldier cracked her head against the wall and whispered into her ar. 'What the hell are you doing? You wanted justice – a head n a plate – and now you're carping that it's undemocratic. Your pinion isn't required. Walk away and know that justice is being erved. He's not going to play around with any more minds. le's done.'

'You are *not* judge and executioner,' she said firmly.

'Don't be naive,' he snapped, an urgency entering his voice. 'ou make your peace with this – or with your God. Am I being ear?'

'Yes,' she said angrily.

He turned her around to face him. The balaclava made any lentification impossible, but she knew who he was. 'There will e consequences if you talk to anyone. Are you clear as to what m saying to you?'

'Yes,' she said quietly.

Handing over her weapon, which had been emptied, h
propelled her through the house and down the path, where h
handed her the keys and, opening the car door, pushed her int
the driving seat.

'There is no other way,' he said quietly.

Eleanor grimaced. 'There is *always* another way.'

CHAPTER TWENTY-TWO

he morning brought blue skies and a shift in temperature. With
orontonian efficiency, the fallen snow had been pushed into car
arks and lay-bys before the morning rush hour.

Eleanor, contrary to her expectations and lack of sleep, felt
onsiderably more relaxed than she had for weeks and put it
own to having had a long hot bath and Minnie's home-cooked
reakfast. She had lain awake for some time despite her exhaus-
on, mulling over the events at Launceston's house. That he was
ead now was a certainty, but how he'd met that end and where
e now lay was anyone's guess.

Eleanor had tried to conjure a scenario that would have brought
stice and retribution without the need for what she believed had
een state-sanctioned murder, but there had been no conceivable
ay to bring Launceston to any kind of trial for his crimes, or
ven to convince the judiciary that there was a crime to answer
r. He had manipulated broken minds into committing murder
nd who knew how many more patients he'd lined up to carry
ut similar massacres?

cob Hareton was awake, out of danger and, having identified
athan Bridgewater as his attacker, he was waiting for Eleanor's
rival. Pulling into the hospital to see him, she was met by
aurence.

'You rested?' he asked, falling into step with her.

'I am,' she said, and meant it.

'I need to talk to you,' he said, slightly embarrassed.

'You *don't*,' she replied firmly, stepping into the hospital atrium

'You've spoken to Mags,' he said, putting a hand on her arm

Eleanor sighed. 'Look, it was simple. Mags thought you didn like the dog; she didn't realise you didn't like yourself.'

Laurence raised an eyebrow.

'I told her you loved Monster and that was enough – we that and the scans of Monster's pups. Timms put her name a the top of the list and she was thrilled to be getting the pick o the first litter.'

Laurence shook his head. 'That's not what I'm talking abou though I'm very grateful to you for explaining what an asshole am to my ex-girlfriend.'

'Not a problem,' Eleanor said and made to walk away.

'Timms spoke to me. He told me what you're planning to d and I can't let you do it! I *can't* let you pay off Mags.'

'I *don't* want the insurance money. It was the payout for bei murdered by Lee Hughes and I don't want to think of myself a murder victim. I'm alive, and keeping that money will alwa make me feel dead. So I gave it to Timms to use as he deems fi starting with giving you and Mags a clean break.'

Laurence looked at her. 'I can pay you back.'

She shook her head. 'It's blood money. Timms has set up a account and he'll use it for causes he deems worthy. I don't wa to know of its existence. Accept it, don't talk about it and kno that being able to help you has been good for me.'

'Thank you,' he said sincerely.

Jacob had the washed-out, grey appearance of the newly decease but he smiled when he saw Eleanor. For a brief moment she fe the familiar trapped sensation that accompanied her fear of bei needed by another person. Determined not to fall into her usual patterns of behaviour, she made an effort to slough it off.

'How are you?' she asked, still standing.

'Sore,' he replied cautiously. 'Your partner says you got him.'

'We did, but not before someone got to him first,' she replied.

'He's dead?'

'Yes.'

'Why'd he do it?' asked Jacob, carefully repositioning himself. 'He was just a kid.'

'He was after me,' she said.

'I meant *why* was he after you?'

Eleanor sighed. 'We don't know that yet. He may have thought I was closing in on him, or he may have been instructed by someone else.'

'A hit?' asked Jacob uncomfortably.

'Hard to explain, but he was definitely being influenced by someone else.'

'But you're safe now?' Jacob asked.

'I am,' she replied.

The call came at 2.45 p.m. Eleanor grabbed her coat and made her way over to the park. The crime scene officers had been working since daybreak, and now that the hard work was over, they were all having a coffee break. One of the technicians greeted her and walked her over to the canvas structure at the far end of the rose garden.

Eleanor surveyed the piles of roots and stones that littered the muddy, unrecognisable garden. A screen was pulled aside and she blinked in the glare from the lights. A woman's partially skeletonised remains had been cleared of mud and looked ready to be lifted.

'Her face is remarkably well preserved,' said the technician, helping Eleanor into the hole so she could examine the body. 'Is that her?'

Eleanor looked at the pale, plasticised skin, noting that the high cheekbones and wide jaw were consistent with the photograph of the missing woman. 'I'm happy to call a halt to the excavation,' she replied.

'Was she blue-eyed?' he asked, pointing to the glass eyes that Toby Adams had inserted and which now stared dully back at them. Eleanor met their gaze and nodded.

'You've been found, Clarrie Eddow,' she whispered.

A LETTER FROM KAREN

)ear reader,

want to say a huge thank you for choosing to read *What She* *:new*. If you enjoyed it, and want to keep up to date with all ıy latest releases, just sign up at the following link. Your email ddress will never be shared and you can unsubscribe at any time.

www.bookouture.com/karen-long

It was during a stay in Toronto that I came across the idea ıat would form the plot of the first Eleanor Raven novel, *Cry* *r Mercy*. I was sitting in a roadside café reading the *Toronto Sun* ewspaper and came across an article about a recent suspected idnapping. Police had been informed by a member of the public ıat a woman had been grabbed off the street and thrown into the ack of a van. When the police stopped the vehicle and liberated ıe victim, they were astonished to discover that not only was this 'sexy red-letter kidnapping' but also the woman was outraged having it spoiled. It was a gift of an idea. All I had to add was leanor Raven, a woman with a twist of her own.

What She Knew is book three in the series. I love the characters ıd the landscape and hope to continue the series in the future. ıope you loved *What She Knew* too, and if you did I would be :ry grateful if you could write a review. I'd love to hear what

you think, and it makes such a difference helping new readers t
discover one of my books for the first time.

I love hearing from my readers – you can get in touch on m
Facebook page, through Twitter, Goodreads or my website.

Thanks, Karen.

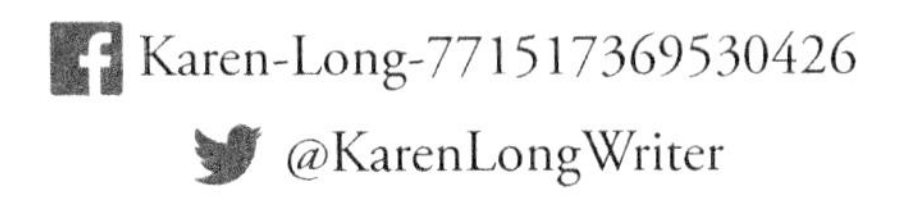

ACKNOWLEDGEMENTS

would like to thank Araminta Whitley, Peta Nightingale, Emily Gowers, Marina de Pass for their constant faith and hard work n my behalf. Likewise all of the staff at The Soho Agency and Bookouture, for their support.

I would further like to praise the extraordinary efforts made y bloggers, readers and reviewers, who make writing novels a oy. They promote, encourage and evangelise, without which few opies would be sold.

A special thanks to my family and Lou Hunter, who have never ailed to read, reread and nag me, when required (and sometimes hen it wasn't).

Printed in Great Britain
by Amazon

64190615R00169